A BOOK OF
Short Stories

THOMAS WARNER

Gotham Books

30 N Gould St.
Ste. 20820, Sheridan, WY 82801
https://gothambooksinc.com/

Phone: 1 (307) 464-7800

© 2023 Thomas Warner. All rights reserved.

No part of this book may be reproduced, stored in a retrieval system, or transmitted by any means without the written permission of the author.

Published by Gotham Books (March 13, 2023)

ISBN: 979-8-88775-238-9 (sc)
ISBN: 979-8-88775-239-6 (e)

Because of the dynamic nature of the Internet, any web addresses or links contained in this book may have changed since publication and may no longer be valid.

The views expressed in this work are solely those of the author and do not necessarily reflect the views of the publisher, and the publisher hereby disclaims any responsibility for them.

Table of Contents

Thoughts for Today 7
Flies 9
Mr Blue 14
Missionary Sunday 18
The Ballad of Young Johnny Jones 22
The Empty Skies 31
Brothers 40
Best of friends 43
Little Mary 46
Song Contest 56
Fear 66
A Walk on the Wild Side 75
Down by the River 85
Brendan Jones LTD Cleaning Services…No Job too Small or too Big…Relieving the Stresses of Life 87
Interstellar Man 93
A Knock on the Door (Its ME) 101
A Time to Live (Ecclesiastes 3) 102
Come Walk With Me Said JC 104
Everybody Said 107
A Simple Truth 109
An Angry Man 112
Fat Black Cat 128
The Root of All Evil 130
Seamus Roach 135

The Man Who Saw Faces.	142
The Boy With The Open Mind	153
The Fisherman's Son	163
Little Henry Rawlings	170
Spooks	176
I Just Love the Music Man	190
The Left-Handed Lawman	193
The Big Girls Brigade	213
YOU	226
Saving Little Johnny	238
Ola	267
Star Ship	273
Train	279
Marie Mc Donnell	285
The Little Robin, The Logger The Moma Bear and The Child	289
White Suit	297
Three's A Crowd	299
Geheimnisse (secrets)	304
Check Mate	308
Puss in boots	312

Thoughts for Today

Today is a good day, a beautiful sunny September day.

I am not in need of anything, I have everything I need,

Food to eat, a nice comfortable home,

A few good friends,

A wonderful family,

I am so much better after my stroke,

My mind is in a better place,

Okay I am living alone now; but I have wonderful memories,

I have put all the not so good ones behind me at last,

I am getting old, but I am happy.

Flies

An elderly man suffering from mild mental health issues begins to see things that are not there, or are they?

Tom Watson always kept himself busy. He worked hard most of his life then retired early to explore the world and enjoy what time he had left. He has survived his second wife Bridget and his partner Marion whom he met eight years later both of whom died from cancer.

He was still on good terms with his first wife Catherine who had divorced him twenty years earlier. He was a part time writer of poems and had even authored a few books. He sang a little in his local church and played a little guitar though he would admit to playing it rather badly.

He also suffered from a mild depression going back to his childhood days when a terrible accident happened involving the death of his little sister Cher.

His depression was mild in the sense that he was never hospitalized or had any kind of flaw in his character except on occasions he would go noticeably quiet. His wife said that it was this that led to their marriage breaking down after 30 years. He had 3 lovely children, a son and two daughters all of whom were incredibly good to him over the years.

So having plenty of time to himself now having reached his 74th birthday he spent his spare time if that term would be used now as all his time now seemed spare; walking in his local park in the afternoon, feeding the wild birds around 3 pm which he loved to do while watching them feed he would sit inside his ground floor bedroom looking out while doing his daily rosary.

He prayed for everyone on the planet, no matter who they were or what they had done. Everyone in his book deserved a second chance or like his Lord and Master Jesus once did say, 'forgive them not 7 times but 77 times' (Matt: 18:22). That is the kind of man he is, even to this day.

So now here he was seeing less and less people except his wonderful daughter June that brought him his dinner every day, and occasionally her husband Matt that dropped her over in his car.

They lived less than ten minutes away from him. It was not a bad old life as every Sunday he would see some of his local friends at mass and have a little chin wag. Then go over to his daughter's house for Sunday dinner. There was even a couple of beautiful ladies living in the same apartment block that were genuinely nice to him always pleasant and charming and if the truth be told they always, without knowing it, brought back some incredibly happy moments of his past life. But that is another story.

He loved his little apartment and kept it very tidy and clean, as he was a painter and decorator in his younger years. He even took to painting pictures on his apartment walls of ships and biblical scenes and animals of all sorts and this he really enjoyed.

Then when he was got ready to try something else, he would paint them out and start painting another subject. Such was his life and for the best part he enjoyed it. Till he had a stroke at 73.

He went into the kitchen to put the kettle on and bang down he went. Thankfully, he got over it, but it did take the best part of 2 years out of his life that knocked the stuffing out of him but eventually he came back to where he was before it happened.

I say almost because a thing like that can never be forgotten not even for a moment. It is always there and the thought of it coming back lingered forever in the back yard of his mind plus he was now on a lot of medication and would be until the day he 'passed over' as he like to call it.

Then one day whilst talking to his daughter in his sitting room he began picking up tiny bits of leftovers from his dinner from the coffee table. Minute specks of food stuffs, and this slowly progressed to doing similar on the newly laid floorboards. Within a brief period, he was going around the home with a small dustpan and brush in his hands. Cleaning: he was always cleaning something or other, whether it needed cleaning or not.

Becoming obsessive about cleansing that he would go about the place looking for something to clean particularly in the bathroom and kitchen, and life being what it was, he always found something to clean. Then one day a Saturday, his daughter brought over his weekly shopping and when she got to the kitchen, she said to him. 'Dad, you want to empty that bin, there are flies everywhere.

So, he emptied the bin and paid no more attention to it, until a few days later he noticed the flies had not gone but in fact were making themselves at home in the spotless little kitchen, tiny little flies, the odd one here and there then they came in twos then threes and they began to get on his nerves. He sprayed everywhere in the kitchen with a bleach solution that only worked for a brief time, in fact in his mind it only made them dozy or drunk for a spell.

One day he said to himself. 'These are fruit flies, very small but small things can grow, one only has to look at children' so he picked up a Punit of pears his daughter had gotten him two days previously and sure enough he could see some tiny flies on a pear so out they went into the compost heap in the back garden beside his neighbour's small but fully stocked greenhouse type shed.

His neighbour, named Shane loved gardening. Then he, Tom, discovered some more flies in the bathroom and in front of his computer screen in his bedroom.

Every now and then one would fly towards the bright light, and this began to drive him crazy, and he would lunge forward and suddenly clap his hands trying to kill the little fuc... eh fly, most of the time he missed, leaving him with sore hands and a determination to get rid of the annoying little creatures.

He called them a lot worse than that but what he truly called them is not printable here. They were only tiny flies but by now were having a significant impact on his mental health. He began scratching himself all over, first his head and face then his entire body became itchy but only momentarily. Not enough to seek medical attention.

There was once an advert on the telly about flowers and it was introduced by the sound of a bumble bee buzzing. The first time Tom heard that sound he nearly had a heart attack. The eyes nearly popped out of his head trying to figure out where the buzz was buzzing from.

Everywhere he looked he thought he could see a fly until it became an obsession with him. And the more he looked the bigger they got. Even at the Sunday morning mass he was watching out for the little blighters to see if one appeared, none did thankfully.

This went on day in and night out. He was on the watch for the dirty invaders and when he saw one which he did several times a day, he would grab the nearest cloth and WACK the little bugger, but if he missed which he did a lot, he would say to the lucky little bas…eh…bleeder, 'I will hunt you down, you're messing with the wrong man here, I will find you and I will wipe you out, that is my promise to you, you dirty little blighter.'

If he was out walking and he saw a black crow which is quite common as most crows are black, he would in his mind, not be seeing a crow but a huge fly. Then he began to think that all flies were out to get him especially the ones in his apartment. He would sneak up and snap on the light and spring into the kitchen or bathroom before they could make a bolt for it.

He caught a good few that way. Blinded by the light they were, and he loved doing that. Then he had a brainwave. A bad one but one, nevertheless. He painted all the woodwork in his apartment and sure while he was doing the door frames he might as well do the skirting boards while he was at it. This he mistakenly believed, would trap the little fuc …eh… bugger's, when they landed on something white as he was now accustomed to seeing them do, the fresh brilliant white gloss would act as a flycatcher like the one he recalled seeing in his childhood home, a fly catcher hanging from the ceiling.

Now he had one in every room. Still, he caught nothing but a headache from the smell of fresh paint. He was however getting the better of them on the swat front.

The little buggers did not know what hit them. But where were they coming from? Then one day whilst standing in his spotless freshly painted kitchen staring in the huge mirror he sneezed and out from his nose popped a half dozen little flies. He sneezed again and out popped some more. He was horrified and when he opened his mouth to exhale out came hundreds and thousands more just like he used to see them doing in the movies.

A long black river of flies was climbing over every inch of his lovely clean kitchen, and he ran all over the place in panic spreading millions of tiny black flies everywhere he went. He ran into his neighbour's garden shed and searched for and found a greenfly solution which he drank down undiluted, and they found him in his spotlessly clean kitchen two days later dead on the floor.

The flies had already laid their tiny eggs on his body and if one listened long enough, one could even hear them laugh.

End

Mr Blue

Mr Pat Short was a postal worker in the sorting office in Tallaght down by the Square. His workmates called him Mr blue because he always had a sad story to tell. He had on more than one occasion left them feeling more than a little blue themselves. He was though, a hard-working man and would do no one a bad turn as he had proved to them over his many years of service and it was this fact alone that made him almost popular with the people of the Postal service in Tallaght, a village that had now grown into a town and would be made a city in the not-too-distant future.

One Monday morning he went into work as usual and found his six work mates four men and two women sitting around the coffee table in a sombre mood. In the centre of the table there was a beautiful vase that left everyone present just staring at it.

He said to everyone there. 'Hey, what's up guys?' has somebody died? why so gloomy, I have not been in five minutes, and it looks like I have been bothering you guys all day,' he did have a sense of humour however misjudged it might have been.

One of the ladies a beautiful heavily bosomed woman called Helena, spoke up saying to him. 'My husband has had enough; he is redecorating the sitting room and he said 'it' pointing to the vase. 'Has to go,'

'God,' said Pat. 'Looking at you guys one might think that you had to go Helena, which would explain all the sad faces, I mean how lucky the guy that was going to let you move in with him. Ha hah' nobody laughed.

Then Helena said to him as she had already explained it all to the others. 'It is my father's ashes! and they have been on the mantle-piece in my house since he died in 1967. Oh, I know I should have done what he wished and threw them into the sea, but I just could not do it, I went a few times but just could not bring myself to throw him into the sea, and watch him float away, I just could not do it'

'That is no problem! said Mr Blue. 'Sure, one of us can do it for you, can't we guys?' nobody said anything. All looked stone faced and turned their heads slightly away. 'Ok then! said Mr Blue. 'I will do it for you Helena…no problem, first thing in the morning. I know the exact place to do it too. I pass it every day going and coming from here.'

Helena was sobbing her little heart out and the other four men were all around her trying to comfort her and themselves. The other woman Mary was powdering her nose and doing her make up.

Meanwhile further up the coast in the BBS 'Booterstown Bird Sanctuary' the staff there were getting ready to release one huge bald American eagle that had been handed into them twelve months previous. It had flown way off course and by some miracle had landed on a boat in the Irish sea then handed into the BBS. By the time the sanctuary got hold of it the big bird was exhausted and in unbelievably bad shape overall.

The staff there had really grown fond of this beautiful bird of prey and were planning on soon releasing it for a trial period and to help build its muscle to see if it were strong enough to fly and if so, would then be put on a plane home to Alaska where it came from and where it truly belongs. Booterstown has a sea front that also runs parallel to the main Dublin to Bray railway track.

'So do you want me to do it or what?' asked Mr Blue of Helena before she had finished her shift at twelve. She replied, 'Do you think you could, I mean I would love to go with you, but I am afraid I might change my mind' she said in reply.

'No that's okay' he said. 'I can do it on my way in, in the morning, I'm on the six am shift so there will be no need for you to get up so early, so can I take it from the kitchen table then when I am finished today? She said to him smiling. 'You can and thank you very much Pat' then almost kissing him on the lips but then turning to the right-hand side of his face she winks and whispers in his ear. 'I owe you one lovey!'

And so it was that very next morning that the BBS staff were preparing to release the beautiful huge bald American eagle for its test flight. They stood the large cage on the clear sandy beach. The first low tide had already gone out, but that was not too bad. It simply meant that big bird could head straight for the water in the distance and with a gentle pull of the lead attached to its right leg the bird of prey would turn and come back to them. They had done this many a time in its recovery and it worked very well, every time.

Except for this morning Mr Blue was also in the equation.

He had overslept and was running late. A simple thing in the life of a simple man. He showered and had breakfast in a hurry and was out the door heading for his car when he remembered Helena's vase with her father's ashes. Even more late now he drove straight to the highest hill on Booterstown Avenue.

Thinking that he would be even later if he went to the beach as he had planned. There was a light wind coming in from the west and thinking it would carry the ashes across the beach and down into the water. Even if they only landed on the sandy shore the incoming tide would then take them up and then in time back out to sea, at least this was Mr Blues way of thinking. It was time to put this plan into action.

It was also time to let the very big bald American eagle loose. Then the wind changed from west to north-west and in his search for the least path of resistance the big bird turned eastward. Toward Mr Blue who at that precise time the bird flew over him threw the ashes into the air, covering the big bird and himself with Helena's father's ashes.

The BBS staff could only watch with horror as the big bird fell out of the air and plummeted to the ground. While Mr Blue made a quick exit to his car, of which the cars windscreen was also covered with the ashes of Helena's father.

He had to return home to have another shower then to the nearest petrol station to have his car washed and he was indeed, very late for work. This time however he kept the sad story to himself; at least for the next six months.

End

Missionary Sunday

'Good morning, Tom, how are you today?'

'I'm fine Lord and you?'

'Fine Tom, thank you for asking, not many people do nowadays, sad to say!'

'Is everything still going well with you Tom? on Tuesday evening you passed me by so quickly I was afraid you were in some sort of bother?'

'Tuesday Lord, I don't remember seeing you, where was this?'

'Tallaght village Tom'

'Tallaght village Lord, what part?'

'It's okay Tom I was a bit hard to see, I was by the side of the church'

'What, by the side of the Priory?'

'Yes Tom, that person you did not bother to see was me sitting there on the steps; feeling sorry for myself, I had nowhere to sleep on Monday night, so I had to sleep there, you came rushing by I thought the place was on fire'

'No Lord, it was not the place that was on fire but myself, at the prayer meeting your spirit was so powerful; it always brings me alive, puts a spring in my step so to speak, I love Tuesday nights in the priory, there is so much love shared in that holy place Lord, so much peace'

'Yes, I know Tom, that's what brought me there in the first place, now though I need you Tom to help me,'

'Me help YOU Lord?'

'Yes Tom, I need you to do a little errant for me, will you do that Tom?'

'Lord I will walk to the ends of the earth for you, I will face the fiercest lion, I will even swim to the bottom of the sea and bring you back all the best pearls, I, I will!'

'Relax Tom you need not do anything so dramatic, you do not even have to push a baby in a pram, no, nothing like that, not even climb the smallest mountain'

'Well, I would Lord for you, I would honest!'

'Tom you can uncross your fingers now; I know you would, in your dreams anyway, no, I want you to be honest with yourself for a while, take time out so to speak, relax and rest in my love, take a deep breath Tom and listen to what I say to you'

'I'm all ears Lord, fire away, I'm listening to you!'

'I want you Tommy to be …are you ready for this?'

'Yes, yes, Lord what is it? I will fight the strongest gladiator I… I will break him in half for you?'

'I want you to be yourself for a change how's that?'

'WHAT!'

'Tommy, why do you put up such a front with people? why put on a show? people, my people, and I consider you to be one, are so beautiful inside that sometimes I wonder it ye all should have been created the other way round, with your inside out and your outside in… no …no…on second thoughts, perhaps not, be who you are Tom not who you would like to be'

'Lord, you have lost me, what are you trying to tell me?

He said to me,

'What I want you to do for me is to be me for this day, this mission Sunday, just try it for the day, you will find it's not so hard and at the end of the day you will have been me and I will have been you and hopefully I will be able to take the next day off and go to the races and you will want to continue to be me or at any rate my disciple, what do you say Tom will you give it a go?'

'Of course, I will Lord, I will give it my best shot I will… 'The Good Lord cut me off saying to me.

'Don't go overboard Tom, just be nice to people, don't go trying to raise the dead or move mountains or give your brother the lotto numbers or anything like that, will you Tom, be me for the day and bear in mind that I too am a missionary, always have been and will always be, so try not to ruin it for me. Just smile a lot and if a genuine problem arises just cross and ask yourself what I would do if I were in the same position and my grace will be with you to carry you through the day as indeed it is every day for, I love you, Tommy Warren. I want you to be at peace with the world and with yourself, will you be my missionary today, Tom? and if you are any good at it, I may make you one on a full-time basis, no pay mind, just room and board when the time comes, what do you say Tom?'

'Er, I thought we were not to do anything but rest on the Sabbath Lord?'

'Your allergic to work aren't you, Tommy Warren?

'Er, no I'm not, not really Lord, I had a job in 1967!'

'1967, and I suppose you still have your wages and your confirmation money?'

'Ah now Lord, don't be like that!'

'You're an awful man Tommy Warren so you are, an awful man, I don't know what I'm going to do with you I really don't; I pour out my heart to you and you go and make fun of me, an awful man, but I like you, so think about it Tommy and rest assured I will be back for an answer, so until then

I'm off on another mission see you Tom, try not to destroy my world okay? take care bye

'Do not be like that I was only messing Lord, of course I will try to be you; and you can be me and see if you like working for a pittance. Brendan Behan was right; work is only for horses, bye Lord bye, love you!'

'Yeah …yeah, love you too, Tom, see you'

End

The Ballad of Young Johnny Jones

The Ballad of young Johnny Jones song (AEA)

Ride on…through the valley,
Ride on …through the glen,
Ride on… through the mountains,
You'll never pass …this way again…
Ride on …over the meadows,
Ride on … over the land,
Ride on … driving cattle,
Here the white man … has made a stand…

He is building for the future: going to raise his family,
Going to build a town of hero's, on this land so wild but not so free…

Ride on … across the rivers,
Ride on… across the hills,
Across the land that once was given,
To the Apache nation that lives there still.

Sheriff's office: a town called Young in Arizona in 1886; sheriff making a pot of coffee in his cosy office.

'I remember that day you first came to me' said sheriff Dan Driscoll to young Johnny Jones, 'The Apache's had just killed your parents out yonder on your ranch, you told me they wanted to kill you too but the young chief, not much older that yourself, stopped them from doing so, I even remember that day …it was raining hard …hadn't rained for months,

Wednesday it was, you were only fourteen, two years ago tomorrow, I know how hard it had been for you John, but you came through it, now look at you, a fine handsome young man …and you can shoot too, I saw you shoot a dollar piece …two holes for the price of one, you were only twelve at the time not many men today can do that son …including myself, but I have to tell you that living by the gun alone means that you won't live long, there is always someone much faster than you out there,

Now you say you want to be my deputy …I'd have to say you are much too young, eighteen maybe …sixteen no way, but you can hang around here if you have nothing better to do and watch how it goes, there is not much doing in our little town, so I see no harm in it if you stop by a couple of hours a day, young fella like you should be out chasing girls, they're much more fun than guns son…'

Young Johnny Jones or JJ as he is known in the town said to sheriff Dan, 'thank you sheriff, I don't mind if I do, I don't mind if I don't, as for the girls, well there is that Johnson girl Emma, wow a real beauty, and educated too but her father is the Mayor not sure he would like me hanging round his only daughter, I will see you tomorrow sheriff,' the sheriff said to him, 'you can call me Dan son, I was a friend of your fathers and I am a friend to you, as for the young Mayors daughter, you could be right there …but sure there are plenty more young ladies in this town, and you do have all the time in the world, but take my advice son, don't be wearing them guns like that, yes it is very impressive, but also very tempting for others aching to make a name for themselves, you can hang them up there on the rack, there will always be there when and if you need them,'

Young Johnny Jones said to him, 'Sure no problem sheri ...eh Dan, but I won't leave town without them, I would not sleep right not knowing there were here and not within reach, ok, see you later Dan'

It was almost four in the evening as JJ mounted his horse and went to ride on home as he still had a few chores to do around the house, then he spotted Emma across the street going into the grocery store and he remembered he was running out of coffee so he made a beeline for the store.

JJ was a handsome young youth as the sheriff had said, blond hair and blue eyes with a very fresh complexion, and tall for his age five eight or nine with his frame well built from all the arduous work he had to put in on his small but study ranch.

He had help of an old ranch hand of his fathers who stayed behind after the killings to look after young JJ and help him about the place. His name was Tucker Warner; but JJ just called him Uncle Tuck. He kept a few of his father's cattle and some horses and it was there that he learned how to shoot and shoot very well. And he revelled in the stories of the James gang and Wyatt Earp, Doc Holiday, and Kit Carson and the like.

His father taught him to read people as well as books and respect others and their way of life whatever that way may be, even the Indian way of life, but he became hard after watching flying Bear and his little bunch of savages kill his mother and father and little sister Janet, and all for no reason whatsoever.

That was one Apache face he would never forget, even if he did spare young JJ back then for whatever reason known only to himself.

Young Emma Johnson was busy trying on a new hat when JJ walked into the store and though she saw him in the mirror she pretended not to notice him. She was a beautiful young lady around the same age as himself, but JJ did not hold out much hope of her ever becoming her girlfriend, but he tried, nonetheless.

'Evening Ms Emma, and how are you today? My you sure do look very pretty in that hat; it really suits you if I may say so?' Ms Emma said in reply, 'You may certainly say so JJ and it is nice of you to say so and how are you today? I saw you coming from the sheriff's office …I do hope you are not in any kind of bother.'

JJ smiled and said to her, 'No Miss, no bother, and I am flattered you even noticed me at all, with all the young men in this town just dying for your attention', she just smiled that wonderful smile of hers and said to him 'And would you be counting your good self among those many young men all waiting in line?'

He was just about to answer yes when the mayor, her father, came into the store. He gave JJ a cold look, staring down at his guns on his hip so JJ turned to the storekeeper and asked for a small sack of coffee which he bought then left the store but not before looking over to see the beautiful Emma smiling back at him.

Happily, he mounted his horse and rode for home. Uncle Tuck would have dinner ready, and he would not be too pleased if JJ was late, but that beautiful smile of Emma's would be well worth the long and painful lecture from anyone, even Uncle Tuck.

'I see those pesky Indians are on the warpath again, seems that chief of theirs, Vicorio, or whatever his name is cannot control his people, especially Flying Bear and his handful of braves, heard tell they hit Mac Kenna's ranch west of here, and I know how you like to keep informed about his whereabouts, if he keep on the way he is going he could be back here in a few days, how do you feel about that JJ?'

JJ replied, 'can't wait to meet him again Tuck, this time there will be only one of us left standing, and it won't be him, he will regret the day he did not finish me off, but I will worry about that when and if it ever happens, that was a great meal uncle, thank you very much, very tasty' after dinner the two men sat on the porch watching the evening fade and continued their conversation about Flying Bear with Tuck saying to JJ

'It was not as if he was brought up to kill white folk, yes, his chief fought and killed them for years, but his uncle and guardian took no part in that, his mother played a huge part in his upbringing and I am told that killing white folk played no part in it, so why he would go wild like that is beyond me, he is smart enough to know that it can only end one way, with him going home to the happy hunting grounds prematurely , if not by you then someone else'

JJ replied to him saying,

'It is hard to know the mind of someone whose history shows nothing but betrayal and killing and burning people's property, we did them no favours, breaking almost every treaty and every now and then it throws up a bad seed that reminds them of that ...and that applies to white men as well as Indians ...Tuck ...I think I will have another glass of that fine moonshine you make so well, it goes down very nicely ...I might even sing you a song' Tucker laughed and said to him. 'Well, if that's the case, I might even have one or two myself'

Back in town the sheriff had been visited by three drifters and they were giving him a tough time. 'All we want to do is pay that little store-com- bank a little visit and we will be on our way, but first we need to remind you of what you will get if you come stand in our way' said the one in charge to the sheriff while hitting him across the face with his pistol.

The other two outlaws just stood there laughing as the sheriff wriggled in pain in his chair, but who managed to say to the leader a scruffy man called Slim. 'My deputies will be here soon then you will have to deal with them, if they don't see me standing at my office door as per usual, they will know something is wrong and come gun in hand expecting trouble'

The other two were called Jed and the youngest one Rufus something or other. The eldest one, the fellow called Slim said to him 'we did a little checking before we came here and we have been told that you have no deputies, not even one,' so he hit the sheriff again across the face breaking his nose, saying to him, 'now we might even come back here and spend the night, might even let you have a drink or two if you promise to behave, Jed here will keep you company while Rufus and I will go and make a little withdrawal before the store closes, just sit tight and who knows you might live to see the morning, watch him closely Jed, if he makes a move, kill him'

The store owner was just locking up when the two outlaws came in and demanded money. The young man in the store called Michael said to them that there was no money, at least not enough to be worth robbing and Slim just shot him dead then searched the office and found a small sum of money behind a small safe.

One hundred and twenty dollars and some change. As most if not all the other small stores had already closed, and the owners gone home, so no one came to see where the gunshot had come from.

The sheriff heard it but all he could do was bow his head in pain and defeat. Tucker heard it too but said to JJ, 'someone out shooting rabbits' to which JJ replied, 'At this time of night, seems to me that shot came from town,' Tucker replied saying,

'Sure we will know in the morning' but JJ buckling on his gun belt said to him, 'I won't sleep tonight unless I know what that shot was, so I best go and find out, it is only ten minutes there and I will be back before you know it and who knows someone might need a helping hand, you go to bed uncle, I will be back soon,'

Twelve minutes later and JJ was riding down the empty street towards the sheriff's office. The light was still on in the grocery store where only a few hours before he was talking to the lovely Emma. He made his way slowly up the wooden steps and into the open door, where he almost fell over the body of the man that served him earlier.

He looked around then went to see where the sheriff was. There were three horses tied up to the rail outside the sheriff's office and JJ knew that Dan was in trouble so he crept round the back to see if he could see what was going on.

He could not see but he could hear them talking.

It was Dans voice he heard first with him saying, 'You killed a man for 100 dollars, that young man Michael was a hardworking man with a young family, and you killed him for 100 dollars, what kind of man are you?

Slim said to him, 'He was a stupid man, all he had to do was give us the money and he would still be alive, it wasn't even his money, what kind of man dies for someone else's money?

And besides 120 dollars is a lot of money to me, I mean ...to us' he didn't like the way his men looked at him when he said, 'to me'. JJ could hear two other voices, so he knew there were three men inside with the sheriff. There was only one thing for him to do,

'You men inside the jail, come out with your hands up' he yelled. The sheriff knew immediately who it was but held his piece. Smelly Slim called out, 'And who would you be?' JJ replied saying, 'I am the sheriff's deputy, so leave your guns behind and come out with your hands up,' Slim yelled back,

'And if we don't?' what can you do? there are three of us and we have the sheriff here and he is in no fit state to join you so that leaves just you, against us, if you don't lay down your gun we will blow his brains out,' then he turns to Jed and says to him, 'Can you see him? can you get a shot at him?' Jed replies saying, 'No, can't see him clear enough, but he sounds to me like a kid, he could be bluffing,' then the one called Slim puts his gun to the sheriff's head again and says to him, 'Who is he, and don't bullshit me,

I have already killed one man today and one more won't make no difference to me, who is he? Then he hits him again across the face.

The sheriff says to him spitting out blood and teeth, 'Jed is right ...he is just a kid, sixteen years old ...but he is more man than the three of you put together' then Slim yells out to JJ 'Ok! we are coming out don't shoot' Jed looks at him and Slim says to him, 'If he is just a kid then he is bluffing, if the three of us go out not showing our guns he will be confused ...and if he is confused we can take him, simple ...like you Jed'

The three of them come out and stand side by side and when they moved their coats JJ can see they are still armed so he yells at them to drop their guns on the board walk. They just stand there doing nothing so JJ yells again, 'I said drop those guns on the floor or I start shooting'

A shot rings out and Jed drops dead to the floor then another and Rufus falls as well and smelly Slim dives for cover firing at JJ while he does so. JJ looks behind him and see's Flying Bear and his braves just sitting on horseback and laughing at him. JJ goes into the sheriff's office and finds Dan hurt but alive then he goes back into the street where two of Flying Bears men already has a grip on Slims arms.

Next moment Flying Bear is standing beside JJ saying to him, 'You want to kill this man; but I want ...to kill him ...more than you do...I know you ...want to ...kill me, and you have good ...reason ...but I make big mistake ...that ...day and this is ...something I ...regret to ...this day, we look for white ...men that rape ...and kill young ...Apache ...woman and her two young ...children, we not find them ...till now' JJ took the chance and said to him, 'Why did you not kill me that day? Flying Bear says to him, 'When I look at you ...I see ...myself... I know you ...hate Flying Bear ...as much as Flying Bear ...hate these white men ...that kill sister ...and her small ...children' JJ said to him 'But you killed my little sister and my mother and father, they did you no harm, why did you have to do that?' Flying Bear said in reply 'Flying Bear ...mighty angry, make big ...mistake that ...day ...braves also very ...angry they ...just shoot ...any ...white people ...they find,

Apache proud people ...admit mistake' the sheriff had come outside and heard everything that Flying Bear had said, and he said to JJ 'It takes more of a man to forgive than to go shooting his way through life, son, your father taught me that, and I know what he would do in this situation,'

JJ looked at Slim who now looked so dejected and said to Flying Bear,

'What about him?' Flying Bear replied, 'we take him ...back to place they kill ...sister and children, two miles from camp ...then let him reflect awhile as ...Apache women stick pine needles in him every time they pass...and then we ...kill him, he not good ...white man ...he must pay for ...what he did' when JJ saw the mayor and his beautiful daughter Emma and all the townsfolk coming close to see what all the commotion was about, he just said to Flying Bear 'Okay! The mayor was very impressed with JJ, as was his beautiful daughter Emma.

And the four of them walked back into the sheriff's office and shut the door behind them.

End

The Empty Skies

John -Johnny boy- Mulligan was a small farmer from Saggart in Co Dublin in the year 1990. He was thirty-eight years old. Blond hair and blue eyes and very good looking. And quite tall at 6-4. A lot of the local women fancied him, but John was not interesting in women since his wife died giving birth almost ten years to the day, leaving him with a mentally handicapped son called Sean. Between looking after Sean and the farm, John did not have too much time to spend with anyone else never mind the women.

Then one day totally exhausted he decided to end it all and late in the evening went into the lake on his land intending on drowning himself and be done with it. He was very very tired and wasn't thinking straight. And he was nearing the point of doing it too when a vison of his young son flashed across his mind. 'Social services will take care of him' he had thought as he entered the deepening waters. 'They will be able to look after him better that I ever could' he let himself go and down he went into the dark waters.

Death was very near to him when he felt something take his arm and shake it. He opened his eyes but could not see anyone or anything. There was nothing in the lake that could have shaken him like that. Nothing that he knew about or could see anyhow. Now he was awake and heading towards the surface. Thirty minutes had passed. He should not be here lying on the bank in the early hours of the morning. He should be dead, but he wasn't. The cold wet cloths made him get up and go home and when he had changed and had a hot mug of tea he went to bed and cried himself to sleep.

That sorry episode played heavy on his mind. One day, not long after, he decided to do something about it. He took flying lessons in a flight simulator in Swords. He loved it so much, so he went on to take to the skies.

It took him two years, but he finally passed and got his licence to fly a small light craft. Like one of the farmer's, he had seeing in a farmer's journal, using a small home-made plane to dust his crops with. He was going to be one of the first famers in Ireland to dust his crops by airplane.

An old green crop-duster called Betsy that someone had found in a barn somewhere and someone else with a knack for restoring old planes had put it together again. John loved the old dear as he called it and most days he could be seen flying the old girl above his farm and roundabout the area, some days he would take his son Sean with him but Sean with his condition could not take it in, and was left in the safe hands of his beautiful carer, Jenny, a lovely young lady with a soft spot for John and his son, so most days he flew alone. John had at last found a new life's purpose and it made all the difference.

He no longer felt guilty about his son or his wife's tragic death. He loved his son and took great care of him but now for different reasons to the ones before where he blamed himself for everything that had happened. Now as he glided gently through the soft clouds, he was happy once more and looking forward to his new life with literally his head in the clouds.

Then one evening whilst simply drifting in the air above his farm he passed through a light cloud and bumped into something. Startled he instinctively looked at his controls thinking that his old dear had hit a bird then from the corner of his right eye he saw something falling from beneath his plane. It was too big to be a bird.

Thinking that the old girl was about to fall apart he turned round and headed back to Baldonnel aerodrome where he found his old dear still in one piece. When he got home twenty minutes later the light was just beginning to fade but he had a quick look about to see what he had thought he'd seen falling from his little plane.

He found nothing and so called it a day. He would take a better, longer look in the morning. He was up early six am as per usual and when

Jenny came in about ten am he met her in the yard and told her about the bang on his plane the evening before and she said to herself she could see a major change in him but there was still a hardness there about him, and it was this hardness she was trying to get through. Please God she said to herself.

Let it be soon.

She said to him,

'What was it, a bird?' he replied saying, 'Don't think it was a bird, if it was, it was a big one, no, it wasn't a bird, it was not a drone either, it wasn't that kind of bang, it was a soft kind of bang if that makes any sense, and there was no damage to the old dear, at least none that I could see last night, I will take a another proper look at her today after I do what I have to round here.'

Later that morning with all his chores completed for the day and having kissed his son as before leaving as was his custom John went back to the aerodrome and gave the old dear a closer look. He could feel rather than see a small dent on the right-side wing, but it was very slight and did not cause him any worry.

Still, it did prove he had hit something all right. But what? He would have to go and take another closer longer look around his farm. This time he found what he had been looking for, or rather it found him.

'Are you looking for me?' came a gentle female voice, Startled, he looked around and saw a young lady laying behind some bushes, 'What, the hell, who… are you, are you okay? I mean are you the thing… oh… sorry… are you the person I hit last night? eh, up there, no… you can't be, of course not… silly me, how could you?' The young lady struggled to her feet and spread her wings full stretch. Shocked he just said to her,

'So!' he shouted. He was so excited he nearly wet himself, 'You are the thing… I mean the person… I… hit last night… with my… eh, my, crop…'

he didn't know what to say. She was so beautiful and charming and said to him, 'So! You are the one that flew into me whilst I was reclining on a cloud,' she stumbled a bit, so he ran to her side and put his arm around her waist and asked her, 'You are hurt? please, here, let me help you, you may need medical attention, here please, come to my house, it isn't far, only a few minutes across the road, I will phone for help for you there, sorry I just cannot get used to those mobile phone things…here put your arm around my shoulders, she did as he asked her to. A few minutes later they were in his sitting room. He lay her down on his sofa and got her some cool water to drink. Then he said to her,

'Where are you hurt girl? eh angel, is it your wing or what is it? show me where you are hurt, please' she tried to sit up and when she did, she took the water on offer and gulped it down.

Then she said to him, 'I am alright, I think I just bruised my wing, silly me, I just wasn't expecting to run into anything last night, I have been hanging out near that spot for months now and never… well, you have a saying here… do you not, always a first time for everything?' I should not have stayed around that area for so long, I never had before, or will again I guess,' he brought her a blanket as she seemed a little cold. Putting it round her shoulders he said to her, 'I have always believed in angels, but I never thought I would ever see one in my lifetime, and here beside me, Holy God, eh sorry, my name by the way is John, do you… have a name?' she replied to him in a heavenly voice, 'My name is Petra, I am from…' he cut her off saying, 'I know, ha… hah… from a Galaxy far… far… away' well he thought it was funny.

'Oh, you know it then! she said to him, He just smiled and said he did. That seemed to placate her. Something else was stirring inside him and it wasn't his inquisitive mind. She was so beautiful he could not take his eyes off her beautiful body.

He managed to say to her, 'So then… can you move your wings? see if they are in working order so to speak. She got to her feet and spread her wings and said to him, 'Yes, I can! It is still a little sore so I am not sure how far I could fly' he replied saying. 'You can rest here as long as you want to, I guess it will take a week or two for your arm …eh, wing to heal …but sure …there is no rush, is there? He made his way to the kitchen.

When he looked back at her she was sleeping like a baby in its mother's arms. He lifted her gently and brought her into the guest room where he laid her down gently and covered her with a blanket. He stood at the bedroom door just staring in amazement at how beautiful she was as she lay sleeping in a bed in his house. He marvelled at the wonder of it all and how lucky he was. He went to find Jenny and when he did, he told her all about the beautiful angel that was now sleeping in his guest room.

'What have you been drinking Johnny boy?' she said raising her hand and feeling his forehead, 'That stuff they put in those plane engines, an angel, hah …here …in your house, boy …that is a good one, the best I have heard yet …so it is' he took her by the hand and brought her to the guest bedroom, opened the door to let her see for herself. She crept slowly over to the bedside and had a look. Of course, she could not see Petra's wings. Moving back to John she said to him. You have lost your marbles oh… she is beautiful alright, but she is no an…' he stopped her and turned her back around to face the bed. There in all her glory with her wings fully stretched out was Petra. With the biggest smile on her face. Naked as a jaybird. John ran to cover her nakedness while Jenny just stood there speechless.

'I thought you said she was hurt, she doesn't look hurt to me,' she said to him over coffee in the kitchen. He smiled and said to her, 'She has hurt her wing, she will have to stay here for a week or so, till she recovers, as my old man used to say when ordering his second pint of Guinness, an angel never flew on one wing,'

'Well! if that is the case, she will need some clothes, we can't have her nursing her broken wing looking like that, and you can wipe that smile of your face Johnny-boy Mulligan,' he said to her still smiling.

'There are still some of my wife's clothes in her wardrobe, Jenny… maybe you will find something to fit her there, and I am only smiling thinking that you sounded a lot like my wife when I heired that young Ukrainian lady, what was her name? ah yes… Mira… Slavanovinski… or Slivinski…or something like that… beautiful she was… to look after the housework during my wife's pregnancy.'

Jenny said to him sternly, 'You can mention her name you know; it is not a sin,' before leaving the kitchen to search for some clothes.

When Jenny entered the guest bedroom Petra was already sitting on the side of the bed, fully dressed. 'Oh, good morning, did John find you some clothes?' the angel smiled and said to her, 'No, we, I, we, always adapt to whatever situation we find ourselves in, how are you today?' can I ask you a very personal question please? Jenny nodded and sat down on a chair beside the bed facing Petra. 'Are you and John in love?' Jenny shifted a little on the chair saying 'I can only answer half that question, yes, I do love him, but I am not too sure he loves me, he did have a wife…' Petra cut her off saying to her, 'Yes, I know about his past, but that is not what I asked you about, I am thinking more about right now and his future'

Jenny was surprised at hearing her say that but went on to say, 'He also has a son, Sean, an adorable little boy…' Again, Petra cut her off saying to her, 'I know also about Sean, and yes, he is an adorable child, but…' this time it was Jenny who cut her off saying to her, 'You know! for someone who has spent the last three days supposedly alone in this room, you seem to know a lot about this family, has John been pouring is heart out to you during the night?

Jenny nearly bit her tongue for saying something as stupid as that. She knew John was not that kind of man, but then again, he never met someone as stunningly beautiful as Petra before. She was not expecting the answer she got from Petra who said to her, 'My dear Jenny, relax, I am here to help John not to snatch him from you, if that is the right word, you see, he didn't bump into me, no, it was I who bumped into him,'

Jenny's mouth fell open and she could not believe what she was hearing Petra saying. It was true that Petra was and is an angel, she saw that much for herself, and it was also true that Petra was the most beautiful creature that she had ever seen, simply out of this world beautiful, now here she is telling her she came her of her own accord with some sort of heavenly plan to help John. After suddenly remembering a little about what her mother and grandmother had told her about angels coming down from heaven to save people all she could say to Petra was.

'I am listening, go on please' Petra said to her, 'I needed a way to meet John and I was sure if I just appeared to him out of the blue so to speak, it might be much more difficult for him to accept my help, so I thought of this plan,' she said spreading her wings up and down lifting her into the air before saying, 'and it seems to be working out just fine, what do you think? and if you don't mind me saying Jenny, he is very lucky to have such a beautiful friend like you' Jenny was almost speechless and Petra saw she was and she said to her,

'Come into the kitchen, I will make you a coffee that is 'literally' out of this world' then she took Jenny's hand and almost dragged her into the kitchen, giggling as they went, like two young sisters about to get up to mischief.

When they had finished their coffee Petra took Jenny's hands in her own and with elbows leaning on the kitchen table said to her, 'Do you believe in me?

Jenny could not help but say to her, 'I do, I do believe that you are sent from heaven, I do believe that, I do,'

Petra then kissed Jenny's hands and said to her, 'Then come with me and see a miracle in the making. Jenny was hesitant and Petra noticed this and said to her, 'Don't be afraid, there is nothing but love in this house, no hate, no jealousy, no bad emotions of any kind, so you have no need to fear, come let us go into Sean's room and see for yourself what love can do'

'But… but!' Petra put her finger on her lips and said to her 'No ifs or buts, no negativity, seeing is believing, relax and believe in the power of love, now you lead the way please'

Jenny still hand in hand led her into Sean's room. The child was still sleeping even thought it was well into the morning.

Petra sat in a chair at the window which was by the child's head. While Jenny sat on the end of the child's bed. Sean's eyes opened when he felt the pressure of Jenny sitting on his bed. Jenny helped him to sit up and made him comfortable. Sean managed to look at Petra as she touched his hair, but he could not quite turn his head. He knew she was there though. He looked at Jenny with fear in his eyes wondering what was going on. She said to him gently. 'It is okay honey, I just brought someone very special to meet you, it that okay darling… her name is Petra, and she is here to help you, if she can!' Petra looked at her sternly and said to Sean, 'Hello Sean, do you mind if I hold your hand? You father tells me it is your birthday tomorrow, he is such a nice man that loves you dearly as does Jenny here,' Jenny knew that the poor child wasn't taking anything in but could see he was totally relaxed and very comfortable with Petra holding his hand and gently rubbing the back of his palm. It looked as if he had falling back into a deep sleep. Then softly and calmly he opened his eyes, that were much bluer than normal… he smiled at Jenny and said to her softly, 'Beautiful Jenny' and sat himself up further in the bed.

Then he turned and looked at Petra and said to her, 'Beautiful Petra' then he moved his legs and Jenny just burst into tears, 'Don't cry Jenny,' he says then leans over to the little locker beside his bed and took a soft tissue from its pocket and handed it to her saying, 'Here Jenny… don't cry please, here… dry your tears,' Jenny looked at Petra with an abundance of love in her eyes, then went to hug her saying to her, 'Thank you so much for what you are doing to this lovely child, you have given him the best birthday present ever, though what I am going to tell his father when he comes home is beyond me,'

Petra said to her still hugging her, 'You don't have to tell him anything, my beautiful friend, he is standing right behind you listening to every word been said' Jenny turned around to see John coming into the room in tears and going straight to his son who said to him, 'Daddy Jenny was crying, like you are now, why is everybody sad? His father put his arms around him, and Jenny put her arms around John, and they were both in floods of tear as Sean hugged them back and said to them, 'Petra' and when they looked at the chair where she had been sitting there was no one there, just a small white feather gently moving with all the air now been circulating in the room. Then all three bawled some more.

End

Brothers

Identical twins Tommy and Johnny Byrne had nine other brothers but these two were the elders of the bunch. Johnny was a very timid youth while his big brother was anything but timid. They also had seven sisters. With Tommy the meanest and hardest of the twins, and with good reason for whatever happened in the area between the other lads it had to be Tommy Byrnes fault and he usually got a beating depending on the mood of the top youth involved. Kenny Jones was his name, and is gang were called the animal gang with good reason. Kenny was cruel and reckless and did not care a toss about anyone but himself.

This constant chasing and hitting him had the effect of making Tommy tough and hardened and it was not long before it is he, that was handing out the pain and punishment. It happened when Tommy was twelve years old, and Kenny had been trying to pick a one-on-one fight with him. Tommy tried his best to avoid that and many a time he had to find another route home. Then of course the day came when he could not do this on account of Kenny standing right in front of him blocking his path.

Tommy was a tall lad for his age, as was his brother Johnny the same red hair and freckles maybe five-seven or eight, six and a half stone but he was wiry and stubborn and once he made his mind up then look out because he was like a bull in the proverbial China-shop and Kenny did not stand a chance against him, the thing was Kenny thought that he was fighting Johnny the milder of the two brothers, the one he had beaten so many times before even if he had a gang of mischiefs around him in case anything went wrong, that was how much of a bully and coward he really was, and so here he was once again thinking he was going to beat him easily too not knowing it was Tommy the other twin he was facing not Johnny, and Tommy beat Kenny almost senseless.

Kenny did not know what hit him and when the dust settled, he was no longer the leader of the gang. Tommy could have been but for the fact that he was a loner and did not like to be at others disposal, in any case he despised the gang and everything they stood for. A few days later Tommy was set upon by three of the lads looking for a reputation, but Tommy left them in a heap on the footpath so anyone thinking of doing the same would think again. And they did.

He was even approached by a big brother of one of the lad's he had beaten fair and square, but when the big brother saw Tommy picking up a rock and putting it into the palm of his right hand and standing there to face him, he backed off.

The word soon spread among the boys that Tommy Byrne was one boyo to be avoided and even the cops got to hear about him. One police officer even tried to get Tommy channelling his energies through the boxing ring, but Tommy Byrne was having none of it.

Then the day came when a body was found by the canal and was so savagely beaten and only one name came to the fore. Tommy Byrne, and there was one witness, but Tommy had nothing to do with it but could not prove to the cops where he had been for the past week until he came up with an idea. If he could find out the precise time that the young man died, he may be lucky enough to persuade his brother to come forward and pretend to be him, because he did, unlike his brother Tommy, have an alibi and it could and did work, the cops had to let Tommy off the hook, until now they had no idea about his twin brother, but all that was about to change, when some friends of the dead mans decided to take matters into their own hands and beat young Johnny so badly he spent six weeks in intensive care.

They did not know about his twin brother either as the two brothers were seldom seen outside together.

When Tommy got the word about his brother been nearly killed, he went straight to the hospital where the doctors let him in to see his brother but only very briefly. He spoke openly to his brother and swore vengeance on the gang that beat him so badly and that he would make every one of them paid dearly for what they had done to his little brother. His little brother that would not hurt a fly.

It was not clear if little Johnny heard Tommy's words but the guy in the next bed heard every one of them. When Tommy had gone, he called in the police officer standing outside and told him everything he had heard Tommy say.

The officer then relayed all the information he had just received to his station sergeant who then passed it on to his Superior that put a tail on Tommy and soon a whole swat team were on Tommy's trail. Following from a safe distance.

They followed him into a bar then waited while Tommy went inside to challenge the gang. Tommy was furious and started swinging in all directions and just as the fight was beginning the Swat team went in shouting 'Armed officers, nobody move!' but one of them did move and pulled out a gun and started shooting and soon the whole place was filled with bullets flying everywhere.

When the gunfight ended there were dead bodies lying all over the place; including two police officers the five men that beat Tommy's brother Johnny, one badly wounded customer and Tommy Byrne, who took two bullets to the chest and died in the same hospital ward as his brother.

Two weeks later Johnny Byrne still recovering in ICU unit in hospital was told the shocking news. He sat up in bed and let out a scream that made every one that heard it very fearful. And the meek and mild little brother was meek and mild no longer.

End

Best of Friends

Patrick and Michael were the best of friends. Had been since childhood. Like brothers they were. Even worked together at the main sorting office in Dublin's City. They even lived in the same area in Tallaght Dublin 24. Though they worked different shifts they always met each other either coming in to work or going home.

Patrick's father was a long-distance lorry driver while Micks father owned a small but busy taxi service in Tallaght, a sprawling suburb on the outskirts of the city at the foot of the Dublin mountains with a population of over eighty thousand souls. They even played pitch and putt together every weekend at the nearby Bohernabreena pitch and putt club near the local cemetery, and often took long walks together to pass the time.

Their wives also great friends for years were extremely glad to get the lads out from under their feet. Mary was Pats wife and Wendy was Micks wife and like the two boys got on like a house on fire. Mary had three children two boys and a girl, well they were adults now of course, while Wendy also had two boys and a girl now also adults. Mary's kids were called oddly enough Patrick and Michael and the girl was called Wendy while Wendy's children were called Michael and Patrick while the girl was called Mary. That is how close they all were.

Now of course they, Pat and Mick were both past their retirement age and in their spare time used to visit the beautiful but now defunct Hellfire club. An ancient ruin where it was said some of the locals used to go play poker with the devil himself. Of course, they did not know it was the devil until one of the players dropped a card and when he bent down to pick it up, he was horrified to see the devil had hoofs instead of feet. Hence the name, Hellfire Club. Suffice to say, he got out of there quick, and the rumours spread like wildfire.

As per usual the two men who looked remarkably like each other they could and often had been taken for brothers, would call into the Mill pub for lunch every Sunday. To give the girls a break and have time out for themselves. The girls were invited but would rather spend the time going through the local shops in Blessington which was only a short hop up the road.

This became the norm of the weekend, but it was one that all concerned enjoyed. Like the lads Mary and Wendy loved being with each other and especially spending the men's hard-earned dosh. Though they were never left short of anything they always had a good laugh about that and if one or the other saw an item that they liked, then money was no object. And so, after the game of pitch and putt in which Mick was nearly always the winner the lads sat down to eat a hearty meal of roast beef with all the trimmings, washed down by a nice glass of red wine. It was during the sharing of this meal that Pat turned to Mick and said to him 'I have a confession to make to you bud,' Mick knowing his best friend only too well said to him 'Oh! And what would that be Pat? You are not going to like it' Pat said to him, and Mick replied saying 'Sounds ominous, but go ahead, and don't tell me you have been sleeping with my wife; ha …ha …hah' Pat blushed but did not laugh he just said, 'You know me so well buddy, I have been sleeping with your wife, at least five times' Mick slightly taken aback said to his best friend, 'how long has this been going on then?' Pat took a sip of wine then said to his best buddy 'Since Michael was born, sorry buddy… it just happened one night while you were on the late shift' Mick shifted on his seat and said, 'and Patrick, And Mary? Pat looked him in the eye and simply said, 'yes! sorry'

Mick said to him, 'So! for at least six years you have been sleeping with my wife?' Pat replied, 'Just on and off bud… maybe twice a year' the Mick said to him,

And can you answer this question? 'Who do you think paid for your three fabulous sea cruises on the Mediterranean within a few weeks after each of my beautiful children were born? Pat said to him whilst scratching his head,

'That was you, I was wondering where Mary got the money, she said it was a credit union loan, well fancy that, you have known all this time'

Mick said to him, 'I could not have children Paddy, my sperm count was far too low, so one day I said to Wendy, go out and find yourself someone you like and do the business with him, I won't hold it against you, and when I found out that it was you holding it against her, well I was really pleased, because it meant she wasn't going to leave me for someone else, so relax pal, you're in the clear, here, have another glass of wine, I need to go take a pee'

Meanwhile the two ladies were enjoying their day out in the luxury Plaza Hotel. They had become lovers over the years and were having a great time in bed together, truly the best of friends.

End

Little Mary

Young Mary Mac Killen had been born just five pounds-five ounces. Small but she was not suffering from dwarfism. She slowly put on weight, but her mother Bridget knew instinctively that her little girl was 'different' not as she should be and told any doctor that would listen her fears and worries. Yet they could find nothing wrong with the little girl. Her mother's fears never ceased not even when Mary celebrated her tenth birthday.

The child was sent to this doctor and that doctor and had dozens of X-rays taken but still nothing could be found that would allay her mother's fears. Soon the medical people were looking at Mary's mother.

Did she have something wrong with her? She was checked out, but nothing could be found wrong with her either. Even the father's medical history was investigated but again nothing could be found. Marys two sisters Brenda and Lucy. Nothing. Mary was a quiet beautiful mannered child, not timed or weak or anything like that, just a little bit different from the other children she played around with. Still her mother's concerns continued.

Then one day her mother was upstairs tiding her bedroom when she looked out the window and saw Mary playing with her little dog Pronto and the dog ran out onto the road and Mary ran after it and her mother could see this car come speeding down the road, but it was too late to even yell at Mary.

The car hit young Mary full on and her mother screamed then in the blink of an eye Mary was standing at the other side of the road unharmed and calm. Her mother nearly had a heart attack as she ran down to her daughter and when she got downstairs her daughter was sitting in the kitchen just like she had never even been outside, drinking orange juice.

'How did you get in here so fast?' she said hugging her little girl. Mary just shrugged her shoulders and said to her mum. 'Oh, I just thought about my drink and here I am!' her mother was taken aback and said to her.

'And how did you manage to dodge that car, I mean I saw it plough into you?' 'Same thing mum, I just thought about it and there I was standing on the pathway looking at the car drive past, simple really, and fun,' her mother was just so relieved that her little girl was okay, and she hugged her tightly even more.

Of course, Bridget told her husband Dermot what had happened when he got home from his job, a supervisor in postal sorting office in Dublin town.

He said to her whist kissing the side of her face. 'You always did have an active imagination and a weird sense of expression, darling, thank God our little one missed that speeding car with that lunatic driver people like that should be taken off the road and never be allowed to drive again' Bridget knew the reaction she would get from her husband, so she did not argue the point with him. He was like all those medical people that just would not believe her when she told them her daughter did not seem right to her. Still no matter; all is well, it could easily have been so much worse. Two days later while walking in Saint Ann's Park with her three girls and their dog Pronto coming near the lake when the dog noticed something near the base of a large tree and went to investigate. It was a young fledgling that had fallen from its nest midway up the large birch tree.

'No Pronto, no, do not frighten it! Mary said running to the little bird's aid. Her mother ran too but the other two girls went straight to the lake to feed the ducks as they always did when in the park on days like this. Mary took up the little bird and looking up was lifted to where the nest was in the tall tree and placed the chick back in the nest and was down again while her mother just stood there watching the whole thing in awe. She was almost traumatised but not quite.

'Mary darling …how did you do what you just did? I mean I just saw what you did but how did you do that? Mary replied saying to her mum,

'I just thought about it mum and there I was doing it, now I am glad we came here, otherwise that little baby bird might have been eaten by a dog, or a seagull, let's go feed the ducks and swan's mum' she took her mother's hand and led her to her sisters who had already used up all the bread. Bridget marvelled at the wonderful gift her daughter seemed to have been given. Little did she know then that her little girl would go on to do such wonderful things before her short life would be ended. That very same afternoon coming home from the walk in the park an incident occurred, involving a pit-bull breed and a smaller dog.

The pit-bull savaged the small terrier type dog and when little Mary saw what was happening, she went straight for the pit-bull, the pit-bull stopped what it was doing and just looked at her sheepishly.

'Naughty bad dog, go home and do not touch another dog on the way, you horrible big bully, no … I changed my mind …stay there!' the pit-bull did not move an inch it just stayed still with its head hung low, its owner and the terrier's owner and little Mary mother watched on in wonder, as little Mary picked up the badly bitten little Yorkshire terrier dog, stroked it, said something to it then kissed its forehead and when she set it down again, the dog was perfect.

Not a sign of any attack and the pit-bull even came up close and licked the terriers face. Anyone who saw what had happened and a good few people did, were amazed at what little Mary had done. They even applauded the young girl, much to her childish and innocent embarrassment. All watching also experienced a feeling of well-being.

Bridget Mac Killen was a from a good catholic family. She had been brought up to love her neighbours. She never did anyone a bad turn and would not hesitate to do a good one. So, it was no surprise then that she went and spoke to her parish priest about her daughter Mary. Fr Ben Collins from Clonakilty.

A middle-aged man with more than his fair share of white hair on his head and face as mentioned above from County Cork. He listened attentively as she told him all that she had seen her little girl do. He said to her gently 'from what you have just told me Bridget, there is nothing wrong with little Mary, on the contrary it seems to me that there is something very right about her, I have spoken to her on occasions and she seems like an ordinary intelligent little girl, now if you want me to talk to her again, you can bring her here or I can come and visit your home, in light of what you have told me today I would most certainly like to speak with her again,' she invited him to her home saying to him 'you do remember where I live, father?

He replied, 'of course I do my dear, you live in Elm House in oh, what's it called again? Kiltalawn right, in… let me see …now …apartment …13 …don't you, or have you moved? She said to him, 'No Father and yes I am still there, father … but I am in apartment 3 and you are more than welcome to visit us anytime' they shook hands, and she left him attending to another of his parishioners.

That same night Bridget went to look in on her three sleeping children. The first two Brenda and Lucy were sleeping soundly but when she got to Marys room there was no sign of her in the bed.

Puzzled she looked here and there still no sign of little Mary until the young girl said to her, 'hello mum,' she was 'resting' on the ceiling and her mother fell onto the bed with fright. 'Sweet Jesus and His Blessed Mother, protect us, what are you doing up there!' little Mary came floating down and lay on her bed 'just hanging around,' she joked, her mother still shaken said to her, 'Don't be scaring me like that darling, I could have had a heart attack or something, where did you learn to do that Mary?

'Oh, I just thought it would be fun! and it is fun, mum you should try it sometimes' her mother asked her, 'can you do things like that anytime darling? Little Mary just floated up to the ceiling saying to her mum,

'Yes, I can mum, as many times as I like …would you like to take my hand and try it too?' her mother declined saying, 'I am a little too heavy to be floating around the place darling, no thanks, my floating days are long gone, try get some sleep now child, you have to be up early for school in the morning,' she kissed and covered little Mary with a duvet saying, 'I love you little one so much' and Mary replied saying, 'I love you too mummy' then closed her eyes and within seconds was fast asleep. Bridget did not go to sleep easily but spent most of the night in prayer.

On the following Monday her good friend and neighbour Wendy Richards was found to be ill in bed. She hadn't turned up at the school with her daughter Rachel. She told Bridget her mum could not get out of bed that morning, 'Is the spare key in the same place?' Bridget asked her and she said it was.

So, Bridget called in on the way home and true enough found her dear friend Wendy in bed with some type of flu like symptoms. She made her drink a glass of water and said to her, 'Will I call Dr Conlon for you Wendy?' he'll be going home in an hour or so,' Wendy said to her, 'I will rest up today Bridget, and see how I feel in the morning, it is probably just a head cold or something like that, Rachel will be home in a few hours, she is old enough now to look after herself so she will be okay,' Wendy looked very tired and Bridget was slightly worried about her but said to her, 'Alright love, you have my number if you need anything before then, and sure I will come back around straight after school, is that okay?' Wendy said it was and went back to sleep. It was twenty past three when Wendy's daughter Rachel rang furiously on Bridget's doorbell. When Bridget answered the door, she found her friends little girl in a very nervous state, 'I …I…can't wake my mother up! she was crying, 'I have been trying for ages, please Bridget can you come and try, please can you come now please?'

Ten minutes later Bridget was beside her best friend Wendy's bed. She looked like she was sleeping but there was no sign of life and Bridget was just about to call an ambulance when little Mary and her friends Rachel came into the room. Bridget did not want the children to see a dead person so soon in their young lives and was just about to usher them out of the room when Mary approached the bed and held Wendy's hand and whispered something soft and gentle into Wendy's right ear. Wendy's eyes opened and she said she was thirsty and Bridget in amazement gave her a glass of water that she took and slowly drank it all down.

If Bridget had not seen and heard it with her own eyes and ears, she would never have believed it. Little Mary just took her young friend's hand and led her out of the room saying, 'It's okay now Rachel, your mum is fine, let us go into the garden and play in the treehouse, with Barbie and Ben'

Wendy was sitting up now and talking to Bridget like she did yesterday. Only this time there was no head cold or anything wrong with her at all. Bridget asked her what Mary had whispered into her ear. 'She told me I was going to be alright and that I was to wake up and let Rachel see me waking up.'

This! thought Bridget, has to be told to Father Ben. This, thought Bridget, is a miracle. This; thought Bridget, is going to shake the world, our world.

The following morning Fr Ben Collins listened eagerly to every word that Bridget told him. When she had finished, she thought that he would come to the same conclusion as she did. She was disappointed. 'Do you have any medical training, Bridget?

Have you ever done CPR on anyone?' her answer to both his questions was no, 'But' she said to him, 'I know a dead person when I see one Father,

And my friend Wendy Richards was dead, and my little Mary brought her back to life, I know she did,' Fr Ben raised his right hand and said to her 'See there you go again! getting all emotional just thinking about it, I am not saying what you said to me just now in your mind anyhow did not happen, it's just that the church demands, and I do not like that word, but the church demands proof of any such thing before it gives its approval, otherwise certain people, we will mention no names but you know whom I am speaking about, would be raising whole cemeteries all over the place, now let us be calm and controlled about this, less than one hour ago that woman you claimed was dead and brought back to life was sitting in my confessional box telling me her life story, now please Bridget, how am I to accept what you have just told me? She said to him, 'I told you because I thought you cared, I told you and not the church Father Ben, but if you don't believe me then that is your problem, not mine' then she got up and left him sitting there looking mystified.

She could see his point of view and had to admit when she told him was exceptional to say the least. As she made the short distance home, she went over and over what had happened that previous afternoon in Wendy Richards bedroom and came to the same conclusion that her best friend and near neighbour Wendy Richards had died and that her little daughter Mary had indeed brought her back to life.

Later that evening Fr Ben called around to see little Mary. He was brought in and made to feel welcome and had a coffee before asking to see Mary alone. Bridget did not mind that in the slightest and was in fact glad that he did.

She left them to talk it out in the sitting room and she went into the kitchen to chat with her husband while the two girls Brenda and Lucy were in the study doing their homework.

'I mean it is hard to believe darling' Dermot said to his wife, 'and if anyone came to me with a tale like that, I would be wondering what they were on, it just doesn't happen these days,'

Bridget said to him, 'That does not mean it can't happen, I have seen it happen, I was there watching it happen, your little girl, made it happen,' he took her hand kissed it then said, 'Okay my love I believe you, even if no one else will, we both knew she was very special the day she was born, you always felt that, remember? all those doctors you brought her too, she is special, and now here we are and here and now she is raising people from the dead, if this gets out she will have to leave school, we will have to move house, there will be hundreds if not thousands of strangers out there in front of our house, wanting to be healed' while he paused to catch his breath Bridget said to him, 'you think I haven't thought of all that stuff? I know what it means, and will mean for us as a family, we might even have to leave the country and go abroad, but it is what it is, it is not my fault that she is gifted the way she is, what are you saying, that we should hide her gift?'

'Look' he said taking and kissing her hand again, 'It has only happened once, let us wait and see how this gift develops if indeed it does, then we will see how things go okay babe? no point in making plans until we know what plans to make' as they were kissing little Mary came into the room, 'Everything okay Mary?' her mother asks, and she said it was and that Father Ben said he would like another mug of your very nice coffee. Then to her mother she says, 'I'm going to my room mum, to do my homework' Bridget hugged her and kissed the top of her head and said to her, 'Okay darling, you go ahead, I will look in on you later, okay?' the priest said to her,

'The reason I came round today to see you and little Mary, by the way, she does know that is what people call her, doesn't she? Her mother nodded her head, The priest smiled then continued saying, 'I was in school yesterday when I overheard some girls talking in the corridor about some dog fight in the park the other day, and when I questioned them about it one of them showed me a video of the fight she had taken on her phone, it truly was a savage attack and what little Mary did was also truly remarkable to say the least, it is true what you told me and I am sorry for not shown more of an interest,

Having saw what she did at that dog fight myself, it would be wise to make a diary of such things you know, for whatever lies ahead, as I say I have spoken to her and she has a wonderful personality and is a beautiful child and truthful in her speech and everything she does, I asked her if she ever did anything like this before and she said yes but did not go into detail, she really is quite remarkable, such knowledge is rare in most children of her age, you must be really very proud of her, and her sisters, Brenda and Lucy, have they shown any similarities to little Mary?'

Bridget replied to him saying, 'No Father, they have not! and I don't honestly expect them too, they are just normal young girls, and I don't mean Mary is not normal but you know what I mean,' He said to her, 'Of course I do Bridget and remember to keep notes of anything she does from here on in, I will talk to one of my colleagues about her if you have no objections, he is deep into such things as these, thank you for your hospitality and wonderful coffee, and I will let myself out, thank you very much Bridget. I will see you soon bye'

Little did Bridget know she would be seeing Father Ben sooner that she thought.

The very next morning she went to wake Little Mary, she found her unresponsive in her bed. Frantic with worry she called for an ambulance and when it came the first responder could not wake her either and they brought her off to the hospital where she was pronounced dead. At the hospital Father Ben came and tried to console Bridget who by now had worn herself out with worry. 'What happened Bridget! I mean, I was talking to her only yesterday as you know, what happened do you know?

Bridget could not stop crying. Wendy and Rachel, her daughter where there and giving Bridget their full support.

A litter later when the panic subdued somewhat and people were standing or sitting around where they could in small groups in the hospital corridor, Bridget got to talking to Wendy's daughter Rachel who said to her, 'I am so sorry Mrs Mac Killen, I am going to miss little Mary so much,' she began crying so Bridget gave her a hug saying, 'We all are Rachel, her whole family, her school friends and her best friends like you and your mother, thank you for being her friend, I know she was very fond of you' Rachel was weeping bitter tears and Bridget said to her, 'Don't cry Rachel please she would not want to see you so upset,' Rachel stopped weeping and said to her, 'Bridget, remember when you asked me what Mary had whispered to my mother that time she was real sick,?' Bridget replied,

'Yes, I do …why do you bring that up now dear' and Rachel replied, 'Well I did not tell you all of it, I'm sorry, it didn't' seem important at the time…'

Bridget said to her, 'What was it she said then? I mean you told me she asked your mum to let you see her wake up, that is what I remember you said'

'Yes', said the young girl, 'but there was something else she said after that…' Bridget said to her hesitantly, 'What was that girl? come on tell me, don't be afraid' Rachel lowering her head said to her, 'she said,

'And I will take your place!' that was what she said, and I will take your place' the two of them were left standing there sobbing and hugging each other.

End

Song Contest

After the terrible news of their three school friends dying in a car crash the pupils of St Michaels Secondary School were left in shock and dismay. Two of them Toby Lobos, and Trish Lovaris both of whom were not only friends but neighbours in the small town of Winston- by- the- Sea, off the English coast. They were Spanish but came here every year to continue their English education, both were sixteen years old and while they were not a couple Toby and Trish had strong feelings for each other.

In other words, they did not have sex, yet. Tony was your typical young student with a mass of dark black hair and a fine physic and five-seven or eight in height while Trish was a beautiful young woman and of comparable size and age but with breasts that made many a man water at the mouth. She also had a wonderful smile and sense of humour for one so young. Toby was sitting on the beach staring out to sea on the Saturday morning after the terrible crash when Trish happened along, she did not approach him right away because he was singing a beautiful song and she did not want to interrupt him. It was a sad song and one that showed the mood he was in.

When she did approach him, he was happy to see her and when they kissed each other's cheek he felt a great sadness coming from her, so he said to her, 'Ola, Trish …you too eh!' I know what happened to that family was incredibly sad, and very upsetting and I feel so helpless, but we just must accept that they have gone, and that we will see them in class no more' he had a tear fall as he said this, and she noticed and said to him, 'Ola, Toby, or not to be eh, sorry… yes, it is, very sad and I heard someone mention that they were a …how you say …eeh …luchando'

'Struggling' Toby replied to her saying, 'We are all struggling Trish, maybe if we had a collection for them or some sort of garage sale, we could raise some money to help send them home'

She moved in closer to him and said almost in his face, 'I have been thinking and I have an idea, a …a…concurso de canciones' Toby laughed and said, 'a song contest' and how will that help anyone? She replied if we can get someone to eh …patrocinador, eh …sponsor it, we could spread the word and other people could join in, that way we can lift our spirits and make money for them at the same time, what do you eh …decir eh, …think?

He replied saying to her, 'I think that is a great idea, of how to lift our spirits but how do we make money from it' she said to him 'We can have a wonderful eh …primer premo…eh …first prize'

'Great' he replied, 'and who can we get to sponsor this great prize? she said to him the whole town is eh… …conmocionado…how you say in English …shocked, they will be extremely happy to help us, Si? He was getting excited as it was beginning to sink in as he said to her, 'YES, it might work, we can print off a few flyers and see how it goes, it might work girl and we already have a few musicians in the class, yes …it will work, we will make it work,' then to his and her surprise he kissed her on the lips.

The school principal was so in favour of their plan to raise funds for the family of the pupils that died so horrendously that he even advocated getting some prominent politicians involved. They all loved the limelight.

Meanwhile at the same time one prominent politician was himself been informed of the contest and having spoken out on many an occasion about the dangers of drink driving was given according to his secretary an opportunity too good to be missed. 'With the elections coming soon in November and with your record on the dangers of drink driving minister… here with this song contest …and with you participating in said contest by means of a donation to a wonderful cause of charity …anonymously of course, though I will myself accidentally let your good name slip in good time for the elections to someone in the know in the press, what do you think minister?

Minister John Mac Callie agreed wholeheartedly with his secretary. 'Most splendid idea James, but how much are we talking about here?' his secretary replied saying to him, '10,000 euros sir …but of course it is tax deductible, and it will help in you keeping your seat, sir, so over all a small price to pay, and the good will …it will create …don't you think sir?

'Mmmmm,' said the minister, 'quite so James …quite so, and it might even help that grandson of mine, you know the one with that gruesome rock band …oh …what are they called now, …ah …yes, the … pig …no …the ponytails, terrible name for a terrible band what…but it would also help my brother to know I am looking after his only son… by letting him enter and win this contest, while he is abroad yes, jolly good show James …set the ball rolling will you, there's a good chap'

Trish was so excited when she heard they had found a sponsor that she positively was on cloud nine when she met up with Toby again later that day, 'We have found a sponsor' she told him almost jumping into his arms, 'and guess how much money will be raised get this, 10,000 euros …that is, 10,000 euros isn't that just brilliant,' Toby holding her by her waist and pulling her closer to him said to her, 'it sure is a lot of money, but we will have to decide how many contestants and how many prizes there will be, but there is enough for everyone to get something, as they will all have to put in a great effort and do we even know what kind of song contest it will be? I mean we don't want a karaoke show, now do we.

She pulled away saying, 'No! we most certainly do not …let us get the school board involved, that way everything will be above board and we can concentrate on your entry'

'Whoa!' He bawled out loud, 'My entry …who said I was going to enter? I am not a singer, I don't play any instrument …or anything, so how can I enter girl?

She replied to him saying, 'But you are a beautiful singer darling' it was the first time she called him darling, and he liked it, but he went on to say to her, 'I am not a singer, eh …darling, and we don't even know what format the contest will take, for example, will all the songs be in Spanish, or a mixture of all contestants?

She replied saying to him, 'That will be up to the organisers, Toby …and you are a wonderful singer, you could even write a special song for the show, I am not saying you'll win or anything but at least you will have done something for those poor souls who perished in that car fire, they were our classmates' then as an afterthought she said, 'and we already have a kind of band with Micky …Manuel, Spikey, and John on drums and we will get others to be the backing singers, oh Toby …it's going to be such fun, can't you just see and feel it …all those people on stage …the sets …the lights …the music, it is going to be the best ever, I can feel it …I can really feel it, can't you?'

'Well! he said taking her hand in his, 'When you put it like that …yeah, I can actually …it will be great and exciting to say the least, okay …let us get the others together and see what we can come up with'

Two hours later they were back together again in Toby's place, and he took up a page from the coffee table and blushing he handed it to Trisha saying, 'look …I know it has only been an hour or so but here…I wrote this, what do you think?' she smiled at him took the piece of paper and read what it said,'

What do I do now (Toby's Song) for contest

What do I do now?
That you have gone, and left me here… all on my own,
I don't understand, …I thought I was your man,
What do I do…now…without you?

What do I tell my friends? what can I say? That all good things…must come to an end,

But how am I …to start again?
How do I tell my heart…to live…without you?

Chorus

What do I see? what does the future… hold for me?
Will I be on my own? …till I am an old man, …without a home …or family,
I never thought this could be true,
Living my life… without you…

What do I do now? you've moved away,
Nothing to do, …no words to say,
This just ain't right, …I can't sleep at night,
What do I do …without you?

She looked at him then back to the paper. He said to her, 'I can change some of the words, I mean if you think I should!

She grabbed him and kissed him and said to him, 'It is wonderful, and so meaningful darling …and it says so much about our friends that have gone away, oh you caught the mood exactly…I think it is absolutely lovely, but can I hear it please, sing it for me now darling …I am sure it is positively brilliant'

So, he did, and when he finished singing, she was weeping gently. He said to her while kissing her hand, 'hey now, don't do that …please babe …I don't want people to cry over it' But she said to him,

'I think it is wonderful song and when we have music and backing singers it will be hard to beat, you sing it from the heart darling …and it shows …it has giving me goosebumps, it is fantastic' He said to her holding her in his arms, 'hey …now …don't be giving me a big head girl, you sound as if I have won already'

She kissed him on the lips and said, 'You have won my heart with that song darling …and in my book you're already a winner'

A week later and after many attempts the song began to take shape and it was truly a good sound and everyone that heard it said it was great song and sure to be in the top five best songs of the evening if it did not win it outright, even Johnny Ponytail the ministers grandson, came up to them and clapped his hands saying how good the song was and wished them luck. They could not stay too long in rehearsal as they were too many acts that had to practice and only had two weeks to do it.

Minister Mac Callie gave his secretary James a small bottle of mineral water to put as he put it on Toby's locker the evening of the contest. In case he gets thirsty before the show. A nod and a wink then continued saying,

'Just a little added precaution, you know to help my grandson win this concert, oh, don't look at me like that James, it won't harm the lad, just make his speech a little incoherent here and there, remember …what we talked about last time, when I asked you to go to some of your sleezy mates and fine a little something to make the lad a little dozy,

And what did you say to me, that 'I' am the only 'SLEEZY' person you know, hah- hah and my reply to you was, 'YOUR FIRED' ha- ha- ha- you should have seen your face, ha-ha-hah priceless, it was' now where was I?

Oh yes! it won't hurt the young lad and might help win this contest for Tony Pony Pigtails or whatever he calls himself these days, now away you go and make sure no one sees you put it there'

James was able to come and go as he pleased as every board member knew that his boss was the one who put up that vast amount of the prize money, so he knew it would be no problem getting into Toby's room on the night. He also knew that his boss would not dare give him anything to physically hurt Toby, it would wreck his chances if it ever came out of him been re-elected not to mention the fact that he himself would lose his wonderful cosy job besides, he may even be given a bonus.

The night before the contest Trisha was over in Toby's apartment going over the song repeatedly as she would now be one of the backing singers. She was doing a fine job of it to and when Toby mixed up some of his lines, she said to him, 'It is okay darling, you are just all tensed up, as soon as you get on stage, those nerves will leave you and you will be great, don't worry, they say if you are not nervous then there is something wrong with you' Toby got up and went into the kitchen for a drink of mineral water and as he was raising the bottle to his lips she came up behind him, put her arms around his waist and said 'Of course, I know another way to ease those tensions, darling, shall we go into the bedroom? Toby blushed and said, 'Oh you do ...do you ...and how do you know these things ...have you been practising more than this song, and if so with whom?'

She laughed as she took his hand and led him to the bedroom where she took her top of then her bra, revealing her beautiful breasts with her nipples standing firmly to attention.

Then she came forward and began stripping him saying, 'Take off my skirt and my panties darling, don't leave me to do all the seducing, then reaching her hand down and feeling his manhood said naughtily to him, 'mmmmmm ...but you are a big naughty boy, and she went down on him.

They spent the night together making love, sleeping shorts spells then making love again. This went on all through the night, and they fell into a deep sleep just as the sun began to rise over the sleepy little town.

Johnny Ponytails came up to Toby as the place was beginning to fill up. It was a large hall that could fit fifteen hundred and fifty people all paying ten-euro admission fee. Johnny said to Toby, 'I wish you luck man, do not be worrying so ...you will do well,' Toby thanked him and said to him, 'You're the one I am worrying about, if anyone should win, it should be you'

The Johnny said to him, 'Look don't ask me any questions but do not drink from any can or bottle that you don't open yourself, a little bird tells me that there may be jealously afoot so make sure you take precautions, in this business nothing surprises me, so good luck and take care, may the best song win' and they shook hands, and promised no hard feeling whomever wins, or loses.

The first three songs went well enough but there was no x factor in any of them. Then it was Toby, and his bands turn. A few seconds into the song and one could hear a pin drop as the whole community was holding their breath in admiration and awe at the wonderful song. The backing singers were positively wonderful in their harmonising and delivery and presentation was very professional all-round. When the song ended everyone stood up and clapped for ages.

Then another four songs that followed were sung beautifully but again had no impact on the listeners. Then it was Johnny's turn and as soon as his band started playing the intro Toby knew that it was going to be hard to beat but as he knew his song went down well, he was not of a mind to begrudge Johnny his due.

As soon as Johnny began singing people started clapping to the beat and stomping their feet. A few even got up and began jiving at the back of the room and in the walkways. Even Toby and Trisha were tapping their feet. It was clear to everyone there that there were only two songs in the running for top spot. The very last song was also very good but long after Johnny had finished people were still bopping and dancing inside, they were feeling that good.

Then there came the break for the judges to make their decisions. Half an hour passed and still no announcement. Toby could see them deliberation and wondered with excited whom they were deliberating about. Trisha was tip- toeing around him like Cinderella, and even Johnny could be seen talking to some man in the crowd, he did not seem in any way nervous. Not like Toby whom by now was starting to bite his fingernails. 'Remember darling 'Trisha whispered to him. 'Last night was just wonderful darling ...imagine we just spent most of it making love, wasn't it so beautiful and exciting, so even if we lose here now, we still have tonight to look forward to,' Toby blushed like mad but said to her 'Icing on the cake baby, icing on the cake' She knew he was nervous so she just pretended she did not hear what he said. She told herself that she was more than icing on any cake. She was the cake, and he was the icing, if he was lucky.

Then the moment came for the judges to give their decision. And they began at the third position and that went to the beautiful Anita with her lovely song about women's freedom in the music business, the second position went to and here everyone held their breath expecting it to be Toby or Johnny, but it went to Marie and James, a lovely duet of a lovely love song.

Everybody cheered but still waited with bated breath, as it was announced that there was a not one but two winners. Toby and Johnny were joint winners of the contest, and everyone stood up and gave them a standing ovation that last three whole minutes.

When the excitement died down Johnny came and gave Toby and Trisha a huge hug and then handed Toby the cheque, he had been giving for five thousand saying 'Here I heard you gave back your money to help the fund, so I want to do likewise, and guess what, there was this guy in the crowd who said he was a music promotor and he has offered to get me a record deal, would you believe that man? Of course, he said I would have to change my name but sure' Toby cut him off saying 'But that is great newsman, you're going to be famous like John Lennon or...' Johnny cut him off saying to him' No man, there is only one John Lennon and ever will be …no… I will think of a good name,' Trish cut him off saying to him, 'how about 'OLA' that is a great name for a band…then on your second album …you can call it OLA AGAIN. I think it suits you even if you are all dressed in black leather' and it will endure you to your millions of fans all over the world.' Johnny jokingly said to Toby, 'Would you mind if she became my manager?

Toby said to him, 'Of course I would, I was just going to propose to her on that stage tonight, you can if you want though ...be our best man, you never know ...we might even let you sing us down the aisle' Trisha blushed and jumped into Toby's arms and the three of them hugged each other and wished each other all the best in the future. And they all, as they say, lived happily ever after.

End

Fear

A young mother of two children is brutally raped one rainy afternoon in the town of Greytown and after her terrible ordeal she grabs her young children, straps them into her car and intends to drive them over to her friend's house at the far side of the city but in her panic is driving too fast for the wet conditions, and as she encounters a young deer on the road slams on her breaks and goes sliding across the road, and hits an oncoming car and her car burst into flames killing the two children and badly injuring herself. She did however survive. Not so lucky were the occupants of the other car. His was a face she would never forget.

There is an old wooden house down the laneway at Abbottstown and the people in the area always told the children to stay well away for it as it was haunted. The story goes that the father of the people that lived there was insane and the young son killed his parent's, brother and two sister's one evening while they slept.

His body however was never found, and it was wildly believed that the father killed his family and buried his son somewhere in the vast vegetation nearby and to this day almost seventy years later, no one was any the wiser of what really happened that fateful night in September in the year 1943. The house had been boarded up since the tragedy and the local teenagers used to taunt each other over who had the most nerve to go explore it but very few ever did.

Michael Collins was one such young man, white haired and blue eyes, very good looking, tall and athletic, the son of a wealthy father that denied him nothing, he was very privileged, and he knew it too, always bragging and boasting to the young females of the group he used to hang around with, saying stuff like, 'my dad is buying me a new jag for my birthday in two months' time, or when our 15 metre pool is built you are all welcome to come swim in it' The other four guys Terry Jonathan Jaz and Jules were much younger and from less well-off families and closer friends to each other than they would ever be to Michael.

The young ladies were Jennifer, Breda, Gwen, and Josie, with Jennifer been two years older that the other three, she was a typical young girl, long legs, and short skirts and busty with a wonderful sense of humour and she was loved by all that knew her. Michael fancied her like mad, but she was not into him or anyone else at that time in her life, as she was studying hard for college next year. Halloween came round and sure enough Michael mentioned the haunted house and dared the gang members to spend the night there. All made all kinds of excuses for not spending the night in that dump but were persuaded by Michael to spend at least three hours there.

And so, the time came when they were supposed to go into the haunted house and all of them knew that Michael would try and pull all kinds of tricks on them, first to impress the girl and secondly to show the girls how scared the boys were. If the truth were known the boys were scared, tricks or no tricks, even Michael was a little scared as they made their way round the bottom of the house where there was still furniture and photos on the walls that shone even more starkly in the torchlight that Michael had brought with him. As did the other guys but theirs was much smaller than Michaels and did not show as much light as his fancy one. Oddly enough none of the girl brought a touch.

Michael and Jennifer were the first to go upstairs and when they entered the main bedroom Michael picked up a small bedside locker and threw it down the stairs and everybody ran to the front door in panic. There were a few broken floorboards in the centre of the room with heavy curtain rope thrown on the derelict dusty bed and before Jenifer knew what was happening someone picked her up and threw her onto the bed pulling her panties off as he did so, and before she could react she was been raped and mauled all over her body and then she was hit full on with a very strong fist and then she blacked out. When the others found the courage to come back inside the house as they entered the sitting room, they found Jennifer hanging from the ceiling beam in the centre of the room. All fled in panic.

Within thirty minutes the place was crawling with police and police car lights were flashing and an ambulance was outside waiting for the cops to do what they had to do before they could take away Jennifer's body.

Captain Tony Hallahan had been in the police force all his life. By now he should have made detective, but his drinking got in the way of any possible promotion. Still, he was a good cop and a through one and loved what he did. Anna Ford was a detective, had been for the last four years and like Tony she too loved her work. Both were in the business of helping to find those who broke the law and put them where they belong, behind bars.

'What do you think?' Tony asked Anna, 'Besides the obvious that is! Anna was standing there looking up at the girl's body and she said to Tony, 'Looks like she had been sexually assaulted, but we won't know for sure till the PM, whoever did this must have been a very strong person to tie her up like that, though he could have done it upstairs and dropped her down through the floorboards, still he must have been strong, have you checked those kids outside, I take it they were with her doing what kids do in haunted houses?

'Not yet, but Nick is out there taking statements' if the photo guys are finished let them take her down and bring her to the morgue, I was going to say where she will be more comfortable but what a thing to say, I mean more dignified, God, even that is the wrong word, and she is so young too, I have two girls about her age, I hope forensics find something to help us get this guy and put him away for a very long time'

The first one to interview was Michael. He was the one that was with Jennifer all the time, it had to have been him, each one told the cops, but rules had to be followed. Michael said to the captain, 'I told you a dozen times already, I don't know what happened to her, I didn't do anything, she was my friend why would I want to hurt her?' Michael's father was sitting beside him supporting his son who was very upset, but he knew that these questions had to be asked to get to the bottom of this terrible murder, so he held his tongue for now.

Terry was next and he told the captain all that had happened last evening, and how Michael had thrown something heavy and how they had run for the front door in panic, all this while Michael and Jennifer were still upstairs. Jaz and Jules told the same stories, so all the spotlight was back on Michael.

'So, you saw your chance and you took it …you had your way with her and then decided it would ruin your life …so you killed her.' Tony said to him, but Michael's father exploded and furiously said to Tony, 'THAT is it, he said he did not kill that girl, and I for one believe him, now …no more questions till I return with my lawyer …you hear me …Captain?'

Tony could do nothing but agree as he knew the rules of by heart. Anna taking him outside said to him. 'We simply must wait till we get the results back from the coroner's office, at this moment in time we are just speculating, we need the facts …so let us wait another few hours, okay? Again, Tony nodded in agreement with her and went to the coffee machine in his office to pour them both a coffee.

Two and half hours later the results came back from the coroner's office. Jennifer had indeed been raped and strangled but much to everyone's surprise it was not Michael that killed or raped her, 'The kid had been telling the truth about been out of the room for those few vital minutes, but that means someone else was there, but who, the other four were not even in the house so there had to have been a seventh person in that house, we need to go back and take another look'

Detective Anna Ford said softly to captain Tony who nodded in agreement. The three of them went back to the crime scene, Anna Tony, and Nick the rookie driver. They went through the house with a fine-tooth comb but found nothing of interest until Anna back in the lab lifted the long curtain rope that was found around Jennifer's neck and put it to her nose, she then gave it to captain Tony to do likewise. 'Smell that, what is it? I got that smell before, on another case we were working on, a young woman, only twenty-six was battered and raped and left for dead after crashing her car, over the northside, not two months ago, that same smell, it lingered on my clothes for days afterwards, it looks like we have a serial rapist on the loose captain,'

'Well if we have, he must be pretty stupid to wear such a distinctive deodorant, or he wants to throw us off the scent, if you pardon the pun' replied the captain and Anna said to him, 'Or works with some kind of oils, it is not a solution for body odour, captain, or any simple body spray no, it's more than that, it is something a French polisher might use, or a shipbuilder, you know a yacht or something like wooden garden furniture preservative, you know, something like that, a special paint or varnish maybe, some kind of oil, we need to find out what it is, can you check this out Tony, I am going back to that house, I know we are missing something there but I need to check it again to find out what it is, now with this special scent we have a possible lead, who knows we might get lucky'

An hour later she was back in the room where Jennifer had been murdered. She went over everything again not only with her eyes but this time also with her nose. That smell was there but very faint and it was not coming from the room but seemed to be coming from downstairs. She cautiously went back downstairs and into the large sitting room, then into the pantry where there was still an old-fashioned washing machine, with some clothes inside, and out the back door into the garden that was overgrown with all kinds of wildflowers and weeds and as she passed a garden shed, she thought she heard something move.

A very slight sound but a sound, nonetheless. Steadily she crept back towards the door of the shed and as she slowly opened the door a large black cat made a dive for the broken window and quickly vanished in the jungle of weeds but not before it scared the life out of her. Someone she could see, was sleeping in the shed, and looking round she could see the odd empty bar of snickers and other chocolate wrappers lying about the place. Whomever it was had a sweet tooth. And there was that smell again, still very faint but also very real. How could we have overlooked this vital clue? she asked herself repeatedly.

Back at the station she went over every detail of the first search of the haunted house with captain Tony and he outlaid the search plan of the house to Anna. 'Well' he said to her, 'There was you and I and Nick, the rookie, he checked the rear of the house and forensics went over every inch of the place but I am not sure if they checked that dirty old rundown shed, I will have to check that with them and see if they did, but if someone is sleeping there as you say, then surely he is our main suspect, I mean who in their right mind who choose a haunted house to sleep in?' Anna cut him off saying to him, 'Someone who did not want others snooping around that's who, or whom'

Anna was at the coffee machine when Nick came over to get a cup. She noticed he was holding a bar of snickers and she said to him, 'Ah, someone with a sweet tooth! I used to love those snickers bars but had to give them up because I found I was eating too many of them a week, do you eat many?' Nick said to her, 'Skipped breakfast this morning, no not many, I find them very filling and a little sickening actually, I won't eat this now, maybe later'

Alarm bells were ringing in detective Annas ears and her nose got a faint whiff of that scent that was by now beginning to drive her crazy. She made her views known to captain Tony and he said to her, 'No way! your way off the beaten track there girl, why Nick is a very good cop and very intelligent in police work for his age, he is also very enthusiastic about this case and only yesterday put some very impressive scenarios to me, most if not all I quickly demolished but it shows he is willing and able, he is going to make a great detective one day in the not too distant future, you mark my words, watch this space girl'

Whatever about watching this space Anna began to watch Nick and where he was going when he was off duty, which was six pm most nights. On the third night she followed him to the haunted house and round to the garden shed where she caught him leaving two mars' bars and a litre of bottled water. Then just before he left, he stopped to feed the cat that was purring and rubbing up against his legs. As soon as he opened the tin of cat food Anna got that scent, she had been getting this past week. So that was it...cat food! Garlic flavoured cat-food. Not many people use garlic flavoured cat food, though it helps to prevent fleas and worms and is excellent for the cat's fur, leaving it silky and shining just like that black cat that was now gulping down its food right before her eyes. He was caught and he knew it. She said to him,

'I never knew you were a cat lover Nick, so much so that you come all this way to a murder scene just to feed one cat, now I find that very strange, don't you?' he replied saying to her, 'It is not my cat...' she says to him, 'Then whose is it? it is certainly not mine or Captain Tony's, or the commissioners, or even the parish priests, so to whom does it belong? ...and why are you looking after it?

He said to her sheepishly, 'It is my brother's cat'

'And what is it doing here then? She asks him, He replied 'Well it isn't really his, probably a neighbour's cat, it just comes and snuggles up to him, he sleeps here you see, he is always having rows with our parents and sometimes it gets so bad he moves out, maybe for a month or so at a time, I know I should have told you about him when that poor girl died upstairs but then you would think that he killed her, and...' Anna cut him off saying to him,

'And did he ...kill her? He answered saying to her, 'Of course not, he is a lot of things, but he is no murderer' she stares him out then says to him,

'And how do you know that? I mean if he disappears for weeks at a time, how do you know anything about where he goes or what he does, seems to me you could be helping a killer on the loose, think about what that would do for you career Nick, you might even end up inside the same cell with him, now wouldn't that be nice? He goes white in the face but stays silent.

She then asks him, 'Where is he then?' he says to her, 'I don't know, if he goes on the town or out of town, he …ring's me to go feed his cat, he calls it his cat now. I don't know where he is or what he is up to or how long he will be.'

'Tell me' she says to him sniffing the air, 'where does that smell come from' he replied saying to her, 'I have to mix it with the tin food otherwise it won't eat it, too much garlic in it…I know why you asking and what you are thinking…it leaves a smell on the hands but it washes off somewhat, it goes after a couple of washes.' She says to him sternly, 'But not if it gets on the clothes …I'm going to have to take you in and explain all this to the captain, till we get to the bottom of this, if your brother rings you, you need to tell him to come in and answer a few questions, okay …let's go'

Captain Tony Hallahan was coming out of his office as detective Anna and Nick were going in. 'There has been a double murder!' He said exclaimed coldly 'A young girl, and a young man, her boyfriend, maybe …found dead in the park.

Grab a coffee and follow me down …the commissioner is going mad, the press is calling for his head, maybe mine and yours too, so don't delay, this is going to be a long night, Nick you drive' Nick looked at Anna who raised her eyes to heaven and nodded her head sideways.

The young girl had been punched about the head and it did look like she had been raped with her bare breasts left exposed and her dress torn, and her panties pulled down but still on her left leg. The young man had been beaten to a pulp and whomever had done this killing must have been in a total rage as both his victims had been viciously beaten about the head and face. It turned out later that the young man had come to the aid of the young woman that was been raped but he was no match for the vicious killer.

Captain Hallahan turned to say something to detective Ford, but she was already heading for the patrol car with Nick close behind. 'You don't think, …you do …don't you! …you think it is my brother, it can't be, he wouldn't do anything like that, I am sure he wouldn't'

When they got to the haunted house Nicks brother was already there, the blood still visible on his knuckles and shirt. He was more than surprised to see Nick and Anna coming towards him and he picked up an old pickaxe handle and came towards the two in a threating manner, 'Nick said to him, 'Put that down, Charles, the game is up, you have killed for the last time, how could you have done such horrible things to those poor people, they never did anything to you, how could you do something like that?'

Charley said to his brother nodding to Anna, 'Just let me kill that bitch, bro, then I will leave here …and you'll never see me again, I promise, just let me do her,' Nick let him get closer then swung a punch and hit his brother in the side of the head while Anna kicked him in the balls and he went down like a sack of spuds moaning and crying like a child that had been sent to bed without his iPad. Pitiful.

Later back at the station after his brother Charles had been charged with five murders and the rape of two women including the murder of the two children that burned to death in that car over the northside, he was sentenced to five life sentences without the possibility of parole. Detective Anna Ford was promoted to Superintendent while Captain Hallahan was moved up to DPC; Deputy Police Chief while Nick was made Captain of his station.

End

A Walk on the Wild Side

Seventeen-year-old Jamie Sullivan was a quite very pleasant young man that would do no one a bad turn. One of a family of five, three sisters and two brothers. Already hard working on the building sites and always helping his elderly neighbours when they had something heavy to shift, or simply running errands for them when it was too wet or too cold for them to go out to collect their pension money themselves. That was how much he was liked and trusted by his elderly neighbours, as like most OAP's hard winters always had them housebound. Unlike his parents who were always going out to one of many the pubs or clubs in the area.

He lived in a large housing estate on the outskirts of Dublin city where the crime rate and drug problem were rife among the young lads of the area. It was not because there was no money around.

The opposite in fact was the case as they now had too much money, gotten no doubt from breaking into people's houses and stealing anything and everything they could lay their drug needle riddled arms on. Violence too was on the increase with no regard for the victims whatsoever. From taking school children's lunch money to old, aged pensioners collecting their pension money.

Long gone were the days when these young and not so young thugs had a conscience but now would use any means, usually a knife, and were not afraid to use it if anyone got in their way or tried to stop them from doing their dirty work. It got so bad that even the drug addicts were selling drugs openly anywhere and everywhere for all to see.

Seemingly even the guards were unable or unwilling to stop them. This then is the place where young Jamie Sullivan grew up and lived in this present day, Tuesday November 12th six pm.

He was coming in from work as usual when he heard a woman scream, looking towards the church he sees a figure running down towards the shops, so he runs up the lane lit only by a single light thanks to the kids around here that had little or nothing better to do. He sees a woman lying on her stomach and when he gently turns her over to his horror and disbelief he sees his girlfriend Marie, her white blouse coloured red from the stab wounds to her chest. He phones an ambulance and then the guards and within minutes they both arrive but too late to save Marie.

One of the guards, a female, took Jamie aside and he told her what had heard and seen and that the body on the ground was his girlfriend. She listened and told him to stand up straight and she shone her torch into his eyes to look for any sign that he had taken something, then she sniffed his breath to find out if he had alcohol taken then she said to him. My name is Jessica O' Toole …you can see my number 32, you will have to come with us to the station where you will be examined by a doctor and as you are a little on the young side you may make a call and have an adult come visit, you, you don't mind, do you?' Jamie said to her.

'You'd still take me in if I did,' he said tearfully, 'I have nothing to hide, that is my girlfriend lying there, I love her, why would I want to hurt her?' she replied, 'Well Jamie, that is what we want to find out, and at the moment you are the only one that can help us with that, I am so sorry for your loss but it has to be done, standard procedure I am afraid'

An hour later Jamie's father appeared and said to him, 'God, this is terrible son! how could anyone do such a thing to that sweet girl, I mean she never hurt anyone, your mother wanted to come but she has had a few drinks and you know what she's like, she'd get herself locked up for sure, how are you holding up son?

Do you need anything? They are not going to charge you, or anything, are they son? Jamie just shook his head and said to his father,

'No! of course not dad, how could they? I have not done anything, why would I? I loved her and planned to marry her as soon as I turned eighteen, but I will swear to you this dad, I will find out who that miserable toerag is that done this, when I am finished with him, he will wish he had never been born'

A few minutes later Jessica came in and offered them a lift home which they gladly accepted and on the way home, she said to Jamie. 'Don't worry, we will find out who did this terrible murder' the word murder set the floodgates loose and Jamie just burst into tears and even his dad holding him tight could not stop the flow

'Leave him be! she said to his father, 'he has had such a shock and crying will release some of the pressure, a terrible state of affairs, I tell you this used to be a lovely place a few years ago now, God, well, you live here …you know yourself? drug pushers everywhere, I pity anyone trying to bring their kids up here, but it's not just here …it is everywhere, every town every county, almost every home now, everywhere' Jamie's father John said to her, 'Well it is not in my home girl, thank God, and never will be …as long as I am alive?

The doctor came and gave Jamie a sedative to help him sleep. His mother was in hysterics, but she had her husband to help calm her down. He poured her another brandy, and one for himself while he was at it, a large one. After all, he had a massive shock too.

Jamie woke at noon the following day Wednesday, and as soon as he pulled himself together, he went out to try find the son of a bitch that killed his girlfriend. He knew a lot of the junkies and for the most part they knew him well enough to trust him. Though not all of them did. One of them a lad called Spiky said to him.

'Jamie man, I don't know anyone around here that would do that to her, I mean everyone here knew she was your girlfriend, I tell you man, I don't believe it was one of our guys, I mean doing that would only end up one way, cops swarming all over the kip, giving us hassle and interrupting our business, know what I mean Jamie? we don't need that crap, no way man ,for f…ks sake, who would be so stupid to do this kind of shit? And I tell you what man, I will keep my eyes and ears open and if I get a sniff of anything I will let you know man, I promise you that much, if I don't kill the low life me self' Jamie thanked him and went on his way, hoping the next addict he met might have more information. He ran into a brick wall, if they did know, no one was saying anything, at least not to him, whether they liked him or not.

It was a little later that Spiky came round saying to him, 'Not sure if it means anything Jamie but I heard last night in the Wilsons gaff yeah, there was a terrible row, world war 3 man, with Taffy ending up in a heap in the front garden, his dad beat the living daylights out of him and left him for dead, didn't call an ambulance or anything, now it might not mean much as that is a regular occurrence in that house but you might want to check it out, maybe it had something to do with what happened to your girl man,'

Jamie thanked Spike and went looking for Taffy whom he soon heard had to present himself at the local A&E. It turned out he had four broken ribs a broken nose, and a left arm broken in two places. He would have to wait until the guy was better again before Jamie could put him back into the hospital or the ground if he found out that he had anything to do with the murder of his lovely Marie. When he found him the next day Taffy was standing outside the local grocery stores, his usual spot despite his many injuries. He went to run but was unable to get away fast enough. He was saying nothing but answered only one question that Jamie asked him, why did his father beat him so badly that same night that Marie was murdered. To which Taffy replied. 'He doesn't need a reason' but that was all he was prepared to say to Jamie.

Suffice to say, the guards were having no luck either in their search for the killer. Then two days later Taffy came looking for Jamie and when he found him still asking question on the estate he said to him, 'Spiky told me where you were, and look …I am sorry about your girlfriend, you know we all fancied her around here but well …the night that she died yeah, …a guy from the northside came to me looking to score a lot more than normal and when I told him how much it was, he didn't have enough money on him, he …he came on the back of someone's motorbike …he told the guy to wait that he would be back soon, he was gone about thirty minutes or so, the guy on the bike went and got himself a bag of chips in the chipper and was stuffing them away when we heard a scream, then this guy came back, he had a wad of notes that would chook an ass and even after he gave me the 250 he still had a stack of money in his hand, then he got back on the bike and off they went. I put two and two together and went to look where I thought the scream came from, I found Marie there and phoned an ambulance, how do you think they got there so fast? Anyway, the thing is, I thought I heard the guy on the bike call him Dunner, or Gunner or something like that, when I got home my dad kicked the crap out of me because my shirt was covered in blood and he thought I was after doing someone, but I swear to you Jamie, I never touched her, I just bent over her to see if she was dead or alive, but I think she was already dead when I got there'

Jamie asked him, 'Could you recognise these guys Taff?' Taffy said to him, 'Dunner, I think I would …but I can't because my life wouldn't be worth living if I did, the other guy, the one riding the bike kept his helmet with the dark face shield on all the time, except when he was stuffing his face with chips, but even then I couldn't get a good look at him, Dunner of Gunner or whatever his f…king name is, would stand out in a line up with his mop of blond hair, I could see that even under his helmet and he had a broken nose, like a boxer…he looked a real nutter, so he did man, I sure wouldn't like to face him up any lane way, anytime soon man …eh …sorry Jamie, I didn't mean…'

Jamie was thinking that if he had to go over to the northside to find this guy, he had better do it the right way and that was to go as an addict looking for a fix so he said to Taffy 'If I were looking for something to you know ...make me look dopier than I already am ...what would I use?

I mean what would I need to take that wasn't addictive, what do you think? Taffy said to him, 'well if that is what you want just go into the chemist and get some paracetamol, are you thinking of going after this guy, you'd be nuts to do that man, let the guards handle him,' Jamie said to him, 'I just need five minutes with him then the guards can have what's left of him, so what do you suggest I take if I want to make a good impression then?'

'Taffy said to him, 'Go and see Spiky ...he will set you right, and please Jamie ...don't mention my name to him or the guards, sure you won't, my dad would kill me stone dead if he even thought I had anything at all to do with that terrible night' Jamie said to him, 'Why does he hate you and beat you so much?

'Because' Taffy replied, 'he caught my mother having sex with some guy in his fancy jeep one night, and he thinks ...and maybe he is right, he thinks I am not his kid'

'And' said Jamie, 'that is what made you what you are ...a drug addict?' Taffy said to him, 'We all have our reasons, man, mostly though because in my case anyway ...there was no love in the house, but as I say ...we all have our reasons' Jamie shook Taffy's hand and went looking for Spike, who wasn't hard to find and when Jamie put his plan to Spike, he was told he was mad,

'Why put yourself in double danger man? you've seen what these kids are like around here, fucking zombies most of them, then this geezer Gunner, and I think I have heard that name before, if it is the same guy I heard about then he is a vicious mean bastard, he would kill you in the blink of an eye, what you need to do is get someone else to do him for you, cost you about five grand but at least you won't get hurt'

'This!' replied Jamie, 'Is one job I need to do myself …besides, where the …f…k, am I going to get five grand? No! This is something I must do …I owe my Marie that much, Spike says to him, 'Well if you are sure then okay …I will help you …but you need to stay on whatever I give you for at least three days and no longer than five days, otherwise you'll be hooked line a d sinker and you will be coming to see me every day …okay man?

And as much as I like you I don't want to see you every day or maybe even twice a day, so don't forget who is the daddy here man, take these and take two a day for the first day, then only one a day after that, and remember you did not get them from me okay? and seeing it is you and why you want them there is no charge, but if you are not careful you will be wishing I had charged you five grand apiece, so, do you want me to tag along and help you set up this crazy plan? I know how it works and if I know him then he probably knows me so it will be easier on you, what do you say man?'

Jamie said to him, 'No thanks ….I will manage, 'Okay then' said Spiky, 'the last time and the only time I met him was in Coolock, over by the northside shopping centre …the back entrance, you never know he might be still doing business there …tell him Spiky sent you, that might help you break the ice …but be careful …if he smells a rat he will break more than the ice …he will break your f…king head .. then go and have himself a Mc Donald's'

When Jamie got home, he took one of the pills that Spike had given him and within a few minutes of nothing happening he went and took another one…then bang, he was in some very dark place lying is some dirty laneway that looked a lot like the one Marie had been killed in.

It was raining heavy, and he could see a huge Anaconda snake make its way toward Marie's lifeless body and opened its huge mouth and begin to swallow her body when suddenly she wakes up and screams. It wasn't her that screamed but Jamie and he woke up in a sweat. His father ran into the room to see if his son was okay and Jamie said he was, it was just frustration and he'd be alright in a few minutes.

His father said to him, 'If you need to talk son, I am here for you, you do know that don't you? Jamie said he did but that he was okay, all he needed was a good night's sleep.

He had anything but a good night's sleep. He went back into that dark place and found himself bathing in a bath full of maggots, with badly decomposing people coming at him every few seconds, and try as he might, he could not wake up.

When he did wake up it was well into the afternoon. Pulling himself together he made his way over across the river Liffey to Coolock and the northside shopping centre where he waited at the rear entrance for well over an hour, going into the coffee shop every now and then to relieve the boredom and keep himself warm.

He was on his third cup when he saw him. Taffy's description of him was spot on and without finishing his coffee he followed him through the shopping centre but even before a few moments had passed he knew Gunner had spotted him.

Out through the front entrance and into the car park when he thought he lost him, but Gunner was standing behind a van and came out and said to him, ' Are you looking for me man?' Jamie said to him, 'I am, I am looking for a little gear, Spiky sent me, he said you knew him…and Gunner cut him off saying, 'Spiky… Spiky, I don't know any Spiky…who are you and want do you want from me? Jamie had to take a step back as the body odour from Gunner was nauseating but it told Jamie that this man was sleeping rough, but he took two pills from his trouser pocket and showed him what he was looking for and Gunner looked at him as if he had two heads and said to him, 'You are either working undercover and trying to take me for a f…king idiot, …I didn't come in with the last bunch of refuges, that stuff you have there …any fool will tell you it's only for kids…so I am thinking you are only new to this shit or you are as I said trying to trick me' Jamie took out his wallet from inside his Jacket and said to Gunner, 'I have money, I can pay'

Gunner coming closer and looking at the money in the wallet Jamie made sure he could see, said to him. 'I don't keep my stash on me for obvious reasons, but if you want to follow me you will have it in a few minutes,' Jamie nodded and followed him across the road and into the little park that was a little on the dark side as it was now well past five pm and made him feel very nervous.

If Taffy was right this is the man that killed his Marie and took her money that she had only a few minutes before she died gotten a loan from the credit union. He did not feel right at all, but it was too late to back out now. He could see many little dark places that a man could hide in and when Gunner suddenly disappeared his fears increased dramatically.

Then he could sense that Gunner was standing behind him and when he turned around he was and holding a large knife in his right hand waving it from left to right at Jamie saying 'The wallet man, toss it on the ground here, and step back, that was a dead giveaway, I know lots of junkies but not one of them has a leather wallet,' Jamie knew it was now or never and as Gunner bent down to pick up the wallet he lashed out and kicked him in the face. He went down but was back up quickly swiping at Jamie and missing his head and chest by fractions of an inch when Jamie hit him with a right hook and knocked him down again. Gunner was furious and got back up to his feet, then fell towards and on top of Jamie who thought his life was over, but Gunner didn't move and when Jamie shoved him off, he looked up to see Spike standing there smiling. Then he noticed the knife sticking in Gunners back, 'What …the f…k! How the hell… you've been following me…'

Spike said to him, 'Lucky for you I did man, you weren't doing so well, anyway …so I thought you might need a little help…my life is shit as you know, so if I went inside for a few years, well it would be an improvement, not so you my friend, …you're a hardworking man, with a bright future ahead, and sure nobody will miss this brute here, not even his family or friends if he has any …which I doubt …everyone hated this piece of shit, besides we all loved Marie as you probably don't know… now if you need any gear, I know a lovely guy over the southside that just might be able to help you, but you have a job so it won't be free buddy,' Jamie came closer and gave him a big hug and Spike with his eyes welling up said to him, 'No one has done that to me in years, thanks man, so shall we get a taxi or what? you're paying, I saw that money in your wallet ha ha ha…lets go man' and they did, get a taxi home.

End

Down by the River

Down by the river-we sometimes go walking- we stroll there together- sometimes not talking- yeah but hey- that's okay- yeah its ok- as long as we stay- together- and not out there doing- somebody in- It's hard going - in this freezing cold weather- to try to stay warm- and happy within- selling gold lockets after picking people's pockets- life is so bad that we're drowning in sin- It's not ok to go out and steal- It's not ok- to have nothing to eat- it's not okay- but this life is so real- it's cold and lonely out here- on the street, I can't feel my fingers- I can't feel my feet,

Yes, it's not okay to be sitting here smoking- broken and battered out there on the street- trying so hard- while your whole world is shattered- people don't see you right there at their feet-they think we sit here for fun- don't see you cry when the long day is done- hell on earth feeling old and cold- you're not worth nothing and you're not yet 21,

But they say it is okay- if you're broken- the say it's okay if your down on your luck- as long as you're not stroking- and causing a fuss- they even smile at you as they hop on the bus- can anyone tell me how the hell do we get out of this rut? People in the know keep on passing the buck,

Down by the river- on a cold Christmas morning- we sit here and shiver- humming and yawning- no one else to talk to- nothing to look forward to- down by the river- it's just me and you with nothing to do- all day feeling cold hungry and seeing fifty shades of blue,

And everyone's happy- yeah, I'm alright Jack- we starve, and we freeze while they smile and say 'Merry Christmas' to you,

But baby it's okay- don't let it get you down- back-to-back we still live in this sack- we sure are lucky to have the best doorway in town,

Down by the river- some children are fishing- I stand there just watching- and- silently wishing- for better days when I'm not so cold and alone- I stand here because - cos my baby's- gone home- and I won't be too long here- cos I'm chilled to the bone,

It's okay if your body is broken- its ok- if you're down on your luck,

It's not okay If you're just sitting there watching - while somebody's choking- with the breath leaving their body- then my friend- it's best not to look- you just carry on stuffing your fat face and go on reading that book,

Down by the river- someone's in swimming- I can hear laughter- I hear children singing-I hope life is better in the here- ever- after- my lucks changing- already it feels like I'm winning,

Angels are coming- with arms open wide- down by the river under the bridge so empty and void- waters so cold I can't feel a thing- nothing to hold on too but my sack full of sin- no use in fighting- this nightmare is over- no more tears to be cried- in a moment or two I'll be with my baby- the storm is over- goodbye and thanks for the ride- this time tomorrow I'll be pushing up clover- my baby' be lying here right by my side- we're okay now- we're together again- we can hold our head's up high- we've made it somehow- to that homeless shelter up there in the sky,

It's now okay- one day- we'll know- the reason why- they say- we had to go so soon- back now together- hey I am over the moon- It's okay to be broken- buddy- I will be seeing you soon.

End

Brendan Jones LTD Cleaning Services...No Job too Small or too Big...Relieving the Stresses of Life.

The girls:

Betty Fields...5-8 45 years old 5-6 in height, the senior of the five girls born in India in a family of five girls...mother and father divorced when she was ten...it took a heavy toll on the little girl...as girls are really frowned on in India.

Kate Hudson...5-6 42 years old...5-9 inches tall originally from Glasgow, if beauty is in the eye of the beholder than she is the most beautiful of all the girls...grew up in her aunt's house in London after her parents were killed in a car crash. She was five years old at the time.

Susan Warwick 39 years old... 5-5 the smallest of all the girls but with the biggest smile and breasts ever a man was lucky enough to feast his eyes on, born in London UK her high hopes of an affluent lifestyle eluded her...both parents were alcoholics.

Brenda Jones...   Welch, blonde and 6-1 in height 39 years old and the smartest of the five girls and the funniest...with big boobs and a bigger dark secret. Well worth getting on her good side...which is any side at all...

Bridget Loftus... 5-5 37 years old came from a very large Irish family from Dublin...ex heroin addict...now five years clear of all drugs...spent some time in prison...for shoplifting...working hard to get her life together. Seems to be working...even if it meant she had to go south a lot.

Angie Burns...   born in the UK, but lived in a lot of countries, now in Ireland 5-11, 40 year of age most wanted of all the girls... even by one or two of the girls, supervisor with a stiff strict heart...but what a figure, so no deal...maybe, maybe not...

The men:

Tom Jones no, not that Tom Jones but this one 55 years old, 6- 4 inches tall., fancied himself a bit of a singer, a fair golfer and hoping to be the next captain of the club. A Family man with three kids and a beautiful wife, ten years younger than he was. Lucky bastard. Handicap 69

Brendan Smith 45 years of age 5-11 also married but his marriage not going to well this past two years, a bit of a comedian for all of that. Spent more time on the golf course than the marriage course. Handicap 68

Luke 'lucky' Barnes: 35 years old and the most handsome of the lads, you know the type, long blond hair and blue eyes, 6- 2 in height, was he gay? not sure but a great golfer so who cares? Handicap 65

Tom Watson 43 years old, 5-7 always moaning about the shortage of money, but nobody listened to him, wasn't a bad golfer, he was the one with the most holes in one. Handicap 70 Welcome to the club boys.

The hotel Melrose in Sunny Wexford Ireland: July, the annual golfer's getaway for the year 2022

Room 21

Luke 'lucky' Barnes is having a lie on one fine sunny morning, when the door opens and Betty walks in into the bedroom, 'Oh' she says softly, 'I did not realise you were still here, I will come back later if you want' Lucky smiling, says in reply, 'No, no need to do that ...you are here now so go ahead, then adds chancing his arm, 'You will have to work around me in the bed though, if that is okay with you' to his delight she says to him, 'that will be no problem, but you will need a bigger bed' then she laughs as he is getting out of bed.

He goes up to her in his shorts, and puts his arm round her and whispers, 'we have the settee, one can do wonderful things on a settee,' she says to him, 'Now it is funny you should mention that, while our main job here is cleaning, we do offer a few little extra's on the side,' Luke, moving closer to her now saying, 'Oh, you do! …do you …and what would they be pray tell?' she says to him, 'Now you look like the kind of man that has been around the world a few times, so you know what I am about to say, don't you?'

'I have an idea, but I would like to hear it coming from those beautiful lips, so, go ahead …I am no prude,'

'Well!' she says, 'if you look at the name of our company, you will get some idea, for example take the first letter from both names B and J yes, what comes to your mind when you see that?' he didn't even blush as he said to her, bj, right?' so let me get this right, you are offering me sex on the side, I suppose you have a menu and everything?' she replies saying, 'we don't have a menu but we do have everything on offer from a gentle kiss to the full Monty, the kiss however is free.'

'I am impressed so go on name your price' he said to her moving even closer,' she moves back a little and says, 'a Brenda Jones special is 25 euro, and extra 10 if we swallow, a massage is 20 euro and that is not you that gets massaged but one of us, for a full feel there is an extra 10 euro but you get a hand job with that, then we have full intercourse, but no holes in ones, if you get my drift, a girl must keep some self-respect, that is 60 euro and no refunds, but if you can pass it on to your mates then you can have the first or the last item for free, what do you say, my…but you are handsome, you not gay are you?

He leans forward and kissed her luscious lips avoiding the question then asks, 'Is it bare breasted with the bj?' she replies, 'not really …but for you I will make an exception' and she takes off her top revealing a sexy red bra and a whole world of pleasure underneath it.

So, five minutes later she says to him, 'are you satisfied with that?' he smiled pulling his shorts back up and says to her, 'Yes, I know I came early I didn't want to keep you too long as I know you have a job to do here, and yes, I will tell the lads all about your lovely bits on the side, thank you …that was wonderful,' It was that good his whole body was trembling. He wasn't called lucky for nothing.

And so, the word spread to the other guys about the little extra services, while they were out on the local golf course. Tom Jones said to him, 'You mean to stand there and tell you that this beautiful woman gave you a bj and she had only met you, what …five minutes before! you lucky bastard …it took me months to get one from my wife, and months more before she would blow me off completely,' the other lads knew there was something going on between the two so they stopped the game and came over for a chin-wag. Tom Watson on hearing all this said to them.

'That is terrible! have you no respect for yourself or those poor women? working hard to make ends meet, you should be ashamed of yourselves so you should.' The others just gave him the blank stare. Then Brendan said to him, 'Will she give me one, do you have to book her in advance or what? I saw her this morning and she is a stunner as all the girls here are, I'm game, but I'll be using a condom if I can find a chemist in the town,'

Tom Watson said to him, I am sure they have their own supply, what about your wife? how would you feel if she was cheating on you? Brendan said to him, 'Ha, she probably is and has been for years now, besides, I don't think a blow job is actually cheating, what harm can it do anyway, as long as you clean it afterwards with a good mouthwash.'

That is how it began and soon they were all in on the act, although not all at the same time for obvious reasons. There was a different girl every second day and before long the lads were telling each other they're favourites and scoring points with each other, making a competition out of it and the girl with the most points at the end of the week would get a 50 euro note on top of whatever she earned on the side, and word got around to the girls and what a performance they put in trying hard to win the prize. With them coming in early and blowing some of the guys before they were even fully awake.

It happened with Tom Watson. The night before he was to get his very first bj, he couldn't sleep, and then he had a heart attack around 8 am when Brenda Jones came in and blew him thinking he would wake up as soon as she put her cool hand on him.

Later that morning as Tom was taken out in an ambulance, the girls were all standing in the foyer watching when Brenda said to them, 'Who is it, what happened?' Kate Hudson said to her, 'it is Mr Watson, apparently he had a heart attack this morning and died in his bed, poor man' Brenda, flustered, said to her, 'What time was that then?' Kate said to her 'around 7 or 7-30, the doctor said,' Brenda's face went red as Angie Burns said to her. 'You did his room early Brenda …what time was then, around 8 wasn't it?' Brenda's face got redder as she realised, she had been blowing a dead man' and Angie giggled as she said out loud enough for the other girls to hear, 'You did, didn't you, you gave him a…hah I can't believe this…she gave him a blow job, is that what killed him Brenda, you were trying to get that bonus weren't you?' Brenda was scarlet and the others were laughing and almost falling about the place, then Angie said to her, 'I hope he paid you up front hah hah ahha,' the other's girl laughed some more as the ambulance pulled away, there was no need for the siren as Tom Watson was already long deceased.

The other lads were very saddened by the loss of one of their members. Luke Barnes said to no one in particular, 'Well, it is not as if we were great friends or anything, still I will miss the old moaner, he's certainly going for a hole in one now, poor soul, ah …well such is life, see you later guys, my little bit on the side is about to be served up on a platter, amazing what 50 euro can do,' as he said the now late Tom Watsons voice came to his mind and said, 'You should be ashamed of yourself, treating women that way.' For once in his life, he felt the shame.

The girls however were back on extra duty that very day. They had lots of time to make up as poor Tom dying like he did upset everyone, even if it was only for an hour or so.

While some of the women were 'resting' not so Angie burns or Bridget Loftus. They were dug into each other in a spare room at the end of the hall. Spent well over an hour going over each other's bodies in slow motion and sheer delight. Bridget asked her during one of her short breaths, 'Do you prefer men or women?' Angie replied saying, 'I don't have to choose, I have both whenever the need arises, I even had the two at one time back in 2010 in a hotel in Galway… which would you choose?' Bridget said on her way back down, 'Right now, you are all I long for, and I am not even going to charge you a cent'

The week went quickly by and when the Saturday came round the boys met in the bar to pick a winner of the 50-euro prize, without a doubt the winner was Susan Warwick with each one pointing out their favourite items on the menu. As she filled all of them.

All it all it was a week to remember and even the death of poor Tom Watson could not put a damper on it. The three of them were thinking to themselves, yep, most definitely going take a few more short breaks in Wexford this year.

End

Interstellar Man

The Commander of the Star ship Discovery Joseph Springer is busy in his cabin when a crew member his navigator, calls him on the intercom to come quickly to the bridge. The Commander having done so says to his flight crew, while looking at the green haze on his video screen to his navigator, Jim Redmond,

'What is it?' his navigator replies saying, 'It is a massive energy field sir, so large we should not go through it … it would play havoc with the navigating system sir,' the Commander says to him,

'Then go round the blooming thing' to which his navigator replies, 'it is fluctuating sir …but that is not the reason we summoned you, watch closely sir, give it a few seconds, it is dissipating sporadically, there it goes sir, now can you see why we summoned you to the flight-deck.

What the Commander was seeing as the green haze was slowly clearing was a fleet of warships staring him straight in the face and he trembled at the sight, 'What the! …do we know who they are and what they want?' at that moment the captain of the ship captain John Mc Million came from sick bay and entered the flight deck just in time to hear the answer to that question. The navigator said to his Commander, 'we do not sir, there is no communication with them whatsoever, we tried but nothing, not even static.'

The captain asked him, 'Do we even know how many ships there are, man that looks like a whole fleet and more,' the navigator replies to the captain, '250 warships sir, and 5 supply ships captain sir, and they are not here to invite us to a picnic, they mean business …big time,' the captain coughs up a little blood, then replies, 'It can't be us they are after, talk about cracking a nut with a sledgehammer,' the navigator suddenly speaks up and says out loud, 'There captain …to the right, warships and plenty of them! they must be why those ships are here, they are about to engage with each other, should we move captain?' the Commander says, 'No not yet! let us see for a moment what is about to happen, but be ready to make a hasty retreat'

Then the battle begins and to use that old cliché all hell broke loose. The Commander yells into the intercom, 'All officers on the bridge immediately, and that means right now' soon the flight deck is awash with men and women watching the battle unfold. With ships exploding and falling out of the battle zone, time after time and at the same time ships were passing in flames right in from of Discovery and the captain gave the order to retreat just out of reach as he was like everyone there on the bridge, fascinated at the battle sight before them.

Then from his right out of nowhere came a ship in flames, 'Steady folks …it will miss us by mile, eh …wont it, Commander? who replied, 'It should captain …but to be on the safe side take us back about 700 km, Mr Miles …no point in taking unnecessary chances,' to which the navigator replies, 'Yes sir, I mean no sir'

The ship in flames and descending at tremendous speed head straight towards them, it came close enough to give everyone watching on the bridge the shock of their lives and when they all breathed a sigh of relief the captain turned round to see a strange man standing behind him. Shocked he looked at the navigator who just shook his shoulders,

'Who are you?' the captain asked the stranger who just stared at all present, that were now all watching him intensely.

The stranger studied each person there slowly and scientifically, as if he were reading their thoughts which was precisely what he was doing. He replied to the captain saying.

'Forgive the intrusion captain …but I had no choice but to beam aboard your ship, I am Captain Zook from the planet Orr, that as you can clearly see is right now been destroyed by the treacherous Muscovites who have been trying to conquer our planet for years now, and it looks like they have succeeded this time.

He looked and sounded the same as the others but was slightly taller than everyone else, I say slightly but he was a good six inches taller than the Commander there who was six- 5 yet looked smaller than that when standing next to captain Zook. Who also had a much larger head than the others. He asked the captain.

'May I ask where you are bound sir? And please can we move away from here it is much too distressing to observe the horrors that are going on …on what is left of my planet, even if it is from the safety of this fine ship'. The captain nodded to his navigator and said, 'steer a course 0 1-50, warp speed Mr Miles'

'Yes! sir captain' he replied and steered a course for 0 1-50. Then turning back to his counterpart, he says,

'Now in answer to your question Captain Zook, first can I say on behalf of my Commander and all present here how sorry we are to have seen the destruction of your planet, and not been able to do anything to help you're people, the Commander here is on his way to Starfleet command centre in Sector 4 to help construct a budget to incidentally increase the Starfleet from 200 ships to double that amount, as you have seen with your own eyes even 200 Starfleet warships here right now would possibly not have been enough to save your people, we will drop you off there if you wish …or if not, then we will be heading back to section 1 which is Earth, to carry on our mission there to see how that new planet is forming. You do not need to decide right now you have another ten days to make your decision,' captain Zook nodded his large head and said to him,

'May I have something to eat please captain? as I am rather hungry after all that action, and I do feel so privileged to be still alive,' To which the captain relied,

'Of course you can, second lieutenant…eh…Ms Marly, please, take the captain to the canteen, and would you please while you are there ask the orderly to bring two large coffees to my cabin please …two sugars, no milk please …yes …I know you know that …thank you oh, and when you can, find the captain here a cabin of his own, thank you lieutenant much obliged, love your hair,'

Having dropped off the Commander and having been told that captain Zook did not want to go with him, captain Zook said to the captain,

'I just want to see my planet one more time, even if it is ruled by those horrible Muscovites now living there' the ship came back around and headed North- northeast and two but Captain Zook stayed in his cabin as he was far too depressed to even look at his former planet, and two weeks later they were entering the earth's atmosphere they found themselves over the Atlantic Ocean heading towards Hibernia and stopped awhile hovering over the country to admire the beautiful scenery the navigator notices a large gathering of humans with one of them big red-haired man with more hair on his face than his head and holding some kind of staff standing in the centre of them addressing his people.

The captain now much better from his bad cold entered the bridge and said to the navigator, 'What is going on Mr Miles, whom are these people and why have we stopped?'

The navigator said to him, 'I saw all these people captain and they looked up to no good, so I just wondered what was going on sir' the captain looked then said in reply, 'I suppose all those bare-breasted women had nothing at all to do with your inquisitiveness, eh … Mr Miles, and wipe that grin off your face and get us out of here,' the navigator looked disappointed and said to his captain,

'Sir captain sir, I was reading up about these people, how crafty they were, and I was just trying to figure out what they were up to sir …captain sir,' 'and' replied the captain 'I suppose you would have us and everyone on board listen in to what they are saying, am I right, Mr Miles?'

'Right captain sir, it might also help us in our report to our superiors on this newly formed planet, to know how its people are managing to survive sir' the captain smiles and says to him, 'you do have a point there, okay …so let's listen in, can we hear them now, Mr Miles? The navigator said, 'we can sir …if we push out the antenna and push up the microphone to the maximum level sir' 'then do it Mr Miles we don't have all day man, can somebody bring me a large coffee please' Ms Marly his second lieutenant, raises her right hand and says to him, 'I will captain, two sugars and no milk,' the captain nods to her and smiling at her says, 'I love your hair, you always look so well …perfect' Ms Myles almost delighted with herself giggles and leaves the bridge.

The very large red-haired man is saying to his people. 'We cannot let this go unpunished, otherwise men from every nation will be coming here to snatch our beautiful bare-breasted women, that king in the next valley will pay a heavy price for taking my lovely Lydia …now why we have gathered here is to find the best way of bringing her back, for even a donkey will know if we go straight in and attack he might just have her killed, now you men that rule this kingdom with me, I want you to come up with a plan, one that doesn't involved me or my queen getting killed, and I want it in my bedroom within one hour.'

The captain looked at his people about him on the bridge and taking off his cap scratches his head and asks the question, 'Is there anyone here who wants to go down there and help this crazy Irish guy? It looks like he is getting ready for a war, God, is there nowhere in this or any other world where men and bare-breasted women can live in peace?' to his surprise captain Zook steps forward and says, 'I like the look of this land, it is a bit like my homeland, I will go and help these women …I mean people' So before he can change his mind he is beamed down and the ship flies off.

So! he is instantly spotted and in record time he is standing there red-faced from looking at the beautiful bare-breasted women whilst trying hard to face the big red-haired guy, who demands to know what is going on.

'My name is Captain Zook, I come from a galaxy far …far way, I have come to help you get your bare-breasted woman back from this treacherous enemy king of yours, in a safe and secure manner, I must add,'

One of the red-haired kings men, a man skinny man called Stumpy on account of his wooden left leg that was savaged by a wild hungry pig itself with only three legs, says to him, 'we already have a plan, we are going right up to the castle gate, eh, myself and Henry here, and we are simply going to ask the king to return her otherwise' he stomps his wooden leg, 'it is war,' the red-haired king said to Stumpy, 'you are replaced …go and prepare the dinner' then turns back to the captain and says to him, 'if you are from a galaxy far …far away, where is the ship that brought you here?'

The captain says to him, 'it wasn't my ship …I lost my ship in a war between my people and a people that is very similar to the ones that took your bare-breasted woman, as for the spaceship …it is by now in a galaxy far …far away, do you want to hear my plan, or not? then maybe after we can go to dinner …I am hungry.'

Over dinner the captain tells the red-haired king his plan to get the red-haired king's woman back safe and sound with no threat whatsoever to the red-haired king or his people.

The red-hard king whose name is Bernard de Great said to the captain, 'I am all ears, …all ears get it' pointing to the captains rather large ears.

The captain who had a good sense of humour for a man that had just lost his county and all its inhabitants, said to Bernard, 'well we …that is I and one of your men mingle with the people camped outside the castle gate and after an hour or so one of us, your man preferably …approaches the guard guarding the gate and bribes him to tell us where the beautiful queen of yours is been held, you with me thus far?

Good, then when we find out where she is been held prisoner having bribed the sentry on duty, myself and one of those beautiful bare-breasted women, disguised as a man out walking with his beautiful bare-breasted wife will enter the castle and make our way to wherever it is she is been held, then I will kill the guard with my bare hands while he is watching my bare-breasted wife then I will grab your bare-breasted woman and myself and my bare- breasted wife will simply walk back out the gate …and you my king …will have your beautiful bare- breasted woman back safe and sound'

The king was very impressed and ordered that the captain be given an extra portion of potatoes and onions with plenty of sour cream sauce before he sets out on his epic journey, to give him extra strength the red-hair- eh- Bernard said whilst knocking back a very large jug of his home-made brew, 'That is a super doper plan,' Then he whispered to the rather large bare-breasted woman beside him that she will have to get lost if his bare-breasted beautiful young wife does happen to return.

The plan worked to perfection with one little exception. Bernard's wife was not held in any prison cell but in the enemy king's bedroom where he was caught in middle of the act of seduction by the captain that had once more, bribed the guard at the king's bedroom door.

The king was simply picked up in the captains two hands and flung out the bedroom window whereupon he landed on a wooden spiked fence surrounding the kings little tomato garden. This was the start of the tradition of hanging the enemies head on a spike; a tradition that Bernard the Great celebrated at every chance he got. Until it was his turn to hang out with his people less than six months later when he stupidly challenged the captain to a fight. For now, though, they had a new king, a very tall, and to most of the bare-breasted women at least, a very handsome king. They loved the fact that everything about him was so big.

End

A Knock on the Door (Its Me)

I have been rescued- I've been set free
I have been taken-from slavery
Now I'm a free man- I'll drink porter no more
Sweet loving Jesus-I have been saved by- a knock on the door

And when I answered- He said to me
I've come here to help you- do you want company?
He sat by my fireside- with a smile on His face
Said He'd been looking- all over the place
He said now I've found you- try sin no more
Holy God- I have been saved by- a knock on the door

I gave Him a teacake and a large mug of tea
He came to save me- I was drowning you see
That teacake was lovely- do you have anymore
Sweet loving Jesus- I've been saved by- a knock on the door

He stayed with me till the teacakes were gone
Then once more He rose and then He moved on
I'll sing His praises- until I am no more
Holy Jesus Christ- I have been saved by a knock on the door

End

A Time to Live (Ecclesiastes 3)

A time to live- to throw off the chains that bind- to open the windows of the mind

To give- to love- to feel- to heal- to be loved by Him who loves us so- to grow- to know His love is real

This time to stay in His love- to pray- today- to lay the past to rest- those memories that never sleep- yet- to keep the ones that's blest- the wounds of love and life- that lie deep within our rest!

 A time to forgive and forget the past- yet not give up the cross- for if we forget and not forgive- another chance may be lost- time to be in love again- with love- with life-to throw off the cloak of darkness and embrace the coat of light-to endless holy blessed- patient- unselfish love- for love is always right- to give and not to count the cost- to care- to share- to be always there- in love with love and life- that life He gave upon the cross- for lovers- of life- everywhere!

 A time to cry- a time of hope- a time to try and learn the ropes and why- to try to understand- how life itself got so out of hand- how hard it is to cope- the ups and downs- the ins and outs- the whereabouts of it all-the merry go rounds- the dizziness of heights- the never-ending fall- the sounds of life- the cry of despair we failed to hear- because the cry within was almost too much for us to bear- while growing up so fast-the search for identity that would last long past tomorrow- the happy days- the sorrow- that never fades- the pity of not knowing- that one never stands alone- and that the pain is real- these are the wounds of life- that only His love can heal- wear them with pride- for it is such as these- that brought me to my knees- Lord- it was on my knees that I found the way to thee- that mighty road that leads to

Calvary- to Him who loves us so- yes the pain is real- the price is high- and is still being paid today- by all who love and reach out- to those- who hurt along the way!

A time for joy- to know that all is not in vain- the winter chill- that heavy rain- the mountains that we have to climb- time and time again- along the way there was some fun- though let us not forget-when everything is said and done-the race is on and still being run- so let us keep this mind set-on our mind- on those who are waiting at the finishing line- with the biggest trophy you've ever seen- and the glorious smile that says it all- welcome my beloved- to the home of love- that God had in mind for us- long- long before the fall.

End

Come Walk With Me Said JC

The sun was shining on this glorious Sunday morning. My mind was on the day before when for some unknown reason my spirit sank into what could now become my waterloo. By this I mean that the depression that I am afflicted with can come and go of its own accord.

Once it was only a couple of times a month, now it has developed a will all its own and can come and go carte-blanche.

It is at times like this when I'm in the deepest-mine. It is also at times like this that I meet my best friend JC.

When one is in hospital isn't it great to see a person you love, come through those hospital doors. Does not your spirit lift at once? Such it is with my forever friend JC. He comes through the door of my heart lovingly and often.

I want you to know at once that He is there for you also, all that you need do is call out to Him 'I NEED YOU LORD PLEASE HELP ME'. It is akin to the blind man calling out.

'Jesus Son of David, have pity on me.' (Luke 18: 35).

The Lord is quick to come to the rescue of those that he loves, and He loves everyone. Amen.

When I call to JC he comes quickly. He knows that I do need a boost of his great love to get me through the day, every day. In my mind's eye I can see him holding out His welcoming arms as He runs up to me. Although I was with him yesterday and the day before He is still so glad to see me such is His great love for me and all of us.

In my minds ear He says to me *Tommy come walk with me awhile"* and He wraps His right arm around my shoulder, and we go walking whatever the weather.

We go walking down by a lake where we sit on a rock by the waterfall. All the little creatures, birds and the like come and sit by his feet. Even the fish in the water stick up their little heads to have a look, such is His outpouring of His Spirit.

I sit here beside Him with tears in my eyes as he sings a song of His love for the world. Again, He sings that wonderful song 'And I love you so.'

I remember Perry Como used to sing it.

My only son David bought the LP for me once a long time ago; I still have it to this day. Praise the Lord. *'My Mother loves to hear me sing that song Tommy; I sing it every day for her bless her.'*

Talk to me Tommy' my Lord says to me and of course I at once go into a banter of what I feel is wrong with the world.

'Tom, Tommy, slow down, I know that you are worried about the state of My world and that's commendable but, Tommy, look at you, you are like a tiny ant in a gigantic world, do not try to lift what you cannot carry, that's My job!

'Is there nothing I can do Lord?'

'Tommy look here …into my eyes, no …no, look straight into my eyes; what do you see?"

'I see a huge mountain range; I see the Grand Canyon filled with Your love Lord!

'Anything else?'

'I can see a Pyramid Lord a huge one!

'You can move that Tom, from where it is; and throw it into the sea. (Luke 17: 5)

That's what you can do, it is harder to move a hard heart but with love Tom, anyone can do it!

'I love you, Lord!'

'I love you too Tom, I leave you My peace Tom and My love and my Spirit Tom, make good use of all three will you Tom?

'I will try hard to Lord!'

'Let My Love do all it wills Tom, you will find that it's quite capable, bye Tommy until next time.'

'I will Lord, bye, love you, Lord bye'

End

EVERYBODY SAID

Somebody said I should have stayed in bed- Everybody said I'm off my head

Somebody said he's not well read- and he's really up the junction!

Everybody said I've lost my mind- Somebody said leave him behind

He's been in the dark so long he's blind and- hell bent for destruction- but

O my Jesus, He loves me- He has me where He wants me to be

No more hopeless days for me- not since the Resurrection

Everybody said see what he's done-He's going to spoil it for everyone

He's trying to take away our fun--- and he'll end up causing friction

An eye for an eye and a tooth for a tooth- That's the natural law and that's the truth

And that's the way it's been since my father's youth

So why now this contradiction?

O my Jesus, He loves me- He has me where He wants me to be

I understand what He's done for me

On the hill on the cross at Calvary

Not many people want to be my friend- They say when your dead- well that's the end

Still, I tell them that's not true my friend- Jesus is waiting here for you

What a wonderful thing He's gone and done

Died on the cross for everyone- So you go ahead and have your fun- Me, I'll live for ever-

But my friend in the days to come- try your best to meet the Holy one- for the time will come when you'll know it's true- and better late than never

For my Jesus, He loves me- life is full of joy love and laughter you see, and He'll do for you what He's done for me- and we'll be happy for ever and ever.

End

A Simple Truth

One thing I love about Sunday is receiving the Blessed host. It gives me great strength to get through the week ahead. I need His strength because I don't have it on my own. In the past few weeks our parish has gone through so much pain and misery with the murders of beautiful children and a few very sad suicides.

I find it hard to comprehend such events, the numbness of it, the pain of it, the shock of it all that may never 'Heal' in the true sense of the word.

The mass in our community as in all communities is the only place where we can all come together as neighbours, of course there are the pubs and clubs but as one that does not drink, I find that Sunday mass is the only time we Christians can come together pray together and yes, even sing together. Then we depart again only seeing one or two people during the week mostly at the local store.

I do not grieve for those who have drifted away from the church. Some have good reason to do so. For I was one of those people in the past though the church never hurt me, and I do believe that these people are more prayerful than most of us that are still in the church today. As it says in the Old Testament there is a time for everything, and everything in its time. (Ecclesiastes 3-2)

I had to look that up.

It is at times of crisis that I pay more attention to the word of God and his Son Jesus though to be honest it is more the New Testament than the old. I find the Old Testament much tougher to follow. I love doing the readings. We have many readers in our church so most of us only have one reading a month.

I used to be in the music ministry, but I had to give it up on account of playing the guitar very badly and my singing voice is no more, but I loved it while I could do it. A time to give that up as well, lol.

I never try to judge anyone as I well know that there but for the grace of God go I. and it is so sad to see so many young people in the poor pitiful condition they are in, because of drugs or other sad and sorrowful issues. if ever the words of Jesus 'forgive them Father for they know not what they do,' really comes to the fore it is then. Imagine one's body screaming out for something or other deadly thing 24-7.

How hard it is for them to 'repent'

It is so good to have one's faith not only in times of troubles but the many happy times as well. I am not sure if you can only have one and not the other because everything has to sides to it. Such is life and death.

I am sure that there are people who never suffer but I don't know of any. I do know some people that seem to suffer much more that others though. I do not know why that is, only that one should only have to bear so much pain.

Having said all that: I have to say I am still a sinner! Not sure about others but for me I am going grand through the week, then bang; I do something I am not even sure is a sin, but it does knock me back a little bit so it must be harmful in some way, therefore I so need the Eucharist at least once a week though in truth I probably need it at least once every day, okay, I know when I have slipped down a rung or two, but I do not beat myself up over it.

Not anymore, why? Because there is forgiveness in Sacrament of Reconciliation before during or after the holy mass and especially in the Blessed Sacrament. Amen.

O' Sacrament Most Holy, O' Sacrament divine; all praise and all thanksgiving be every moment Thine.

End

An Angry Man

The mission

Senator John Mc William's from his mansion in Arlington between Fort Worth and Dallas, was looking through his binoculars at the rider that just turned onto his property. It was the hottest time of the day. He knew that large figure of a man was his old friend James Russell.

He himself had got the Marshal appointed on his recommendations Marshall of Coates County in Minnesota then of the whole United states. If anyone could help him with his problem, it was James Russell.

He was still watching when the rider leaned sideways and fell of his horse, hit the ground hard and came back up shooting… accidently killing his horse, 'what the hell…?' gasped the Senator not believing what he had just seen, happy to see his old friend getting back to his feet,

'Asleep, drunk, or both, just the man for this job' he muttered aloud.

The Senator rang a bell, and, in a few seconds, a colour servant appeared and was standing in front of him. 'Did you hear those shots Mo? His real name is Joe Mathews?'

'Yes sir, I did that, Lucy said the man fell from his horse down by that old birch tree, Senator, you want I should go take a closer look?'

The Senator replied. 'Sure, go bring him one of the horses from the corral, make sure someone takes that dead horse away, get cook to feed him to the ranch hands tonight and be careful he does not shoot you; the man might be drunk or worse, out of his head with all this sun, go quicky now and bring him here'

'Yes sir, sure thing boss'

It was still a long way from the house, and the Senator still using his binoculars to see what was happening, watched as old Mo rode up to James with the spare horse. James was now nursing his left arm whilst kneeling by his horse's head, saying under his breath,

'I am so sorry old girl, I didn't mean to do that, so sorry' he rose when he heard old Mo approaching. Mo dismounted and asked him if he were alright. 'Sure, I am, just fell off my horse,' then added, 'She stumbled and threw me, poor thing I had to shoot her, broke her front leg an all,' old Mo was around long enough to know better than to argue with the man, even if the Marshal was lying through his teeth. he just said.

'The Senator sent me here with this one, try not to shoot it' James was just about to ask him what he meant by that remark when a pain shot through his left arm, so he didn't bother just gave old Mo a funny look.

Five minutes later he was dismounting at the Senator's porch.

'You alright?' the Senator asked him, as he watched him rubbing his sore arm, the Marshall replied, 'Sure just a touch of rheumatism, is all, nothing to worry about' then the Senator said to him,

'I am happy to see you James, come inside and have lunch with me' he threw his right arm over his old friend's shoulder and guided him in through the open door, James looked down at the binoculars on the Senator's seat and wondered just how much his friend had seen.

Inside the massive hallway James was surprised to see so many doors in a huge circular hallway. The Senator could see how impressed his old friend was then turned right and entered a door into an oval shaped room.

Before going to his massive mahogany desk, he went straight to his drink's cabinet.

'Like one' he asked the Marshal who declined the offer. 'I always have one about this time, so what do you think of the place nodding his head left to right? James replied saying.

'I have never been there, but I've seen a picture of it somewhere, but isn't this the same type of office the President Grant has in the White house?'

'It surely is' replied the Senator who then said, 'As you know or, may not know, I will be running for the Presidential office come early-November, now about this problem I am having up north, a place called Provo ever heard of it, Jim?

The marshal nods and says,

'Sure Senator, it's on the trail to Salt Lake City, Spanish fork' then the Senator knocking back his drink continues saying, 'that is precisely that reason why I picked you Jim, you know your way around those parts,

…my problem is this young man called Billy What's is going round shooting people for no reason, up there, no reason whatsoever. The Senator slams his fist down hard making the marshal jerk awake.

'He fancies himself as the next Billy the kid, or some kind of hellish ghoulish kind of gunslinger, he is everything they say he is Jim …a pure savage murdering low life …and any kind of argument …that he himself starts Jim …ends up with someone getting killed,'

He slams the desk again then carries on saying 'and many people have gotten killed, James …far too many …and this killing spree cannot go on, so I want you to head up there and take him out, any way you can'

The Marshall sees the Senator's face redden somewhat and asks him. 'Why doesn't the local sheriff handle this, don't tell he too has been shot?

The Senator replied, 'Not just the local sheriff, but his two deputies as well, I tell you James …this young man needs to be stopped, he has taken over the town and people are too scared to do anything about it, you have been chosen by me to bring this bloody young man in, dead or alive, and I do not care if he is shot standing up, sitting down or even in his bed,' the Marshal shifted somewhat on his leather seat and again notice how red the Senator's face was getting.

Then the Senator cooling down somewhat, reaches into a drawer and takes out a white envelope and throw's it across the desk to James and says,' There is 5000 dollars in there …just in case you might have to stay a bit longer than normal or get additional help plus all the information you need, it's all in there'

The Marshal replies. Looking at the photograph of a young man, 'mmm half Indian, looks to me like he is, that is a lot of money Senator, to bring in one man, whatever his age!' and if any bounty hunter gets wind of this it could make my job twice as hard' the Senator cuts him off with a wave of his hand and say's,

'That is not going to happen James, I promise you that, I cannot trust those bounty hunters, James …they could and have done brought in bodies with they're faces smashed in, claiming to be this or that outlaw, when it could easily have been some poor sod on his way home from town after having a few drinks,

Are you sure you won't have a one? Again, the marshal decline's as he rises from his seat, picks up the envelope from the desk and follows the Senator across the ovel office and heads for the front door.

Along the way before he can ask, the Senator says to him. 'You can keep that horse outside James, and I know you won't let me down, I don't have to tell you …you know I need to be seen dealing with this problem so I can depend on those people up there to vote for me, in the up-and-coming election' the Marshal replies saying,

'I will do my best Senator, I won't let you down' The Senator replies saying 'I know you won't James, that is why I picked you for this job' then walks with James to the front door then raised the whisky glass in the marshal's face then says,

'If you need anything, anything at all …just send a telegraph to the local office and I will respond at once, don't worry James, just get this done for me please' James replies mounting his horse, 'Nice horse Senator' then turning the horse north-west bound says. 'Don't worry Senator! I will not let you down'

Mapleton: a small cattle town with an ever-growing population and large enough to considered for a railway-station is the next stop for the Marshal who heads straight for the sheriff's office.

'Yep' said the sheriff after listening to the Marshal's story, 'Heard about that kid running riot up there,' offered to go and arrest him myself but someone pulled the brakes on that one, so you're going after him? Huh, well I wish you luck marshal, if half of what I heard is even half true then you're going to need it,'

Then as an afterthought said, 'You can take Henry there, a fine young deputy, and as honest as the day is long,' the Marshal replies, 'Its nearly November, the days aren't so long, thanks but no thanks' the sheriff says to him. It's a bit late now Marshal …best get yourself a room in Aunt Maggie's downtown …she does a great steak, best I ever had, and cheap too' the Marshal looking at the sheriff's thin frame says to himself 'don't look like you had too many steaks to me' then says he will, thanks the sheriff then rides on.

Marshal James Russel, 56 years old white haired and lean and mean having spent 20 years in the army in Fort Worth, spent most of his army life chasing renegade Indians all over Utah and surrounding lands even as far south as New Mexico, risen to the rank of Coronel before becoming a sheriff in Elk Ridge on retiring from army life and after his many successes in bringing wanted men to trail and mostly to the hanging tree in some town square somewhere was recommended by the Senator and accepted by the Governor and made United States Marshal.

Now here he was on the trail of some young thug that for some reason known only to the Senator himself wanted dead and preferably buried in some unknown grave in some unknown graveyard in some unknown little town, somewhere up north.

The marshal did not buy that 'You're the man for the job Jim,' story that he had been told. And why had the Senators face reddened so?

Was the man suffering from high blood pressure? Or was there some other reason on his mind that he wasn't telling his old friend? These were the thoughts of the Marshal as he rode westward towards the large town of Hope.

From earlier trips he knew it would take him at least five days to get there as the countryside was wild and rugged with mountains to the left and right and only one watering hole that he knew off, two days hence, and even that was off the long tortuous trail. No, he had slowly concluded that there was more to the Senators story that he had been told.

It was on the road to Salem that he came across the Reverend Berkely, formerly of the 22nd rifle brigade of the confederate army in New Orleans at the time shorty before the civil war in 1861.

A man of many talents good and bad but now had turned to making his living by promising redemption and ultimately salvation, for a price, everything he had done and always would do was still for a price.

He was standing by the wheel of his pony and trap when the Marshal came upon him and offered to help, 'That is very nice of you sir, and no doubt but the God that brought you here will reward you for your kindness,' to which the Marshal replied.

'I haven't done anything yet,' the Reverend laughed and said, 'it is not what you did or did not do kind sir, but what is in the heart that matters, everything else will follow, now this wheel, the spokes have broken, and it is driving me crazy with its wobbling, can anything be done to restore it to its original condition?'

The Marshal got of his horse then dismantled the rig from the horse then threw a blanket over the shivering horse then said to him,

'There, that is the only thing I can do for you, you will find it a little bit uncomfortable for a few hours then you'll be wondering why you hadn't thought of it before, I know you have ridden a horse before and you will soon get used to it again,'

The Reverend disappointed that he hadn't thought of it first said to him,

'Thank you kindly, Marshal, I can see your badge from here, yes thank you and do you mind if I ride along with you for a while? the road here is so long and a man needs someone to talk too' the Marshal says to him,

You're not going to try and save my soul are you now, cos if you are then we part company right here and now'

The Reverend replied saying, I can see sir that you are in no immediate need of saving, although I am not saying you are perfect or anything remotely like it, but on the face of it, I can see you are a good man'

The Marshal said to him, 'Goodbye Reverend! what have I just said to you about preaching to me?' then he trotted on ahead only to be followed by the Reverend who was sitting a little sideways on his horse. 'Hah, hah …you do have a sense of levity …but I promise not to preach to you, so I won't'

When the Reverend heard that the Marshal was in the opposing army he went on to tell him about his many skirmishes about the time he and his company stole some Yankee gold and were headed across the mountains on a stolen enemy rig to get back to his camp that was based across the Mississippi River on the southern side when they were held up crossing the mountains at some point by bandits, killing four of his men and stopping him in his tracks, and when he saw that the four out of the five bandits were on horseback behind the rig he reversed the rig and sent them over the edge to their deaths below and before the other bandit could react shot him between the eyes. The Marshall asked him,

'And the Yankee gold, what became of it?' No, don't tell me …it went over the edge with the rig and was never seen again, except maybe by some Apache that was looking for somewhere to answer a call of nature and found it, that is why every Indian from here to the Canadian border was wearing chunks of the stuff'

The Reverend said to him grudgingly , 'Ah …an unbeliever, oh …well I promised not to preach to you so I won't …but suffice to say, that if I can raise enough money and men I will one day return to that place in my head that pinpoints the exact spot …well who knows …reclaim that gold and as I say who knows …I might just run into such a person any day now'

And thought the Marshal. Horses might grow wings and fly. I am going to shoot this man if he doesn't shut the hell up, anyway; won't be long now till we get to Salem then he can go wherever he likes, just as long as he goes in the opposite direction to where I am going.

It was in Salem that he meets the young Molly Springer. A singer in the local saloon. She overhears him telling the barman he is on his way to Provo. Where she tells him later she is on her way to marry a very nice young man that has been writing to her this past six months, then she shows him the last letter and says to him, 'he is like you Marshal, a lawman, a sheriff in some time called HOPE, and he writes saying that he hopes, ha -ha …to meet me there sometime before spring, so do you mind if I tag along with you, as there is no stage due for another four weeks,'

Instantly he agrees, as now he has a good reason to get rid of the Reverend Joseph Berkely, and besides she is such a pretty lady, and the Marshal would be only too glad to go for a long ride with her.

Any red-blooded man would.

On the day of his departure, he and Molly got up before sunrise and left the Reverend sleeping soundly in his bed. He found out soon enough that she had at least one tiny fault.

She would often burst spontaneously into song, she was a singer after all, it was nice at first then him and his horse got a little weary of it, so he asked her to stop doing that and she did.

They were now two days from the town of Hope, and she said to him one evening. 'Are you a married man Marshal? I don't mean to pry but do you have family? cos I don't …I lost mine in a house fire when I was six, a man passing by managed to run into the burning house and grab me, I lost my mother and father a brother and two sisters, I don't know anyone out here and…'

The Marshal said to her trying to cheer her up, 'That is because there is no one out here, look around you, but, then again, you now know me'

She came right out and asked him 'Will you lead me down the aisle, I have no one else, would you do me the honour please?' he went red in the face as he was only thinking of someone else walking the two of them down the aisle, any aisle.

'I would love to' he politely answers, 'I will look forward to that, thank you, Molly …that is an Irish name, isn't it?' he asks her, and she replies saying, 'It is, my family are …I mean were …all Irish, the whole family…the singing Springers is, was what they were called, in a place called Clare in the county Mayo, up the north-west of Ireland' she stopped when she saw the

Reverend riding hurriedly up to meet them. Then Marshal wiping his brow said to her.

'O' Christ forgive me! not that two-face old bragger again!' said the Marshal on following the direction of her pointed finger. Who said to them, 'There you are at last, why did you leave without me?

Then looking at Molly's beautiful long red hair and smiling face said to him, 'Not that I am surprised, when I heard that the two of you had left at the same time, in the middle of the night, well, I guess I would have done the same thing, Marshal,

Ah well! we are together again that's all that matters now,' the only thing the Marshal had to say was, 'You are riding that horse like a true professional, we didn't want to wake you and as far as I can remember you said Salem was where you were headed, anyway as you just said, we are all together again. I can always shoot myself, thought the Marshal.

The only good thing about the Reverend re-joining the small group, was that he, seeing how close and cosy the Marshal and Molly have become rode a few paces behind them plus the fact the Marshal did not want anything to do with him at all. So once more settled down for the night; The Marshal laying not too far away from Molly so he could keep an eye on her, didn't notice the Reverend creep up behind him and put a gun to the back of his head saying softly,

'I know what you're up to with her and you can have her, but I want that fat envelope you cling to so tightly, I am guessing it is full of Yankee dollar bills, hand it over or you're a dead man,'

The Marshal went to take out the envelope with his right hand then suddenly grabbed the gun with his left hand and pulled the Reverend down and there was a scuffle, and the gun went off shooting the Reverend in the head. Dead.

The sound of the gun going off woke Molly and she jumped up and when she saw what had just happened, she threw her arms around the Marshal's neck saying,

'Oh my God! he could have killed you, oh are you alright, oh, that terrible man ...and him a man of God, do you mind if I sleep beside you? ...I am shaking all over,' Of course the Marshal didn't mind, he was only too happy to have her lie beside him, but he figured he wasn't going to get much sleep either. Unbeknown to him the shot also woke up three Apache Indians sleeping nearby.

'You have got to be joking! said the Marshal to Molly Springer now that he had her alone and shaking in his strong hairy arms and asked her what was the name of her soon husband to be,

'William What's' she replied wondering why the Marshals face just turned white as he said to her bluntly.

'And he is the sheriff of this town called Hope, that's what he told you and how old is this man?'

'Twenty- three' she replies, and you, young lady, how old are you? 'Twenty-four,' then continues what she was saying, 'and he has a small piece of land just outside town.

The Marshal is thinking. The only piece of land he owns or will ever own will be in the local cemetery, this can't be the same man, don't tell me she and I are going to meet the same man? she to marry and I to kill, this just isn't happening, it just cannot be.

He went quiet whenever he was around her from then on. She noticed and put it down to him been tired, after all he was an old man and had been a long time on the trail, and even I she told herself, was tired and weary. Not to mention he had the night before just killed a man. It might also have something to do with the three Apache Indians that were now following them and moving up close.

'Should we run?' Molly asked the Marshal who replied, 'no point, their horses could outrun ours every day, just relax and don't let them see you are afraid, they might just be friendly,' the three young braves came along side and the one nearest the Marshal said, 'you the one that killed that man back there?' the other two were more interested in Molly's long red hair. The Marshal showed him his badge and said, 'I am ...he tried to rob me then he would have killed us both, so I shot him', then the Marshal, working on a hunch slowly moved his hand inside his waistcoat and took out the envelope with the picture of Billy What's saying to the Indian next to him,

'Have you seen this man? And the Indian nearly fell off his horse and took the photo and showed it to the other two.

They had a quick and heated discussion between them. Then without even looking back at them they quickly rode off. Molly asked him,

'What is all that about? They looked like they had seen a ghost, who was that person in the photograph you showed them?' the Marshal said softly, 'Just some young troublemaker I have to bring in, judging by their reaction I think they knew him and have probably gone to warn him I'm coming, anyway we will know soon enough another four hours and we'll be there,'

It had been a long arduous journey and if it hadn't been for the beautiful Molly Springer springing herself on him like she did back in Salem, he might have turned back. Luckily for her and himself he was a man with a moral compass that saved him from making a complete fool of himself on more than one occasion.

Still, he thought to himself, we are not there yet, we still have a long way to go.

Three and a half hours later looking down from the hillside, they could see the large town of Hope, ahead, 'Oh' Molly giggled to herself as she realised her future husband was only a stone's throw away. As the crow flies.

The Marshal on the other hand frowned at the very thought of spoiling her beautiful dreams and decided there and then that he would retire as soon as this job was over.

As they rode into town they got some strange looks from the townsfolk, some nice ones and some not so nice as the Marshal followed her to the sheriff's office where she jumped off her horse nearly breaking her neck she ran into the sheriff's office with shouts of joy and tremendous excitement.

This was the moment the Marshal had been dreading since he found out who her husband was going to be.

He needn't have worried because the young man now standing in front of him was anything but troublesome. In fact, he was polite and charming even to the point of embarrassment. He was so delighted to finally have met the beautiful Molly Springer that his smile almost reached from ear to ear as he said to the Marshal.

'Welcome Marshal I heard you were coming, I hope you like our little town, well …it's not so little now that the railway has brought hundreds of new people here, I want to thank you for looking after my darling bride, she told me how well you looked after her, isn't she just beautiful, I hope you can join us for dinner tonight and can stay for the wedding next weekend?

Molly snuggled into his Billy's arms as she said to the Marshal, 'Maybe Marshal, you might think about giving me away, you know …walk me down the aisle?' the Marshal responded 'I will be honoured to do just that, thank you Molly, now can someone please direct me to the nearest motel? I am all tuckered out,'

Later over dinner the Marshal asked Billy What's how he managed to get the sheriff's job. Billy said to him, 'You mean because, I am half Apache? The Marshal replied, 'No, that is not what I meant, you are so young and must be very good with those guns of yours, I mean there are other, older men here, I have never seen a sheriff so young before, so how did you get the job?'

Billy said to him, 'because not so long ago this town was a lawless town, good folk been killed every day of the week, innocent people that weren't even wearing firearms shot down like dogs as they made their way home, so one day I decided to do something about it, I closed the saloon and that did not suit some people so they challenged me on the street, calling me all kinds of horrible names …but I was faster than they were, and so it took off from there and here I am with the most beautiful woman in the whole wide world by my side and I could not be happier' the Marshal raised his glass to him and said,

'And this is one fine meal, she can cook as well, very nice indeed, you're a very lucky young man' Molly said to him, 'Oh! I didn't cook that, I can't boil water, no …he has his grandmother to do that for him, but I am sure she will teach me how to cook in time' and she gave that lovely little childish giggle of hers.

Later, when they were alone Billy said to the Marshal. 'So! you have come to take me in, back to Texas …you must be very fast with those guns of yours, I guess you have a job to do, and I won't try to stop you, but can I ask you why you are here to take me in?

I mean I must be some kind of terrible bandit for you to come all this way, lots of gunmen have tried before and failed' the Marshal told him all about the Senator, and he listened intently to what he had to say.

When the Marshal had finished young Billy What's went to a desk in the room and took out an old photograph of the Senator holding a badly beaten young Apache woman and smiling like a man that had just been elected President of the United States.

'That monster that you work for is my father, he raped and beat my mother repeatedly until she could no longer stand on her own two feet, there in that photo your holding he is playing the hero, to the drunken hordes of white folk, true, the Apache's were on the rampage back then, but the women weren't, and he was running for office at the time, and got elected on the back of that picture,

I am thinking of becoming a Marshal, but I believe it must go through him, so I don't fancy my chances, he knows who I am, someone, and old friend of his, sent him a copy of that picture and I believe that is the reason you are here to kill me Marshal and get me out of the way' the Marshal took off his badge and placed it on the table before Billy and the young man took it up and ran his finger over it, then looked at the Marshal who said to him.

'I have the power to make you a Marshal and not even the Senator can block that, only the governor can do that but won't, not when I tell him what you have just told me,' Then the Marshal took out the 4000 dollars from the envelope and gave it to Billy saying,

'A wedding present, courtesy of the Senator, and if you play your cards right you might even get him to build you a new church or schoolhouse, or a bigger railway station, with what you know about him, maybe a whole new town, don't worry about that badge young fella, I don't need it anymore, I just retired'

Ah well, thought the Marshal just before he went to sleep, at least I get to walk her down the aisle.

End

Fat Black Cat

My black cat is getting fat- she eats everything-no matter what- or where she's at

The vet said-if she doesn't lose some weight- then she will soon be dead as a door mat

I can't have that- so I didn't hesitate

I took her to the track- the dog track- and let her loose thinking that- the dogs would see her on the track and think she was the rabbit they were suppose too chase-she would have to run like mad and thereby lose some weight- but she just sat there- looking fat- and the dogs never even looked at her- meaning of course that not even dogs like a fat slob of a cat

Then I took her to the park-on a lead- and tried to take off running thinking that-this fat black cat would run beside me- not a chance- she just did some kind of snotty dance and sat her fat behind down on the ground and wouldn't make a sound- moved not a muscle- not even a little moan- just a tiny little groan- more like a mouse squeak-bleeding cheek of that fat black female cat

So I took her up a mountain- it nearly killed me to do it- but I did it- only to find she somehow managed to jump onto my backpack without me knowing it- to be honest though I was so concentrating on getting up that bloody mountain and I had only to carry my heavy backpack with all my goodies in it- i.e.- plenty of coca cola and lots and lots of sugary stuff- mars bars- etc. etc.- to give me energy you see-as I knew I would need substance if and when I got to the top of the mountain- which I did- though only just- it was a hard slog- I should have brought my dog- at least he would have pulled me some of the way up that bloody mountain- he is a St Bernard- and he is very fat as well- but he looks great-like a bear-only bigger- he also loves those mars bars and Lidl's chocolate- so do I- mountains of it-lovely food- lovely stuff but enough already

My fat black cat is dead- I woke this morning to find her in my bed- she was after eating all my slimming pills and hormone tablets that the fat lady doctor with the moustache and smoking a smelly cigar had giving me these past ten years- I mean they taste horrible so they do- so I just never took them- but my fat black cat did- don't know how she managed to open so many bottles but she did- oh I remember now- I opened the bottles myself- so I wouldn't feel so bad if the huge fat doctor asked me did I take my anti-eating pills- so I mustn't have tightened them back on again- silly me- I'm having trouble getting in and out of bed these days- forgive me my southern drawl

I've tried all sort of ways- but the bed is just too small.

End

The Root of All Evil

Tom Robinson was not a young man, he often said that although he was seventy-five, on the outside, he felt twenty-five on the inside, the same I suppose, can be said of most people.

A man with simple needs. He did have a reasonably good life up until the death of his second wife Jennifer, in 2006 then, eight years later his beautiful partner Rose, died as well, both of whom died of cancer.

There were other women in between but none that he wanted to come live with him. He had grown used to living on his own. It was while living on his own that he had a stroke, on his way into his kitchen down he went and not having his phone with him he had to crawl on his belly back into the bedroom where he phoned his daughter who upon seeing the condition he was in, phoned an ambulance.

To make a long story even longer it took two years out of his life then truth be told he is to this present day still recovering from it. Thankfully, his mind and body are still in working order, if indeed his mind ever was to begin with, as his wonderful daughter Josie often said to him, 'you are much too soft dad, don't be giving those people (beggars) your hard-earned money, they are only going to spend it on drugs or drink.' he was however a sucker for a sob story. With his sending money to this and that charity.

He once even sent nearly 3000 euro to someone in Canada to help get her and her family out of a tight spot and home. They made it as far as the UK where they got into another tight spot.

Once while he was down to his last 28 euro on his credit card, he responded to someone in India looking for financial help in caring for her son and whilst in the process of donating 20 euro a window popped up saying that most people donated 200 euro to this very sad cause, so that was it, he packed it in and to this day he hasn't donated a red cent to anyone.

Though he was in his mind anyway, still a good Christian man. Loved his weekly mass, singing and reading the word of God. A few weeks after his stroke he felt no longer safe driving, so his four-year-old Nissan Juke had to go.

He loved his ground floor one bedroomed apartment on the south side of the city, close enough to the Dublin Mountains where he walked every day in his local park, a park he loved dearly.

His neighbour every now and then would come and ask him for a loan of this or that amount, and he mostly gave it to her as he liked her and as also stated above, he was a sucker for a sob story.

Anyway, it was only small amounts of money. At first. This then was the character of the man called Tommy Robinson, until the day he won 500,000 on the lotto.

The brand-new Nissan Juke in his car-spot kind of gave the game away. At first, he said he had won it in some raffle, the near neighbours bought it at first then when all his fancy new sound system arrived one or two put their finger on it, and soon the sad stories began knocking on his door.

He had been warned about this and he planned not to touch his winnings for at least a month, longer if he could hold out. Of course, his children got 50 grand each straight away, and his ex-wife got 20 grand for just been his ex-wife but overall, he never touched his money other than that already aforementioned.

His neighbour a good-looking woman half his age would come in sometime slightly intoxicated and would sing his praises and generally flirt with him in the hope of getting on his softer side, even offering to give him a BJ and although he was tempted, he did not fully accept her kind offer, but gave her the 50 euro anyway.

Word began to spread and soon there were strangers coming to his door with stories of bringing their half blind legless elderly parents back from Australia so that they could die happily with their families, in their own country.

Or they had a wedding coming up in the Seychelles and they had no way of getting the bride and her six bridesmaids there in time and would now have to charter their own small plane within the next two days if they were going to make it on time. Or they simply wanted to send their four children to college, but only had enough resources to send one.

Then there was the one about the father dying of cancer who had great difficulty going up to the local HSE care centre's palliative care unit to see his wife. Although Tommy was a soft touch, he held out against most of these sad made-up tales of woe.

Though the one about the lesbian woman lost on the mountains in the Siberian winter almost had him until the said woman phoned her partner who had accidently and unintentionally put her on speaker said, 'well! did he buy it? are we going to Rome this weekend or what?'

Now here's the thing. Tommy wasn't sleeping well anymore, or eating well, or enjoying his daily walk in the park anymore. Not even his favourite TV show Judge Judy could he enjoy anymore, his little apartment that he loved dearly was now fast becoming his prison.

He was now thinking of moving out and buying a bungalow somewhere on the Dublin Mountains which only six weeks ago, would have been unthinkable.

Then the boys moved in on him. The tough bad boys that he knew where out there but now they were in his face, right here in his home.

Threatening to smash his face in if he didn't give them the money that they said, was rightly theirs. F…king cheek.

He refused point blank.

Not even when they punched him several times in the head and beat him about the face. They wanted his credit card and pin number, but he told them to f…k off and get out of his house this was a different Tommy Robinson that then one before.

This new man had balls of steel.

One of the four thugs was a little more compassionate than the others and Tommy played on that saying through his broken nose and broken teeth that if only their mothers could see them now, beaten up an old age pensioner.

The shame she would feel. The other three beat him some more, saying things like, 'If you don't give us the money, and not all of it mind, we will let you keep some of it, but not a lot of it, we will kill you before the morning comes,'

Then one of them took out a cutting tool used to cut thick locks from closed factory gates, and shoved it in Tommy's face saying, 'we will start with your toes, then your fingers then your ears and then your willy, then your nose, I am telling you your own mother won't recognise you after we're finished with you neither will your dog,' He didn't have a dog'

The one with the little compassion said to him, 'Give them the money man, it is not worth your life, and we will be gone out of here in a few minutes'

Tommy said to him very slowly on account of the pain he was in, 'You dumb asses actually think I keep a lot of money here, in this place, maybe under my bed or in the wardrobe, use your thick skulls …the money is in the bank where it belongs, the taxman has frozen my account on account of them claiming I owe them a lot of back taxes, they said that I was working while claiming the dole, so you see, even if I wanted to I could not give you any more than the four hundred I have in my wallet, so take that and welcome to it, you fucking morons'

Once more he was hit in the side of the head by the one claiming and willing to cut him to pieces who said. 'I don't buy that, and if you're lying, we will find out, we will come back and tear you a new asshole, you get me …old man?' then they moved towards the door when the mean mouthed one stopped, came back, and took the money from Tommy's wallet, then left without even a thank you or goodbye.

It took a while, but Tommy managed to free himself from the rope that they tied him to the chair with and then phoned himself an ambulance. He had a broken nose in two places, fractured jawbone on both sides and a torn lip that needed ten stitches, not to mention his broken full set of false teeth that they deliberately stamped on. He had to have reconstructive surgery on his face.

This was going to cost him a lot of money. Money that he now wished he'd never won in the first place. However, a two-week cruise in the western Mediterranean with his beautiful young female neighbour soon changed his mind, as did his beautiful villa in the south of Spain, that helped a lot as well.

End

Seamus Roach

Seamus Roach lived on an island off the coast of Innishsmall, about ten nautical miles from the fabulous Cork harbour where the Titanic dropped in to collect some passengers, of course it was called Queensland back then and the ill-fated ship was so big it had to anchor offshore. On a good day, according to Seamus you could swim there and back with the weekly shopping, so you could. There were about twenty people left living there as most of the once busy little island was no longer viable and sure there was hardly a cow left in the place.

Never mind people.

The once busy little pub that at the height of the tourist season was so full to capacity, they had to put the sofa outside the door, and it was the first pub in Ireland to offer an outside service so it was, but was now only open once a fortnight and even then, was only serving bottled stuff, God there was more alcohol in the washing up liquid than some of them bottles, so there was, according to Seamus.

'Why haven't you left, Seamus? Some nosey tourist once asked him back in 74, to which he quickly replied saying, 'Sure where would I go man? or are you a female?

Tis hard to tell these days, you know, where would I go? and why would I go? Sure this beautiful little island is my home, and my wife's home and we are as cosy here as we would be six foot under, she is still living you know, a fine strong woman, a bit like your good self, no matter if you are a male or female, tis hard to tell these days, we raised a good family of heifer's and goats here, with two fine children, one male, and one female, sure …why would I leave here when rich people all over the world are buying up little islands like this one just to get away from the busy towns and cities? no thank you kindly …sir, or madam, tis hard to tell the difference between the two nowadays, so it is, if it weren't for the fact that some women wear lip stuff, sure it be nearly impossible so it would to tell the difference so it would, thank you for asking that stupid question now f…k off back to where you came from. He could be rude at times could Seamus.

Yes, it was a sorry day when his good friend and nearest neighbour Frank O' Mahony went and died. They had been the best of friends since childhood, and would, when they got married on the same day at the same time, no, not to each other but to Shelia and Nancy that the lads had no qualms whatsoever about sharing their wives every other Friday night, with the two girls spending the night together every other Monday, and it was not to go play bingo.

They did everything together except die. Nancy still came over to see Shelia from time to time and Seamus still went over to see Nancy from time to time, but it was never quite the same since Frank died, because Seamus now had to milk his own cow.

He told this tale to some stranger he met on the island one fine summers evening. When asked if he ever went on holidays, where would he go? It was a good and fair question as he had everything he wanted where he was, scenic views, sandy beach. Wind surfing if he had a mind to, which he most certainly did not have a mind to go windsurfing. Ever. He said to the stranger who was sorry he stopped and asked such a stupid question.

'Where would I go? Now tis a secret mind, but as you won't be here long enough to tell anybody, I will tell you, sir, if you look towards your right, you can see one palm tree on the very edge of the island, well a few steps back from that tree, under the rocks there, are two very fine caves, oh, about forty yards in length and two yards wide, well, tis there myself and my missus Shelia, would go every year for four or five days, sure you might as well be in the south of Spain watching all those fishing boats coming and going, with just the two of us and sometimes Nancy might, if she is not too busy come and join us, she usually came at night when I'm out strolling along the beach, and when I'd return and see her there and sure it would be a lovely surprise to know they spent a few happy hours together, so that is where we go for the holidays my friend, thank you for asking, now f…k off and leave me in peace' he could be quite rude when he had a mind to be.

He often had a mind to be rude. He loved to hear himself talking and would on occasion have the odd local about turn and hastily retreat when he or she saw Seamus coming towards them.

Then there was that tall tale he once told to two unsuspecting tourists about the islanders woken from their sleep by a huge container ship ramming into their little island on the eastern side and pushing it roughly three kilometres out into the wild Atlantic Ocean, thankfully for the islanders there just happened to be a Tsunami coming in from the western side an hour later and thankfully pushed it back into place again. Causing on account of the islands size, little or no damage but rather as Seamus put it, quote 'Cleaned the place up a bit' unquote.

If you're still standing there wearing your clogs, he might even tell you the one about how he, eh, once kissed a mermaid. It had happened he said after having a few of his best friends Franks home brew. He said that he wanted to have a pee…eh catch some fresh air before he went home to his darling Shelia.

He was about to when he saw this his words beautiful mermaid standing in three feet of water just watching him, and that he had had a good long chat with the female, 'You could tell the males from the females back then so you could, the fact that this mermaid had rather large breasts told him it was a female.

A beautiful female mermaid. He had he said walked into the water and kissed the mermaid goodnight. It had been said Seamus, a long passionate kiss, cold, but sure, the water was cold.

The very next day, sadly, the body of one of the elderly islanders, a rather large female, from the north of the island was washed up on the shore. Her grieving husband said that she took her own life after having two glasses of Franks home brew that he had bought the night before from someone called John, and it had sent her spiralling down into the depths of despair, but Seamus would not mention that to anyone. Not even his beloved wife Sheila. He could be very devious, could old Seamus.

Then one night back in the heydays when hay was not delivered by rowboat, Seamus was in the company of his wife and others when challenged to a weight-lifting contest in his local bar. 'God' he had said, 'Sure I can't lift myself out of bed in the afternoons, but I will nom …nim …nomin eh…tell you someone sitting not a thousand miles away from me that can lift a heifer under each arm while milking a cow at the same time with her false teeth,'

He looked at his beloved wife that was built like a Russian T34 tank and said to her, 'fine girl you are' She stood up, red-faced, then lifted him up by the scruff of his neck with her right hand and kicked him out the door with her wellington booted left foot as any decent Kerry footballer would do all the way home into his back garden, where she made him sleep in the outside shed whilst she went and made Nancy some supper. He could be a two-faced f…k…eh, so and so at times, could Seamus.

He would not tell you about the twenty-foot crocodile he once found on the beach one cold winters day. At first, he thought it was a replica, a play toy of some child's sorrowful upbringing somewhere on the planet; and that it simply got washed up on his little island by the strong riptides and currents that surrounded the island.

Then it opened its eyes and took one look at Seamus then turned abruptly as if to make a hasty retreat back to wherever it had come from, but the waters were too cold for the poor weak creature. It most certainly did not like the patting of its head by this weird looking Irishman.

Even after Seamus took off his long winter coat and wrapped it round the poor thing and took it home to sit by the fire to warm itself despite the ranting and raving of his beloved wife, the creature had great difficulty keeping its natural dignified position, of not moving until it was ready to move.

It was only after the large puffed-up pet dog called Alijah suddenly went missing, and then his beloved wife Shelia suddenly moving into Nancys house, it was only after the cat went missing and Seamus found the reptile having a bath that he had just run for himself that he noticed something was amiss in his daily routine.

Gone was the joyful sound of his wife's singing, while Alijah howled in accompaniment, gone also was his twelve your old cat's habit of tripping him up every time Seamus went to the kitchen. Only then did he realise that since he brought the creature home had things changed in his life, and not for the better either.

So, he called the local vet to do a house call and as soon as the vet arrived, she went back out to her car and came back in with a double-barrelled shotgun and shot the poor thing in the head, right in the bath. There was blood everywhere. Even on the ceiling.

Then she had the nerve to charge him twenty-five pounds, for the visit and cartridges. Seamus could be very stupid at times, all other times he was just stupid.

on the other hand took delight in her short hiatus from Seamus and was only too glad to spend some quality time with her dearest friend Nancy and after doing what great friends do together, she told Nancy about the weird sea creature Seamus had brought home and made it more welcome there than she was.

At this point in time, she did not know about the sharp shooting vets visit to the house.

It was only after the word quickly spread through the village that Seamus had shot himself with the vets double-barrel shotgun that she returned home with Nancy in toe and they both were somewhat disappointed to find that the rumours weren't true. Seamus was quite rightly left in Coventry while Shelia and Nancy played house.

Then there was the one he bragged and boasted about the Russians knocking on his door in the middle of the night. Apparently the three of them came from a submarine that lay just off the coast.

All dressed in black, that left Seamus not seeing them at first when he opened his front door and then they smiled. 'Isvinite' one said meaning 'excuse me' but we have collided with a …how you say? Kosatka eh, …killer whale, and have lost eh …lost, eh, poterly…contact …'the one in the middle cut him off saying, in perfect English,

'We have collided with a very large whale of the eastern coastline and have damaged our communications antenna, and having done so, have lost contact with base, so we were wondering if we may use your phone, please? we know the Irish are very welcoming and always have an open-door policy when it comes to visitors'

The third one was playing with a bunch of notes in his hands flickering through them to get maximum attention from Seamus, oh, those Russian navy people, always up to no good.

Having got Seamus's attention, he allowed them the use of his phone, while one was on the phone Shelia came out of the bedroom wearing nothing but a strange look on her face wondering what was going on in the middle of the night.

'Kosatka drugoi 'gasped one to his mate who had the decency not to laugh. Translation read 'another whale'

As the lads were leaving Seamus rubbed his fingers together, meaning of course money and the one with the wad of notes handed him a monopoly

20-dollar bill. So, such was the life of Seamus Roach, some people liked him, some called him a cockroach, while others tried not to think of him at all.

End

The Man Who Saw Faces.

Mary Dunne woke up screaming from a bad dream she was having. Her husband Tommy lying beside her was sleeping like a baby. A travelling salesman now retired, up with the setting sun usually but now the complete opposite. Then he was on a lot of medication after his stroke last year 2021. They have been married now for well over forty-five years. With two sons and two daughters now with families of their own making them grannies and grandads much to their delight.

A third daughter Helen never married and was renting her own apartment in the city, rumour had it she was living with another woman, supposedly a former Russian nun she met in Italy.

They're eldest son Tom junior is a landscape gardener, had himself a son called Thomas, now both living in Cork, the other son Timothy now with two daughters of his own Shelia and Jennifer had bought a house in Wicklow on two acres of land and had a small car repair workshop on his property. They're eldest daughter Eileen married to a Scottish man named Luke also with two daughters Sarah and Jane and two sons Johnny and Jimmy had moved to Scotland and remained in contact only on birthdays and other occasions like the odd holiday in Ireland, or vice versa, the second eldest daughter Clare also never married after been badly beaten up by a former boyfriend. They all had one thing in common. They all loved their father and grandfather Tommy. He never, thanks to his faithful beautiful wife, forgot anyone's birthdays with mostly a phone call on the day in question.

He always remembered his wedding anniversary, mainly thanks to his eldest daughter Eileen, with a fair-sized bunch of red roses for his wife and a meal out in her favourite restaurant An Potin Still, and for the most part was an easy-going fun loving, generous kind of man, that everybody loved. Then one Monday evening just as they were about to have dinner, Mary coming in from the kitchen heard Tommy mumble something whilst waving his left hand about in a particular manner, 'Who are you talking to?' she asked him but again he muttered something unintelligible.

So, they got on with having their dinner when again Tommy mumbled something, and this time Mary heard what he said,

'Go away Scottie!' Scottie had been their little Jack Russel terrier that Tommy had to have put down on account of him biting one of the neighbour's children, even though it turned out that the child had wacked the little dog across the back with a heavy stick.

Tommy had felt terrible having done that, and he never had another pet in his house or would go anywhere near any of the families pet anywhere else for that matter.

Mary assuming, he was having another turn, gave him his medication and put him to bed. Then two weeks later it happened again, just before supper she heard him say to himself, 'Not now, Ann Marie, go away!' she had never heard him mention that name before, there was no one by that name in the family circle and when she asked him whom Ann Marie was? he just muttered something and brushed her off and went to bed sulking.

The third time she heard him mention some man called Gerry, 'I never said that Gerry,' she decided it was time to pay their doctor a visit, but before she did that, she rang her eldest daughter Eileen in Scotland to know if she had ever heard these names before to which the reply was negative.

Doctor Joe Conan assured her that in was unusual but not uncommon for such behaviour in the elderly, that they start to remember bits and pieces that they had buried years ago, a bit like suddenly remembering a line of a song long forgotten, he would look again at his medication and if he could change any part of it, he would send a note stating such a change to her local chemist.

'Don't worry Mary,' he told her, 'I see lots of OAP's just like your husband, it is just a phase they go through, and it soon passes, so relax, it won't help him to see you stressed out'

But Mary did worry especially when she heard the next name that Tommy muttered in his sleep. Sarah Ferguson. That name sent shivers up and down her spine because Sarah Ferguson had been brutely murdered, she had been sexually assaulted, almost ten years ago in Co Cavan, a town where she knew her husband had spent the day, she knew that for sure because she went with him to see an old friend of his, while she went into the town to do a little shopping as par usual. So, she worried herself sick and went back to the doctors to see if he could do anything to relive her suffering.

'You poor thing!' he said to her and gave her some anxiety pills, 'I am not sleeping Doctor Joe, do you think I might be able to take one or two of Tommy's sleeping tablets? they work great on him,'

She replied, 'Better not' he said, 'but I can give you some of your own, but only take the anxiety ones during the day, otherwise you might be going around all dosed up, and we don't want that what with you looking after that poor but lucky husband of yours, I wish I still had my darling wife, she was like you, beautiful and caring,' a little inappropriate maybe, but she enjoyed the compliment just the same.

She thanked him and left for home with her mind all over the place. She began to change Tommy's medication around slightly to see if that made any difference, and a few days later, she changed it again, and again a few days after that. Nothing seemed to work because within two week's Tommy was muttering again.

Shelia Holmes, another familiar name. Shelia Holmes was found dead in her bed suffocated with her own pillow and sexually assaulted. Mary could come to only one conclusion. My dear gentle husband is seeing faces from his past, could he possibly have killed these women whilst he was travelling up and down the country? No surly not, this loving and caring and helping man.

Then again it is possible! but what to do about it. Should she go to the police or leave things the way they are? He was never going to harm anyone again; she will have to make sure of that.

Then Tommy went quite for almost two months and she, as best as she could put going to the police out of her troubled mind. Then that first name he mentioned Ann Marie, she remembered now, Ann Marie had been found dead in her bath, it looked accidental at first, she recalled then it came out that Ann Marie was bi-sexual and may have been in the company of unknown person that fateful night, but no such person was ever found.

Then Tommy came up with another name, this time a man called Gerry; Gerry Boyd had been found stabbed to death up a dark and lonely laneway in Cork, on one wet winters night, Saturday it was, and it was on a late Saturday night early Sunday morning that Tommy had returned to Dublin.

She remembered it well because she was with him. It was obvious to Mary that the change in medication did not help at all. So, she upped it adding two anxiety pills and two of her sleeping pills that oddly enough seem to make him more aware of what was happening around him.

Then one Monday morning on her way out the door, he called after her, when she came back to see what he wanted he asked her for a cup of tea. When she brought him the tea and biscuits he simply said, 'Thank you, Breda' Mary was shocked to hear that name after all those years. Breda Hemmingway was found dead in a lake, just outside Roscommon. She had been hit over the head with a blunt instrument and left for dead, disorientated she had crawled into the lake instead of away from it. Mary with her mind now made up decided it was time to take some drastic action of her own.

Detective Sean 'Spiky' Mulligan was nearing retirement age from the Garda Crime and Security office in Dublin Castle; he got his nick name 'Spiky Mulligan because of his unwillingness to let go of unsolved murder cases, better known as cold cases.

So, when Mary Dunne came into his office one Wednesday morning two weeks before his retirement party with the lads in the crime squad and told him about her husband Tommy's ranting and raving about murder victims, he was all ears.

For two hours he listened to how Mary described her ailing husband's poor health and all the things he said and what the doctor had told her about how old people react and say stupid words about stupid things sometimes. He said to her while rising from his large mahogany desk.

'Can I come and see this elderly gentleman? That way I can access his mental condition and ascertain if there might be any truth in what he is, to use your words Mary, mumbling to himself' Mary gave him her address and he said he would be out before the day was over, roughly six pm.

He arrived at five-thirty precisely and was greeted by Mary at the door. When he was brought into the main bedroom, he was surprised to find Doctor Joseph Conan attending her husband.

'How is he, doctor? he doesn't look too good' he said showing the doctor his identity badge, as the doctor was straightening up from the bed, he replied, 'I give him another hour ...maybe two, no more'

Sean turned to Mary and taking her aside said to her, 'I am so sorry Mary, I am too late, if he did have any secrets then he is taking them to the grave, forgive me for been so blunt, have you anyone you can call to stay the night with you? I am free if you just want to talk, one way or another it is going to be a long night, eh, em ...these names you gave me, I have been researching them online and they are of people that have been murdered, you say your husband occupation was a travelling salesman, do you think you could find his work dairy and let me check it for any details of where he was and when he was in such and such a place, I would be most grateful to you if you could drop it into the station …as soon as you possible can, will you do that please Mary? Mary said she would as soon as she could giving the circumstances' he said to her 'Of course my dear …please forgive my insensitivity',

He had not been gone an hour when Tommy died and she was furious with herself for getting the guards involved, she should have handled this whole mess herself. Now it was too late, but at least now that smart ass detective would know it was Mary Helen Dunne, that had brought her husband to their attention. Still, she had totally forgotten about his diary, that would crucify him. The facts and figures were there, all written in her husband's own handwriting, thankfully, he was a demon for details. As she herself was a stickler for details.

Two weeks after her husband's death she was back in the police station going over and over the same information she had already given twice to Detective Sean Mulligan, but he needed to hear it all over again. I have been going through his diary and noticed, the time and places all match up with those grisly murders and I noticed that you were with him on single every occasion …is that true Mary? were you with him every time he went on a job of work? And if so, why were you with him? I mean the odd occasion yes, but every time, come on, even you must think that rather strange?

Mary replied within a fraction of a second. 'Because I loved him, I wanted to be with him everywhere he went, I loved the traveling and the excitement of going to new places and see the county side and meeting new people' he cut her off saying, 'but yet,' he said smirkingly, 'that while he went about his business, you usually went shopping, and that could last anything from an hour to three or four hours, that is a long time to be away from, as you just said, someone you deeply love, isn't it?'

She replied,' Maybe, but I never actually went into the place of work, I mean how would that look to the man or woman he was trying to sell his equipment to, seeing me there practically sitting in his lap, come on detective, use your two celled brain, and why all these questions, you don't think that I was his accomplice, now do you?

He straightened up from his desk chair and said to her. 'Of course not, someone as beautiful as you, certainly not, no, no way, but I simply have to ask these questions, it is my job to do so, you understand?' please can I call you a taxi or maybe if you do not think it too insensitive of me, I might drive you home?

She responded by saying to him. 'On the contrary detective Sean Mulligan, I thank you for your sensitivity, it is so rare to see such a tender and sensitive person these days, especially in your line of work, no one seems to want to show their true feelings anymore, not even friends, but I know how busy you are so I will just take the bus, it is only a twenty-minute journey, thank you very much for your kind offer, will that be all? He walked her to the station entrance, and there they said they're farewells.

A week later he phoned her saying he had just got the autopsy report back from the coroner and that he would like to call round and discuss a few things with her if that were possible.

An hour later he was sitting in her living room drinking a very nice mug of coffee. 'Was he self-medicating or were you the person in charge of giving him his medicine?' was the first question he asked her after she handed him his coffee. She replied, 'What! more questions, I am beginning to think you are stalking me detective, I mean, it sounds so serious, the way you put things,'

He said to her, 'this is a very serious business, Mary, do you mind if I call you Mary? I'm sorry, I should have asked you before' she said she didn't mind him calling her Mary, that is my name she said,

'It is just that there was a lot of sedatives, in his system, eh, too many as a matter of fact, can you, account for that please, eh, Mary?

'Well,' she said, 'I gave him his morning afternoon and night-time pills I usually leave them in his bedside locker, I suppose he could have gotten confused and taken some himself, what other reason could there be? surely you don't think I killed my own darling husband?

I don't think anything of the sort, it is just that there were a 'lot' of sedatives, too many as a matter of fact, and we, I …deal in facts Mary, and the simple fact is, your husband died from an overdose of sleeping pills, could you maybe have given him too many, by accident of course, I know how draining and tiresome looking after someone can be, I do know …I had to do it with my own dad in his last year of life, there were days when I didn't know if I was coming in or going out, believe me …I know how easily it can happen.'

'No way! She replied, 'If there were too many pills in his system then, only he could have put them there, you don't think that he …no …he wouldn't, I mean you don't think he might have taken them deliberately?

He said to her, 'Mary at this particular point in time I don't really know what to think, however it is possible, I suppose …that he may have committed suicide, what was his mood like in the week before his demise, can you recall?

'Well,' she said, 'He was …as I told you …continually muttering something to himself, his appetite was not too good …otherwise he was his normal happy self'

He said to her, 'Happy self, you mean that old man on a lot of sedatives was 'happy'?

'Well yes!' She replied, 'insofar as that was possible, I mean he wasn't on any king of uppers or anything …so for me to actually say, how he was feeling, you would have to speak to Doctor Joe about that … more coffee? He responded saying 'No thanks, as much as I've enjoyed been in your company I do have a busy schedule ahead of me today, thank you …I will let myself out, you have been very helpful …thank you, I will be in touch, even if it is only to ask you out to dinner sometime,' blushing he then says, 'sorry, didn't mean to say that, I was thinking out loud'

She replied saying to him, 'I am free Sunday, if you want, but just for dinner …no more serious questions alright?'

He was back around ten to three on the Sunday afternoon and they went to An Poitin Still restaurant on the Nass Road and had a very enjoyable dinner, she then had a very nice red wine before during and after the meal.

She instantly knew what this detective was up to, A, to get her to open her mouth and talk or B, to get her to open her legs, or maybe a little of both, she kind of liked the B option better. Mary was no experienced little teenager, no, she was a woman of great experience with more than her share of steel nerves.

And she still was a beautiful blonde woman that a lot of men, if not most men fancied, and with a wonderful figure that women half her age would dearly love to have, okay she was in her late sixties but most certainly did not look that age, but if this man, now sitting in front of her in a fancy restaurant and stripping her with his eyes thinking she was easy prey then he was sadly mistaken. Whatever was to happen today tomorrow or never would be her decision full stop. Much to her surprise detective Sean Mulligan was anything but a female predator and dropped her straight home saying, 'that was a most enjoyable afternoon, Mary it really was, I am stuck in that office morning noon and most nights with my backlog of cases so it is good to get out, thank you very much, and perhaps we can do it again?' Mary a little stunned said to him, 'Won't you come in for a coffee Sean? its early yet …and I do enjoy your company, when your head is with me …and …not in your office'

He replied, 'I have a meeting with my Super at seven, every Sunday night if he isn't going anywhere, to discuss the weekly ongoings, thank you again Mary…it really was wonderful, I will phone you if I may, and maybe next Sunday' she cut him off abruptly saying, 'to what? discuss the weekly ongoings, I don't think so, thank you for an enjoyable dinner, good evening' she left him standing there in no doubt that she expected more than just to be dumped on her own door step. For him however everything was going according to plan.

The following Monday he phoned Mary and asked her to come into his office to 'discuss' certain matters. He now had the time to review some more pages of her husband's diary and there were a few things that he needed to talk to her about. He had told his female colleague to give him ten minutes with Mary then bring in the file and leave it on his desk. Mary got there at ten past ten and apologised for been ten minutes late, 'No worries' he said to her, 'what's a few minutes between friends huh? would you like a coffee? nothing like yours I'm afraid, but it's not bad' she thanked him but said no thanks, 'can we get on with this? because I have an early afternoon hair appointment and they don't tolerate people been late'

'Of course, we can, no problem!' then he takes he diary from his desk and lays in front of him and pretends to go through the pages, 'What is this about?' she asks then says 'I thought we've been through all this stuff?

With that his fellow detective Joan Molloy knocks and comes into his office and lays a folder down on his desk then retreats graciously nodding to Mary. He takes the folder opens it so that Mary can see enough to know that they are photographs of murder victims, he says to her,

'There has been a mayor development, a solicitor came by this morning with this folder, have you even seen it before?' she says 'Never! what is it?'

'It came with a letter from your husband, to be opened only at the time of his death, well that was two weeks ago this coming Wednesday, that's tomorrow Mary, are you sure you haven't seen this folder before? because it has been in your house in a suitcase understairs this past nine years, or so, you can see the date there very clearly, about the same time you started to join him on his many trips, you said so yourself, remember?'

She said to him quite calmly, 'So! what has this to do with me? It's his folder not mine' I told you I have not seen that folder before this very minute,'

For the third time he asked her, 'Are you sure?' then he took another plastic bag from under his desk and said to her again, 'have you ever seen this before?' he takes out a light brown lady's dress and places it in front of her and she goes a little pale but says to him, 'No, I haven't seen that before either, what is this! Sean?' she never called him Sean before, and he notices that fact.

He says to her,' If you take a look at the inside of this lady's dress, you can still see small bloodstains, see here …and here, and here …small yes …but still strong enough for us to take DNA samples from when mixed with another chemical, it is as we speak been tested in the lab…together with a glass I managed to take from that restaurant you and I went to last week, so do you want to tell my anything, …Mary? anything at all? I will give you a few moments to think about it, because if this is you're dress, and those blood matches up with any of these victims then you're going on a very long holiday' she went quiet as a mouse.

He had placed the folder with the photographs besides the diary, they were all mixed up yet when he came back into his office, they were all in order, from the first killing to the last. A complete lack of concentration of the act of someone who is a stickler for detail. The game was up for her, and she was arrested for the murders of ten people plus two more before those ten in her own locality. Given life in a women's prison without the possibility of parole. Three years into her sentence she was stabbed to death in the prison kitchen by some lesbian lady killer. According to some in the know. Justice was finally served.

End

THE BOY WITH THE OPEN MIND

Wayne Rogers was twelve years old when his parents' house went up in flames. His parents perished but he was rescued by a very brave firefighter and rushed to the local hospital with second degree burns to his face and upper part of his body, he spent six months in the burns unit was left with scaring on his face and upper body.

No matter what the doctors tried to do in terms of skin grafts there was one part of his forehead that never seemed to heal properly with the results of him having to wear a special type of plaster that made him look well, different from the other kids, and what with the red blotches on his face and neck that drew some close unwanted attention from anyone that saw his disfigured face he took no part in any further schooling or activities and in short withdrew into himself. **Deeply.**

He was now living with his uncle Bill up north in Helena in Montana on a large open ranch with forests and lakes and mountains and apart from his uncle Bill Williams, his wife Melinda and they're two sons John and William and three daughters Mary Madge and Malissa, there were not too many people around which suited young Wayne as he had become very introverted. No amount of encouragement from the others seemed to have any effect on him.

'There must be something we can do?' said Melinda to her husband Bill one day while watching Wayne head down to the river to fish.

He replied ,'We have tried everything, babe, the kid just wants to be alone, hopefully he will come to terms with his past and accept what has happened to him, I know if I looked like that I wouldn't want people looking at me the way they look at him, even weeks after having met him our own kids can't bear to look at him, you and I both know how hard they tried …but he just doesn't want to know, just let nature take its course and hope for the best, darling …that's all we can do for now' Milina nodded in agreement but with great sadness in her heart.

Then for his up-and-coming birthday his uncle decided to buy Wayne a little Yorkshire terrier. He was over the moon with the pup and the pup returned his love and affection by following him everywhere, and the two became inseparable.

He still however, remained distant from his fellow piers and try as they might his uncle and his beautiful caring wife and family could not make the break-through they wanted with him.

He had his own room with television and video games and all kinds of young people's gadgets like the mobile phone which he never even turned on since the day it was bought for him.

Day after day from early morning to setting sun he spent down at the river or simply walking through the woods. Alone with his little companion Sheba, despite the many warnings of danger by his uncle, 'There were' he had said to Wayne, 'many dangerous animals like snakes and wolves and even crocodiles, and alligators, coming from the swamps down to the river; so, he must be always aware of the dangers, and always home before dark. Which he was. At first.

Day after day week in and week out he would follow the same schedule while taking different paths to relive the monotony and one day whilst out walking he noticed a little blackbird that seemed to be following him as he sang as he walked along. The little bird did not seem to mind the little dog walking beside Wayne as he continued to sing and whistle a merry tune, as they made their way through the thick bush towards the river.

One day while he was sitting by a log near the river Melinda came by to see what he was doing but stopped as she watched in amazement at the wonderful sight she was seen. Wayne with his little Yorkie at his feet and the blackbird perched on his shoulder was petting a young deer that had come to the river to drink. 'You should have seen it darling! It was as if he was talking to those lovely little creatures, I wish I had brought my phone, I could have taken a picture.

Bill replied saying, 'Talking to animals! Impossible darling' it may have looked like it, but that stuff only happens in films and fairy tales, how can a 13-year-old boy talk to animals? why, he can't even talk to his own family, impossible' she said back to him.

'Well! how can you explain the way your horse knows everything you say to him? or our old Shep? that old dog knew what you were going to say to him even before you did, remember? Or that little budgie in the cage, he could talk back to you' Bill replied,

'It is not the same thing babe, budgies only mimicked what was said to them and as for my horse and my Alsatian memory played a huge part in their interaction with us, but to say a young man can go out into the wild and talk to the local creatures is just a step to far. I don't buy that at all'

And that was that for another week or so, until Melinda saw Wayne appearing to be talking to a young tree sapling growing by the river, and it ended with him hugging that same tree.

She was again amazed but this time kept what she has seen to herself, fearing ridicule by her husband.

Then the boy disappeared and was seen no more. Fearing he had been killed and possibly eaten by a wild animal she phoned the police who came and for three days combed the area and found nothing, the officer said to her,

'Mam, he could be anywhere, if as you say he was a reclusive young man, we found no traces of any violence, no traces of anyone sleeping rough, we searched for any signs of animal kill, again nothing, if he is out there, then he knows how to look after himself, we have already put out an APB on him, you say he has a nasty open wound on his forehead, has had since he was rescued from that fire, that sounds really strange, we will be checking that with his doctors, it should make him easy to find in a town or city, but of course by now will have grown his hair to hide it, sorry we could not have been of more help, Mrs Williams, but we will spread the word and keep an eye out for him, okay?'

She thanked him and went back inside to shed a few tears, though safe in the knowledge that at least he wasn't found dead, or half eaten by some savage beast.

Still no sight or sign of the young man for weeks, then the weeks went into months into almost a year; then Bill called in his brother Tony, he was a hunter of some experience both at home and in Africa from where he had just returned. He said he would arrive on the next plane out of Idaho.

He was picked up at the airport by Bill the very next day and on the way home Bill told him all about young Wayne's story and when Bill finished Tony said. 'It seems to me that he is running with these animals ... half of what you say is true, then he could be another boy Tarzan, or Mowgli,

No ...don't laugh! You want to hear some of the stories I heard in Kenya, and it's the same all over Africa, young boy or in some cases a young girl goes missing and everyone presumes he or she has been killed and eaten by some wild animal only to have him or her walk out of the jungle a week or two later hungry and thirsty with a few minor scratches but otherwise okay, but none quite like what you've just told me! a wound in the head you say, the frontal lobe perhaps?' that 'is' different ...I never heard of such a thing, maybe it's connected to what has been happening to him, as you know Bill ...we don't use all of our brain ...only 10% of it ...who knows what the other 90% is capable of doing, we might even be able to fly one day, now wouldn't that be something? They both laughed then Tony said to his brother,

'How old did you say this kid was?

Bill replied, 'I didn't say ...but he be almost 14 now' his brother nodded, then said to him,

'Seeing as how the police with their dogs and all they're men, could not find anything, but rather may have walked any evidence under foot then I will head directly east towards Yellow Stone and will continue eastward towards Powder river ...then well ...stop at Broadus, where I will phone you with any information I may ...or may not have, it will take me three or four days ...so do not worry if you haven't heard from me till then, if I pick up a trail I don't want to be distracted by having to make or get a phone call, unless of course he has been found, understand Bill, and don't worry, if he is out there ...I will find him.'

At the end of the third day just before bedtime, Bill got a call from his brother Tony, who was all excited telling him, 'I found him brother, and you are not going to believe the footage I got from my secretly recorded cameras, unbelievable, this kid is something else, he is fine and healthy and get this, he is living with the most dangerous of animals ever, and I will be back to show you this film in a couple of days, hope I don't spoil your sleep bro, but this is wonderful news for me and hopefully for you guys,'

'What do he mean living with the animals darling? surely you heard him wrong? no one can live with wild animals, Bill ...it just isn't possible ...is it? Melinda exclaimed; remembering that those were the exact words that Bill used to her when she first mentioned Wayne talking to the little animals.

Bill replied to her saying, 'At least we know he is alright babe, and from what Tony just said to me, he is not in any danger ...that's good news ...right? so let's try get some sleep, he has some film to show us when he gets back, wonderful stuff, he says, so let just focus on what that can be, okay babe?...and try to get some sleep' it took a long time for either of them to fall asleep. It was only after making long passionate love that relieved the stress of everything that they fell soundly asleep in each other's arms.

Tony arrived on the Thursday as he said he would. Arriving with his friend Alberto, a cameraman from his safari days.

Having introduced him to his brother and wife and young family he set his laptop up on the kitchen table and got it ready to roll saying, looking at everyone there, 'You not going to believe this brother, but look at these, and he started the slide show. There was a photo of young Wayne on a high ledge with not one, but three, mountain lions beside him, a mother and her two cubs. Amid gasps of wonder and amazement. The next slide came up. It was a picture of Wayne standing in front of a large boulder with a pack of wolves around him.

The third was even more amazing, it was picture of crocodiles swimming in a river with Wayne bang smack in the middle of them, his little head bobbing up and down, laughing his head off. Between the ooaa's and the aaaaagh's in the kitchen Melinda put the kettle on to make coffee. Bill said to Tony, 'That is absolutely incredible, I mean we were right, thinking that he had gone to live with those animals, but they are fantastically wonderful photos Tony, well done man'

'We! were right' Exclaimed Melinda, 'I seem to remember you telling me it was impossible my darling, doubting husband' she kissed him gently on the lips. Tony said to them,

'That is not all, there are two more, here look at this one, the more placid of the two' they moved closer to the laptop and saw Wayne staring into one of the cameras. He looked more mature, since the last time they saw him, with a mop of hair under a cap of some kind on his head including a full beard with moustache. Yes, he had that wild look about him what with his wearing some animal jacket and shorts to match.

'Good God' extoled Bill, 'He is only a kid yet in that photo he looks like a mountain man, how is this possible, I mean only last year he was a shy as any 13-year-old kid, only more so, now here he is a brave and as fierce as any wild mountain-lion in a bad mood ....what the hell is happening here guys ...can someone tell me please?'

Tony jumped in saying, 'that is why I brought my friend Alberto here to see you, he is a wonderful cameraman ...we want ...with your permission, to do a full documentary on this kid, I mean it is a fabulous story, everyone will want to know about him ...and it might make the world more friendly to animals and the planet we all live on ...what do say guys? can we go ahead? of course there will be a lot of money coming your way folks? and will be for years to come, what do you think? but before you answer that question take a long look at this last photo...brace yourselves, the world is going to want to see this...' Everybody gasped out loud, with coffee cups falling to the floor in astonishment.

It was unbelievable. Wayne with his arms wrapped around the neck of a huge Anaconda in the most playful manner the likes of which has never, ever, been seen before. The Anaconda seemed to be enjoying the experience also.

And so, it was, contracts having been signed and with Tony and Alberto heading off into the great beyond; seeing them laughing and giggling together leaving Bills home, Melinda says to him,

'Do you think they are a couple?'

Bill laughs and said to her, 'After watching those photos in there nothing will ever again surprise me' she responds saying to him, 'At least we no longer need worry ourselves sick about Wayne, he is having the adventure of all lifetimes, don't know about you baby ...but I am feeling very horny, what do you think? Is there any chance of the ride?'

It was two months later when they had any word about Wayne, not from Tony or Alberto, but from Wayne himself. It was when Melinda was changing the batteries on the C.C.T.V. when she was shocked to the core. There, staring right into the camera over the main entrance door was Wayne, all alone and looking somewhat frightened. This was three days ago.

They were told later that Wayne had killed a man, a poacher who had just shot a mountain lion. The man was not expecting to find him not far behind the animal and as he was standing over it, Wayne came up behind him and hit him over the head with a heavy stone, killing him instantly; that was about two weeks before he was seen on camera outside his uncle Bills house.

So where was he now then? he had not returned to Powder River where he was last known to be. So where has he been in the last two weeks? Where is he now?

Then Tony and his friend Alberto rang Bill to see if he had heard anything about Wayne. Bill told Tony about Wayne appearing on the CCTV, and the state he was in. 'That explains a lot' Tony replied then told him what had happened just before Wayne showed up at Bills house roughly two weeks ago, 'We have him on camera four days before he turned up at your place,

Tony said to Bill, 'it was a strange thing to see, but once the facts were known, it was understandable, the two mountain lion cubs whose mother had been shot by that poacher, well, when Wayne approached them, they ran away, they had not seen their mother been shot so it wasn't anything to do with them fearing man as such. But we figure it was the state of Wayne that frightened them off. He had become very angry, walking around with a weapon like a baseball bat, and they weren't used to that, so they ran from him, now Bill you might want to sit down for the next part, maybe brother, even have Melinda by your side,'

Bill sensing the bad news called Melinda who came beside him and holding her hand he simply said to Tony, 'I'm listening' Tony said to him, 'two days after the cubs ran from Wayne, we were out checking the camera's when we hear a gunshot, it was far away but close enough for us to hear it, so we searched in the direction the shot had come from and we, ...well ...we ...found Wayne, ...dead ...sad to say ...he had been shot through the heart, it was a direct hit, he would not have felt a thing, ...are you still with me Bill? There was a slight pause then Bill said to him tearfully,

'Yes, we're still here,'

Tony said to him 'Now here's the thing Bill, that open wound on his forehead that you told me he had for years, that wouldn't heal, well, there was no sign of it ...just a tiny little scar, it had completely healed up, now I was thinking could that have been the reason the cubs ran from him? they could not communicate with him anymore, just a thought, another thing brother, do we bring him home or bury him here with his furry little friends?

Bill said to his younger brother, 'Can I ring you back in an hour or two Tony, we need to discuss it with the family, it won't be more than a couple of hours?'

Ninety minutes later Bill was back on the phone talking to his brother Tony saying to him 'We want him home Tony, we couldn't look after him when he was here with us, but now we can, we will bury him on the same hill that we buried Mom and Dad, he is family after all, did you at least get the documentary finished'

Tony answered, 'we did bro, not the way we expected ...but yes ...we will have enough footage to finish it, and if you don't mind Bill ...when we come home in a few days with his remains ...can we get that screen shot of Wayne at your front door? that sounds rather dramatic,' Bill replied, 'Of course you can brother, and thank you and Alberta for all your great work, and I look forward to seeing the finish product when its ready.'

Two weeks after the funeral when everything had calmed down, Melinda while doing the dishes at the kitchen sink just happened to look up towards the hill where Wayne had been buried and she was surprised to see a little deer kneeling by the graveside and his little Yorkie Sheba sitting on the grave. Excitedly she called her husband Bill to come see ...and he came ...and he saw ...and they both wept at the beautiful sight.

End

THE FISHERMAN'S SON

John Wains was a fisherman out of the small fishing town of Howth on the northern side of the Irish coast. He was not always in the fishing business; just part time helping out an old friend with his lobster pots but he got to like the sea and when he took early retirement he bought a little boat, twelve metres long and took up lobster fishing mainly to give him something to do that did not require a lot of effort as John was a big man, six-four in height and carrying a lot of weight 215 pounds which is nearly sixteen stone and the first thing his only son Johnny junior said to him when he saw the newly bought little boat was 'we're going to need bigger boat' yes, that great line from the film Jaws.

They both worked to get the boat ship shape as there were a good few bits and pieces that needed doing, small things but sometimes, too many small things can take up a lot of time.

There were the charts to learn and the radio frequencies to get to know and other small but vital things if you are living off and on the sea. Like weather forecast and such. It was an old wooden fishing boat with some lathes needing replacing and the small cabin in the back of the boat needed some new sheeting that would give some shelter from the wind and rain. But it was in good shape for its age and the shape it was in.

He had hired a man name of Phillip Mc Mahon, to help him with the lifting and lowering of lobster pots which they would be doing three times a week if things were slow and double that if things were good, nowadays of course the sea was not as productive as it once was, mainly due to overfishing.

Two weeks later after a few small trips around the harbour the small boat was ready to sail. It was now Monday morning seven am.

'Do you have to take little John with you John? I mean he is only a lad out of school, and I don't want him working on the sea, it's far too dangerous' his wife Paula had said to him that morning.

To which he replied. 'Now Paula honey, we are not going out too far girl, and who knows, he might want to become a fisherman in his own right, when he finishes school, and every job has some kind of danger honey, and there are thousands of fishing men and women, and yes, I count myself as one, working on the sea every day of the week all over the world, so relax, you think I will let anything happen to my pride and joy? I will make sure he puts his Bulldog on to protect his pretty face and don't worry I will make sure he is always wearing his lifejacket, even if he is on the loo, and he will keep it on till we get back,

I will look after him, and Phil will keep an eye on him as well, we will be gone for roughly six hours a shift so if we are not back by eight pm ring the coastguard and give them those coordinates, but we will be back before you know it.

I have just written them down for you in case, we need to be prepared for any eventuality,' he took her hand pulled her toward him and kissed her on the mouth saying softly, 'it's just in case honey, will you do that babe? and stop worrying.

It is not as if we are going to fish crab in the Baring Sea or anything remotely like it, it is a lovely calm day out there with no sign of any strong wind till tomorrow morning at the earliest, I will ring you on the hour every hour, if that will ease your mind'

He did not bother to mention the busy shipping lines they would have to cross or the sudden gales that can blow up in an instant, or the crazy tricks the sea can play on you in a sudden crisis, no point though, in worrying her any more than she already was.

Not that he had any experience of such things, he had heard of them from his old friend Martin, an excellent sea fisherman, now deceased.

He followed the same route his old friend did, and it had taken two and a half hours before they were at the same spot. It was a lovely day with slight westerly winds, a day out at the seaside really but an excellent first day for John and his little crew. It was now mid-April, well into the lobster season.

At first the fishing was good with some fine big cod caught for dinner and even a good few seatrout that should keep some of the neighbours happy for a while. The following few weeks were along the same lines, with one good pot up or and the next two not so good such is the life of any fisherman, and he was happy enough with the numbers and beginning to get his self-esteem back.

Who knows in a couple of years he might even get a bigger boat and go further out into the ocean where the fish are much bigger and so are the rewards.

Then everything changed. Instead of lobsters on the radar there were bigger fish, like sharks and octopus with only the odd lobster venturing out along the seabed. So, he had to follow the other lobster boats out further and this made him somewhat uneasy for, he did not know any of the other boats. He kept well to the right of them, but they knew he was there and for the most part didn't mind him been there. He had heard them say to one another over the radio 'we all are' they had said 'only trying to make a living and feed our families, he isn't, any different, so welcome buddy, whoever you are'

So, over the next few days the fishing was good and on the fourth day one of the other boat owners came and introduced himself as Marvin O Mahony and said to John 'you need to keep an ear to that radio, this is a great spot for fishing but it is also a good spot for drug smugglers, they hitch their gear onto a Buoy that could be anywhere within a two mile radius, this spot right here, where you are right now, is a hot spot, that is why I have come to warn you,

They appear out of nowhere in they're very hi-powered speedboats, and within seconds they're gone again. The guards try to catch them but with boats that are much slower than theirs, so if you see a Buoy spring up like a red carrot head, leave it alone, even if it is there for a whole week, you don't want those guys coming after you, they're the real sharks of the sea, and if they happen to see you, don't try to run, you'll never outrun them…'

Little John said to him, 'How come you know so much about them? He replied 'even out here son, where there is nothing to see, you see things, okay John, nice meeting you man, and you guys' then before he leaves turns back and says to John, 'your safer in a group John, your welcome to come and join us, the fishing is good too, ok, see you guys' then he was gone, back to the others.

John and Phil and little John were using their spare time fishing for anything that would sell to make a little more money on the side, there was a good three-hour gap between the dropping and lifting of traps. So, they would move closer to land, and fish along the coastline. They often caught plenty of fish and seafood like crabs and oysters and brought them into the markets before going back out again to check their pots. Not strictly favoured by the other fishermen but was done by the few, rather than the many.

Sometime a large restaurant owner might meet them at the dock and offer them more money because the fish would be the freshest ever, but the market owners did not like that and threatened to bar anyone caught doing business with the likes of those guys. So, it was seldom done, but there were other ways of doing it but were not legal ways, but it was done, nonetheless.

Then a couple of days later when they got to their spot, John noticed they were alone, not a lobster boat to be seen in any direction, but it didn't bother him as he was a loner at heart.

Then with the last pot been laid John grabbed his chest and little John saw him drop to the floor 'Phil, look …at dad! The lads rushed to his aid and Phil feeling for a pulse and finding none began to give him CPR. It was only then he noticed his cut right hand, he must have caught it from on something in his haste to get to John, He was still doing CPR when a speedboat arrived and tore into the side of their little boat, almost cutting in in two, little John followed his father into the water and it seemed like forever before he looked over at Phil but when he did he saw a huge shark take him underwater, and there was a fountain of blood sprouting to the surface, horrified he scrambled his way onto the bow of the broken wooden boat in time to see another shark take his father and bite him in two, there was blood everywhere, the speedboat had gone a few hundred yards away, stopped and came back. The next thing he saw was a man reaching over to offer him his hand. Reluctantly he took the man's hand and was pulled into the speedboat and away they went heading south towards the shore.

A man in a business suit came gave him a blanket and sat beside him saying, 'I am sorry you had to see that son, it was an accident, we only meant to tip your boat over, to see what fell out or if our Buoy might just spring up and surprise us all, then we got a phone call saying the gear was recovered and back in our hands, some guy thinking he was Marvellous Marvin …now I know what you people think of people like us, but me… I am and honest hard-working man when I mess up, I admit to messing up,

Now here's the thing, any other man, might just throw you back to the sharks and leave it at that, problem over, …but me! No way, I have a son about your age, looks a lot like you too…' Little John cut him off saying, 'I know …you're a man of integrity,'

The business man looked him straight in the eyes and said, 'Integrity, integrity won't put a loaf of bread on the table or feed a hungry house cat, you're thinking that this is some kind of play or film you have found yourself in son, that I'm the villain and your maybe the hero, but this is reality lad, this is the real world, in the movies men like me would think nothing of killing a kid like you, but me I'm …' again little John cut him off, 'a man of integrity, yes, I know,'

The businessman replied, 'Don't get smart with me kid, you …young farts think you know everything! when in fact you know nothing …how could you? You only five minutes on the planet,' they were approaching the landing spot when the businessman stepped ashore followed by little John, he said to him 'Here's the deal son, I made a huge mistake thinking that you guys had stolen my products and as I have already said, I admit that …and I am willing to compensate you for your tragic loss, if you are willing to forget what happened out there, I am not asking for forgiveness, just forgetfulness, if you are willing to just walk away and get on with your life, then I am willing to …as I said … not fix everything …I cannot do that but I can compensate you…

'Blood money! Said little John, the businessman said to him, 'I am trying to put things right here son, you say blood money …well I saw a lot of blood in the water back there, so yes …it is blood money, your friend's blood, and now it's their money if you accept…' again he was cut short.

'One of those men was my father…' little John began to weep, The businessman said to him putting a hand on his shoulder, 'Then I am truly sorry son, I really am, look, give me your address and I will send a courier round sometime tomorrow with a package for you and yours, it's a lot of money son, 250,000, if you accept it, if not, nobody wins? remember, once you do accept my generous offer you will never hear from me again, I promise you that, and believe it or not, I am a man of my word, but you must not say a word to your mum or anyone else, you will find a way of explaining the money, and you will also be able to help that other man's family, so do we shake on it or what?

Little John took the outreached hand and shook it hard knowing that at least his mother will be better off financially and so will Phil's mom. Anything else would all have been for nothing.

The businessman took John's address and gave him a card saying, 'Hurricane Express Courier Service'. 'Be home about three pm, and again I am so sorry son, but I wish you all the best for the future, any idea what you want to do?'

John Wains simply said to him, 'I am a fisherman's son'

End

Little Henry Rawlings

Was the kind of man that always had a smile on his face even when he had not much to smile at. He had worked most of his life on the building sites as a housepainter in Dublin and had travelled all over the country doing the same thing.

Yes, house painting and he was particularly good at it too. A man with a heart of gold, who would not think twice of knocking money of the estimate he had just given if he thought for a second that the house owner was struggling in any way.

Even one time on getting paid at the end of the job, handing back some of the money he had just been given. He was a good man most of the time, he was a happy man, most of the time, always trying to make people laugh, which he did, most of the time. He could though if he thought for a second you were taking him for a mug, render you speechless with a tirade of strong words, too vulgar to mention here.

Overall, though, he was a decent man, never refused to lend if asked and would never go looking for the money back. His daughter thought him foolish; his wife thought him foolish, but he thought of himself as Christian, and believed strongly in his Lord and Master Jesus.

In truth he had seen his mother struggle all her short life trying to raise a family of eighteen. Yes! There were a lot of exceptionally large families back in those days. One of his neighbours; an exceptionally large woman who shall remain nameless, lol, had a family of twenty-three. A small army.

Henry himself was the eldest of eleven brothers, and seven sisters, a lot of siblings indeed. One must remember in those days in the early fifties things all over the world were unbelievably bad on account of the war, and despite been neutral in WW2 Ireland was particularly hard hit by recession so there were no luxuries like television or video players, so early to bed nights were quite common. Such was the background of little Henry Rawlings, but it made him tough as a youth, and he had many a scrap in his teens and most of them he won easily. Even on one occasion of been picked on by a much taller bully, out trying to impress some local girls standing around the shops, after been picked up and shaken like a rag doll in front of the young ladies.

Henry once set back down managed to kick the said bully in the nuts and when he bent down in agony Henry headbutted him and the bully fell backwards like a sack of potatoes. He did not know it at the time, but his future wife was one of those schoolgirl's watching from the shops. Her name was Marie Conlon.

He married her at seventeen on account of her being pregnant, they did that in those days. A not insignificant matter of honour for the ladies, and they stayed together for almost forty years raising a family of six, three boys Seamus Sean and Eamon and three girls, Patricia, Marie, and Evelyn, all much taller than he was, eventually of course.

The first few years were brilliant but then ten years later he lost his eldest son Seamus in a joyriding accident, he was a passenger in a stolen car when it ploughed into an oncoming car and the two in the front seat were killed outright while the two in the back seat died two weeks later from multiple injuries. It was to become all too common in most working-class areas, at that time, the early sixties, despite better living standards and better and bigger and faster cars on the roads.

That whole episode really shook Henry and Marie tremendously and things were never quite the same after that as Henry began to suffer from depression where he would just go into a quiet corner and closed down inside himself, going down into the mine, he himself called it.

Marie herself, like most women of the time, proved to be the strongest of the two and she pulled Henry along until he seemed to recover somewhat from his depression. Even when the second eldest girl Susan died from a drug's overdose it did not shake him as much as Seamus death did, not because Henry loved him more and her less, no, it was because by now life had changed him and Henry had become, I know this may sound rather silly, but Henry was no longer a teenager in the mind but now a fully-fledged man in the flesh. And real life was hard, very hard, with huge real responsibilities. It showed him how weak he really was.

It was not as if parents didn't care for their children, they loved them all dearly. No, it was just that at that time there were far too many kids from working class parents, working night and day, day in and day out to provide for their families, that who for the most part were running around with nothing to do, and of course the pied piper syndrome became quite evident with one young man in the area, then another and another in terms of anti-social behaviour on a very large estate in the heart of Dublin. Joyriding: on a nightly basis even progressing to a daily basis.

A black wolf among the many little white lambs that had too much time to spare when they should have been safe inside doing their homework. The devil makes work for idle hands.

Not all youngers were like that of course but there were quite a few and they were a barrelful of trouble to others, especially their parents and neighbours not to mention the bad name they made for themselves. Then the mighty demon drug called heroin moved into the area, all areas of the city and towns of Ireland, killing hundreds if not thousands, and ruining families everywhere.

Like the time a tractor and trailer full to the brim with loose cabbages came to make a delivery to the local vegetable shop. The cabbages weren't bagged in those days. The driver said to one or two of the children outside that if they gave him a hand to bring some cabbages inside then he would in turn give them a lift up the road in his trailer. Well, withing minutes there were dozens of children of all ages helping him shift his load.

With the result the trailer was full to brim with children climbing all over it. As soon as the trailer moved back out onto the road there was a scramble for places at the back of it, with the terrible result of one young boy of eight falling and getting himself killed.

He was to make his communion the following day, Saturday. Henry had been one of those young boys scrambling for a space at the rear of the trailer. He was at the boys wake two days later in the parlour of the little lad's house. The driver himself died the following year; it was said that the poor man never got over the shock of that terrible incident. Henry's father Bill Rawling was himself a painter and would on occasion bring young Henry into work with him, and that is how young Henry became a housepainter, or as they are called today a painter and decorator.

Henry loved it as the economy began to grow and people began to earn more, the building trade flourished in the cities', and at twelve years of age, after having a bad accident while coming out of school when he fell down an open manhole he was out of action for a whole year and truth be told he never went back to school, not after the headmaster and principle had written him off the school roll book.

Though he did his junior and leaving years later, much later when he was 56 in fact after he went back to Adult Education, even getting a place in Trinity College for a short spell, again his depression kicked in and spoiled everything, but although he was very proud of the fact, that he got there though be it on TAP program, college wasn't for him, much too long and tedious studying.

His first job started with him cleaning out the houses on the building sites and getting them ready for the painters to come in and finish off, then he progressed to knotting and priming the woodwork, then to filling and undercoating then glossing, and he became very good at it and very fast. He took great pride in what he had done and in the fact that he was now a person with a trade. And after a while a trade union member. As the old saying goes,

'If you can use your hands, you will never be idle' and so it was, until he met and married Marie Conlon. They met at the sea resort in Bray Co Wicklow one fine summers day and like himself she was only five feet-two inches, and she was picking up a coin she had dropped outside one of the amusement halls.

He met her again inside the Star picture house in Drimnagh that same night and as they say, the rest is history.

They were married within two years and despite been told she was pregnant the first year their first child Seamus didn't arrive until the following year, a phantom pregnancy, then the other five in two-year gaps.

Most of the time they were happy, then came the double tragedy of the deaths of two of his children, and life became very hard and for a long time they would argue like most people do then one day out of the blue Henrys depression returned, leaving him as before, isolated from the family for long periods of time. Even though he was still in the centre of things in the home. Then after 28 years Marie applied for and got her divorce. Because he still loved her, he didn't contest the divorce. He still loves her to this very day.

Signing over the house to her, he left himself homeless but within a short space of time he moved into his father's house about twenty minutes away, where he stayed for over a year and a half then is father died. He met his second wife Catherine, who unfortunately died three years later from complications from a breast cancer operation, Henry was devasted, she was the only joy in his life apart from his remaining three children who by now had kids of their own.

Making Henry a grandfather and a great grandfather. With still time hopefully to become a great-great grandfather, a true honour indeed.

It was after the death of his second wife Catherine that he met Monica, ten years after, but he was lucky enough to meet her at some church meeting or other, like his other two wives Monica was beautiful and loved travelling like he did, and this fact brought the two of them even closer.

Two years later Monica started getting daily headaches and Henry was telling her almost daily to go to the doctor and get it checked out. She was eventually sent to the hospital where she was diagnosed with a rare brain tumour and died a year later in palliative care in Harold's Cross. They had planned to get married that year.

Yes! Henry Rawling was a small man, but he did and still does carry a lot of weight around. So be kind to your neighbour, you just don't know what he or she is going through, or indeed, it might be even your good self my friend in need of support. I sincerely hope you have a good friend in life. Someone to listen to your worries and your woes, for everyone needs one or two of those. God bless you and yours. Amen.

End

Spooks

So, you call yourself a loner huh? been alone all your life huh? and you claim to know it all, seen it all, been there, worn the tee-shirt? And that you have forgotten more than I will ever know! Ok, maybe I accept what you say, but, only about this world, but what about the other world? what about the spirits that move about in our world, both clean and unclean spirits? what! cat got your tongue?

A lot of us know what a concept of a clean spirit is! Friendly and in some case can be even playful. An unclean spirit is a total bad ass spirit that can drive a sane person insane very quickly, that can move things about, that man make sound that would send shivers up and down your spine. It matters not if you are religious or atheist, once one of these unclean spirits or in some cases even more than one, invade your home then you have a problem indeed.

Though even if one or more do invade your home all is not lost. You know the old saying, 'if you can't beat them join them'

It started for me when I first moved into a new house on the outskirts of Dublin. My wife and I were watching a movie in the sitting room, and I got up to go into the kitchen to get a coffee. On my way back out of the kitchen something caught my eye over in the right-hand corner.

I looked over and saw this large black shape standing there, not sure if it was watching me as there did not appear to be any facial features, like eyes mouth nose etc, so I guess it wasn't watching me for who can see without eyes? But it was standing there facing me. That much I could tell.

A large black hooded shape.

The hairs on the back of my neck were tingling but I went back into the sitting room and said nothing to the wife, not wanting to scare her. When the film was over, she went into the kitchen and came running back out saying, 'there is someone or something in the kitchen Tommy just standing there in the corner, will you go and see what it is?

I went in expecting to see the same thing but there was nothing there at all. But she had seen something I know that much. This made us go to the local priest to get the house blest which we did, but lo and behold it made the whole situation even worse.

With wired voices and lights even spinning round our bedroom leaving our little dog Sheba barking its head off while the four of us lay frightened on the bed. I put it down to the wife on going to her father's grave to see her mother been buried that day, she brought home handles of her father's coffin, and God knows what else she brought home that day.

That is just my opinion.

And so, we contacted the Tallaght Historical Society that quickly became the Tallaght Hysterical Society with the woman on the phone telling us to get out of there at once.

That horror film the Exorcist had been out a few years and people were still saying and seeing all kinds of things creeping round in the bosom of the night. I confess, it affected me somewhat three days after watching it, now back to my story.

What we heard and saw was during daylight hours. Another time the wife's sister who lived just a few doors away came round to say that the devil had been trying to pull her out of her bed. I could assure you, if the devil had wanted her out of bed, then she would have been out of bed, even if it meant she ended up under the bed. Again this was a few days after her watching the Exorcist.

The whole thing drew me closer to God, and still to this day, nearly fifty-years later that has not changed.

What I am about to say did not, and I repeat, did not happen, just in my head it did, and for years it has been in there while I was too afraid to let it out, until now.

We have all felt that muscle in the leg that moves after you get into bed and cover yourself with the blanket. How it seemed to move more than it should move, and for a few nano seconds you stiffen up thinking that you might have an unwanted visitor crawling all over your bed. I think this is what happened to my wife's sister.

It starts with small things, like 'I swear I closed that kitchen press door', or 'I know I left it on the table,' or when using the bathroom the shower curtain moves slightly, and you instinctively know that you had pulled it further across than it now was, and you know in your head that it was only the slight breeze of the toilet door opening that made it move, and ok, you shrug your shoulders, but you get still get out of there faster than you normally would.

Then you begin to think things like, 'I need to get the screwdriver and fix that hinge or put an extra screw in this or that door handle,' you been thinking of doing it for years, then hey presto, there is the screwdriver in plain view, on the table or on the sofa, or right by your feet. Then sometimes when you sit down to have dinner, you get the feeling that there is someone sitting beside you.

Did I tell you I live alone? Another quite common thing is when your just about to drop off into slumberland and you hear a voice very clearly saying something to you, suddenly your wide awake, wishing you had someone there to hold and cling too. When, it is yourself probably just saying goodnight to you, or you simply might just be breaking wind.

One day mid-afternoon, I was sitting at my kitchen table about to have myself a coffee, I poured the hot water in, then the sugar then the milk and was after returning the milk to the fridge and was about to sit back down when the spoon in the mug began to swirl around and round.

I could not believe my eyes as it went round and round and all I could say was, 'What's going on here then' it stopped then started going round again, I removed the spoon from the mug and laid it on the table whereupon the spoon was lifted, and the wet table was wiped with a tissue that lay nearby.

I am a strong person most of the time, I don't scare easy most of the time, and I don't panic, most of the time, but I just grabbed my coffee and hid myself in the bedroom for well over an hour.

I also do some writing and stuff on my computer in my bedroom and the next day whilst sitting at my desk and stuck for a few words to say when click up came this,

'Hello, my name is Nina, I am your new house guest, I must say you are a very nice and clean person, not too sure though about your mind, it seems to be all over the place,' I was almost struck dumb, and it took me some time to reply to her when she then said, 'What is your name?'

I replied shaking somewhat, 'Tommy eh …Tom what the f…k …who are you? What are you? Was that you with the spoon out there in the kitchen? She said it was, and that, 'You need not fear me, for I am a good spirit, not as holy as you are, but I am a good spirit'

I replied saying, 'What! like a genie or something, why can't I see you? She responded, 'I can only be seen in exceptional circumstances, and only if I allow it, but you can see what I do and feel what I do, again only if I want you too, so for now you will have to be satisfied with that, now may I also say I have seen better looking men but, I have also seen worse,'

'Why are you here pestering me?' I asked her to which she replied, 'Pestering you, you think I am pestering you; I am here helping you, I mean, I tried to stir your coffee, and what thanks did I get, you were so rude, I tried to tell you what was going on, but you just ran away from me'

'What do you look like? I asked her, and she said, I am spirit, when I was like you I was a beautiful woman, that lots of men fancied and wanted to be with me all the time, but I am …I mean I was a married woman, with great wealth, I am …I mean I was a princess, married to a great prince of wealth, from Jamaica, I was also a singer well known in the musical business,' I asked her what her name was and she said, 'I told you ...Nina'

I could not stop myself from saying, 'Not ...Nina Simone? There was a short silence then she said to me, 'No, not her, but as famous in my own little world, my husband died from cancer and hanging out with too many other women and my manager had me killed and stole all my money, which was a considerable amount, believe me,' I said to her with some feeling, 'I am sorry to hear that, but what do you look like now? and can you speak? and ...' she cut me off saying to me, 'That is one too many questions, as I said I am spirit, a clean spirit, I am rather very small in terms of what I used to be, I was almost six-foot tall, a real Jamaican beauty, all men used...'

I cut her off saying to her, 'Yes I know, all men fancied you ... but that is no big deal, it's been like that since the world began, I mean, like most men always did fancy a beautiful woman' she replied, 'I am new to this spirit world, I can see other spirits and to be honest they scare even me, I was led to you by a helpful spirit called Peter, do you know of him?'

I had a brother called Peter died in a motorcycle accident in the year 1989, I think it was, yes it was that year my poor mother died the following year 1990 from the shock of it all, could it have been him? I wondered.

Then she said, 'He told me to tell you he had red hair when he was young as most of his many brothers did,' 'My God,' I gasped, it was my brother Peter. He was the one next in line after me, then I had nine more brothers and seven sisters. 'That is enough for now ...Tom dear, I need to take some rest, ...do you mind if I take your bed for an hour or two? That drawer in that wooden unit smells of old socks, ...you don't mind dear ...do you? I just shook my head from side to side and left her to it.

Then of course it came time for me to go to bed, and as I could not see if she were still in my bed, I said out loud, while getting ready to turn off my computer for the night, 'Well! are you still here in my bed?' I was not expecting the answer I got when she replied on my pc to me,

'Do you want me to be, I don't mind if you do? I don't mind if you don't?' all I could say was, 'Stop messing me about, that is my bed and this time yesterday I was living here alone so yes, I do mind thank you very much' she typed back, 'Ah, Tommy, you thought you were living and sleeping alone! but what do you know, isn't life surprising?' then there was a slight pause before she continued saying,

'I must say I never thought I would see the day when a man, and a not too good-looking man at that, would rather have slept elsewhere, but life has changed dramatically for me so, ...so be it, though you have to admit for a dead person I am not doing too badly, and as they say, the best is yet to come, would you like a blow job?'

I nearly fell of my chair when I heard her say that, but I managed to say to her, 'No thank you very much ...and we will have none of that kind of language, this is a Christian home' then she said to me, 'Oh yeah! well what were you watching the other night, and it wasn't the cartoons, what with you sharpening your Chinese pencil with?

I blushed and said to her, I was doing research for a story I am thinking of writing, that's what I was doing. She typed in, 'well if you change your mind, I will be in the top drawer of that kitchen unit, good night and sleep well ...oh, and if you feel even the slightest movement in the bed...don't try to kill the bed bug, it just might be me lol, then again you can't kill me, I am already dead, night'

Suffice to say, I could not sleep, it took me hours before I finally drifted off into never-never land. Lying there thinking all kinds of things, like how on earth could this be happening to me?

Then I thought well, why not me? I mean there can't be too many men in the world with their very own lady spirit, especially one that constantly boasts of how beautiful she is or was. One with her own peculiar sense of humour. Blow job indeed.

She was a fast typist too. A couple of nights later I thought I had left a radio or cd player on in my apartment, and I got up to turn it off, but there was no radio or cd player on. I discovered to my surprise that it was Nina gently singing in my room, a very beautiful song about lost love, well most songs are about lost or found love, but it was beautiful, and I was very impressed, she was right about one thing, she could sing, so why couldn't she talk to me then? And why couldn't I see her?

I asked her those two very questions but all she typed was, 'When the time is right, you will see and hear me, but not yet, I am not ready, and you need time to adjust to me being here, I do not want to scare you away, you only heard me because I wanted to sing you too sleep, as you weren't sleeping well, these past few nights'

She would play jokes on me at least once a day, like when I was about to pour hot water into my coffee cup, she would move it slightly. It was on such an occasion that she did this when suddenly everything on the table went flying in all directions, it seemed that I had burnt her with the hot water, so I quickly turned on the cold water tap and told her to get under it.

Not sure if she did or not but I did not hear from her again for the next few days. I even thought that she had gone. Moved out. It was only then that I realised how glad I was that she was here, with me. I missed her been around. I need not have worried as she surfaced before the end of the week.

'Are you alright? I asked her then, 'where have you been?' she replied, 'I am now!' that hot water nearly cut me in half and it is taken all this time to mend together, man, I've been in hot water before but never like that, and thank you for your concerns, telling me to get under the cold tap like that, that was quick thinking'

Then it hit me, 'we were talking, 'We are talking, I said to her excitedly, 'Yes, we are Tommy, I had time to think and now I think it's time we had some quality time to ourselves!'

I exclaimed, 'but that's wonderful, a talking spirit, I heard of talking in the spirit, but never of one answering back' I was so thrilled I really didn't know what to say. She said, 'and now are you ready for the next 9th wonder of the world?' she appeared right there and then the most beautiful of women, stunningly beautiful she was, then as quickly as she appeared she vanished into thin air, I mean she was already thin air, O God! what am I saying?

She said to me, 'I can only do that for a very brief period, what do you think? was I telling you the truth or was I telling you the truth?' I said to her pouring on the charm that I was gifted with in my day, 'You lied to me, you were ten times more beautiful than you said you were, absolutely beautiful' but why only a quick visit? she said to me, 'a spirit is energy Tommy, to do what I just did, takes a lot of energy, I don't have enough to keep displaying myself or indeed anyone I conjure into view, I can only do for very short amount of time' I wasn't sure I liked what I had just heard her say and I pulled her on it, 'You mean you can come in all shapes and sizes, I mean as different people?

She says, 'Yes! Anyone and everyone that's in my memory bank, and I did retain my memory bank, any person good or bad I can become, thankfully for me and you, I am a clean spirit, I would never want to be anything else in this world I find myself in still, well, living is not the right word, …being …is probably the right word,'

I said to her, 'So if you met some horrible human being in your past life, you could take his or her shape in this one, you can do that?' she replied, 'yes, I can! Tommy …but let's not go there, as I said before, I am a clean spirit, in my world now it is not good or bad, it is clean and unclean, are you glad I am still here? If you want me to leave I will, and never come back,' I was happy to see her even for that short time and I told her so.

I was happy she was back. She seemed glad to hear that and said to me, 'Then in time, I may be able to help you with that 'story' your 'researching' I could not think of an answer to that, for did she not say on numerous occasions that she was a 'clean' spirit? So, I didn't say anything because we Irish can and often do see the funny side in everything. Still why wasn't I laughing?

On another day I asked her, 'how long have you been here, in my home?' she said to me very quietly like, 'Eh, …a time …a time and half a time, I think, yes two and a half years,' I said abruptly, 'Two and a half years! And you only coming to me now, why is that? Nina, she answered me saying, 'that is two and a half years in my time, my spirit time, in your time, it has been only two and a half months'

I said to her, 'and my brother Peter God rest his soul, where and when did you meet him, or as you say, his spirit?' she replied, 'well it must have been about then, two and a half years ago, I was finished off by a very jealous woman, whose wealthy husband would not leave me alone, he was spending all her money on me, she came at me from behind and stabbed me repeatedly in the back, the whore, just when I was getting into the hang of it...eh ...well that's another story, but where did I meet your brother?

Well! all I can tell you is it was on the way down; I mean ...I don't know where we were heading to ...all I do know is, it was downward, what's with all the questions? You getting bored with me or what? I said to her, 'no ...no I am just fascinated by whom you are and what you are and where you came from, that's all!

Looking back that was another red flag I missed along the way to the slippery slope to nowhere. But she was fun to have around, and it did do away with that dreadful feeling of loneliness that gripped me from time to time. And let's face it, she was really cheap to keep, with no extra food bills, or new clothes, true she didn't have to pay rent but sure one can't have everything.

I once said to her, 'Whatever happened to your great wealth? her answer shocked me to be honest, she said, 'How the f...c would I know? once I was gone ...I was gone from everything I held sacred,' all I could say to her was, 'I'm sorry, I wasn't trying to pry, I just wondered that's all, I am sorry if I upset you!'

I did not see her go but I felt her go off in a huff. Another red flag was rising, and I began to wonder what I had let myself in for. This was beginning to remind me of an ex-girlfriend whom I had great trouble getting rid of. Yet get rid of her I did.

Later in the afternoon of the following day, she made her presence known. She was back and she said to me, 'I am sorry for the way I treated you yesterday Tommy, I forgot that you people still think in terms of money, but you made me think of what I am missing most, my home comforts and everything that goes with that, but I will make it up to you soon, I promise, do you forgive me?

Now I am not one for holding grudges, not even with my own kind so of course I forgave her and told her so. 'I am so glad to hear that Tommy, it is not very nice in Coventry ...having no human to talk with, never mind been intimate with'

I thought I was hearing things there for a moment. Intimate with? She quickly corrected herself by saying, 'I mean ...we ...eh ...I mean I have missed you Tommy, your fun to be with, and life eh ...such as it is ...can only get better,' I heard that word and it stung me a little, no, it stung me a lot.

'We! how many of you are there Nina?' I asked her, and she replied, 'that was just me thinking in general terms, rest assured ...there is only little old me ...and you, together in this lovely ...cosy little home, I wish I had known you before in my life' she hissed at me and I said to her, 'you would not have looked twice at me, not even once, I could never have moved in your circles of riches and pleasures, I am a simple mean with simple means and...'

'Yes', she said, cutting me off, 'I can see that, even from here, but that was then, and this ...is now, and I am in the mood for a little pleasure, how about you, you sexy beast? Another red flag perhaps?

All I could think of saying was, 'I need to put my dinner on, one of us has to eat to live and I live to eat! Well, I say stupid things when I am all flustered. And I was very flustered.

I could feel the heat from my red face all the way down to my toes. And back up again. She took it well though I will give her that much, but I think it was only on account of the way she treated me the other day. There was something else in the air I could feel it and it wasn't her.

Then just before bedtime as I got ready for bed, I pulled the duvet down to reveal the most beautiful woman I have ever seen and will probably ever see this side of heaven.   Even in the moonlight I could see how velvet her skin was, her beautiful breasts like huge grapes ready for the sucking, eh ...sorry ...plucking, her slender body with her long lets and things began to stir within me.

But I was hesitant to touch her expecting her to vanish at any moment, leaving little Tom bewildered and bemused and me kneeling there looking like a fool.

'You're wasting precious time' she whispered suggestively opening her legs wide enough for me to see the valley of delights.

I was just about to touch her when poof she vanished again and left me sitting there like the fool I was. All I could sigh was Nina. 'Nina, who the f...c is Nina?' Came a very rough voice and I looked down to see a horrible, bearded man with a face like a Parana fish staring back at me.

'What are you f....k…g looking at? You f..k…g wanker, you f..k…g moron, this is my f..k…ing house now, so get the f..k out and leave me and my f..k…g family in peace, you f..king F..k face'

I now am renting a room in my sister's house over the northside.

End

I Just Love the Music Man

Ever since I was kid, I loved music, my son David bought his son Aaron a plastic guitar and a dummy microphone on a stand and even an Elvis cape like one the king wore. And even when he was a wee child of about five of age. He was giving concerts to us captive families whenever he came over from Scotland.

I was more into Bob Dylan than Elvis, at that time in my life. Still am though Dylan's raspy voice, doesn't sound so good these days but fair play to the man, his bell still rings.

Later when the Beatles and the Rolling Stones came on the scene I changed or rather broadened my taste for music, who didn't at that wonderful time of wonderful music.

Abba and Mama' and Papa's and so many wonderful singers and musicians out there, but the one thing I loved about Dylan and Elvis was the fact that they stood alone. Most of the time.

At that time of wonderful song writing and melody's and such, like 'the times they are a-changing' to name just one. I suppose everyone at one time or other wanted to be a singer or musician of some kind.

I know I did. I was always singing at work on the building sites in the empty houses I was getting ready for the painters, of which I later became one, people said I could hold a tune and had a good voice, I don't know about that, all I knew was I liked singing.

Then one day I bought a small acoustic guitar for my daughter Tracy, she never took it up, but I did, I had heard some guitarists make their guitars almost talk, like Jimmy Hendrix, Phil Lynott and Rory Gallaher, and so many more, to many to mention here. I wanted to do that.

At first, I could not take to the female singers who stood alone, I honestly don't know why that was, until the great Cilla Black, Kath Bush and of course Dolly Parton, but she could hardly be ever accused of standing alone. Lol. They were always there but had a different beat to the men so I suppose that might have been it.

Now I know how fabulous they all were for their time. Mary Black, Dana winning the song contest, Bonny Tyler, Sinead O Conner, and thousands more wonderful female artists, each and every one of them great in their own right. Anyway, I got to learn sixteen chords and to make a long story even longer, I played in my local church choir. At first with my good friend Wally Maloney from Tallaght in St Mary's priory and it was good but not great. Wally on the other had knew what he was doing which was more than could be said for me.

I had taught myself how to play, but badly, and could never master the finger picking style that you need to know if you want to play guitar. Luckily for me I never wanted to be a star because I knew from early on that was never going to happen. I was just too nervous playing in front of everyone and I once heard Brendan Grace say to his audience,

'Youse are all looking at me' he was a real comedian.

I know some will say that is how all beginners feel but I feel like that to this day, and I'll be 75 next birthday. Christy Moore just must get a mention here, for he is one of my favourites, what an entertainer that man is, wonderful, and I had the pleasure of meeting him once and he is a lovely human being, so he is. So let me finish where I began, young Arron Warner is now 16 and for the last two years, man, can he make that guitar talk, he is brilliant, and I believe a star of the very near future.

So, in a way him with having some of my genes and all, I will get to make that guitar sing, and I am more than happy with that. Me! I have written a lot of books of all genres and poems and short stories, like this one. Amen.

End

The Left-Handed Lawman

Dan Gayle's was the sheriff of Salem town and district in Orange County, a small-town northwest of Montana. He was forty-five years old and was originally from Ireland. Came over with his father in the year 1897 after his mother died from cancer. His father a farmer with 200 acres in a town called Fannad, in the beautiful County of Donegal up in the northwest corner of Ireland, sold up and moved everything except livestock over to that great land everyone was talking about, the US of A.

The land where even a poor farmer can become President. But only if he had rich friends. His father never got to become President, but he did get to become sheriff in a town called Provo. He was a game shooter back home and could hit a target from almost 400 yards.

His father a man called Daniel Gayle gave his son the choice of staying or going with him across the deep Atlantic Ocean. Dan was 20 at the time and he jumped at the chance of starting a new life in a new country. Then ten years later his father was shot in the back while trying to break up a fight in the local hotel, two men fighting over a woman, that sad old story that keeps repeating itself over and over.

It took his father two weeks to die and that left Dan once again pondering his future. He kept the ranch because of a friend of his that had just lost their home, the bank foreclosed on his small farm, a man with a wife and three children, to look after, and as Dan always told himself, 'A man always needs a second chance' so he let him use his 500 acres at a fair price but took over his father's job of sheriff of that ever-growing town.

One Monday afternoon two men came into town looking to rob the bank. It was their hard luck that that was the very day that Dan used to visit the bank manager to discuss expanding his ranch a few hundred acres more. He was in the office when the robbers came in shouting and screaming and waving their guns about.

The bank manager jumped up and stood behind Dan pushing him forward to go out here and do what he was been paid to do. The next moment there were two gunshots and two dead bank robbers on the floor. Dan was a good shot with either hand, he seldom missed whatever he was aiming at.

Dan with his guns already in his hands could not miss and did not miss, both men were shot through the heart. It was all over in seconds and the bank manager praised Dan to the heavens promising him all kinds of high office and other benefits of the town, meaning of course, free meals free haircuts, and so on.

But Dan had never killed a man before and now here he was after killing two men, and it shook him up a lot. It was in this state of mind he met a woman called Molly Fergusson originally from Scotland but had come to Chigo and like a lot of country people came out west for its wide-open spaces.

A red-haired beauty of beauties. Dan had an inkling that the bank manager sent her over to cheer him up and it most certainly did cheer him up, a lot. She came into his office with his dinner, a pot full of Irish stew a couple of days later and as soon as he saw her, he fell in love with her.

She had been there that Monday afternoon of the robbery and was she said, 'So impressed by how calm and cool you were facing those two wicket men and shooting them down like the dogs they were.' after that little speech he was up and about just like before. In fact, he went about the town with his head held high and his chest sticking out further than it normally was. But only for one day as it all got a little tiring.

They fell in love with each other, and life was good then for Dan Gayle but life such as it is, is always full of surprises as he was to learn two-weeks later.

He was walking down the main street as usual when he saw the stagecoach rolling into town, at the same time he noticed a young child walking with her mother. She saw a little white dog in the road and letting go of her mother's hand ran out to greet the little stray dog, when at that precise moment the stage approached at a high speed and if Dan had not run and dived to pull the little girl back from danger she would most definitely have been killed or crippled at most.

Dan however was left lying there with the coach's front wheel resting on his right wrist and the horses very restless. It took four strong men to raise the wheel of the stagecoach just high enough to free Dan's right arm, but his hand could not be saved so had to be amputated two days later, and it was two months before he could even show himself again in public. Molly once again lifted his spirits with talk of their up-and-coming wedding.

Which of course had to be put back a couple of months. Dan, trying hard to even practice with his left hand holding his gun, and for a while it looked like he was never going to make it, losing his temper at every attempt to even draw his gun. Slowly though over the next few months he got the hang of it and the more he practiced the faster he became. As they say, practice makes perfect.

The fact that he lost his hand on the job, and saved a little girls life, the townsfolk decided he could stay on as sheriff of the little sleepy town of Salem, at least until the date for the re-election of sheriff, which was in four months' time, in November, after all what could possibly happen in that one horse town in the next four months?

As it turned out, everything that could happen did happen and much more.

It happened that there was a man called Jacob Mac Callister the 3rd living in Provo. He wasn't royalty or anything like it, but he was the third of his three brothers, each one a miserable and cunning as he was. A very fat middle-aged man that had the appearance of everyone's idea of an adorable uncle, but he was a man hungry for power and he didn't care how he came by it; he was mean and vicious but never did the dirty work himself.

Always hired at least six to ten outlaws ready and willing to kill, for a price of course, any farmer that didn't do what he wanted, i.e., sell him their land at an outrageous price. One man in particular, his front man called Ray Barnes he overpaid to keep him out of the limelight, as Jacob had ambitions to become a politician.

He dressed very well always in black clothes, wearing on his hip a double set of matching revolvers, an indicator perhaps of how he must have felt inside, Ray Barnes was every bit and even more vicious and deadly as his boss, Jacob Mac Callister the 3rd. Moreover, he loved his job.

Tommy Tucker Mellick was fifteen years old. He was born and raised in Provo but moved to Salem two years ago when outlaws killed his parents then set fire to his home, a modest wood cabin five miles east of town.

He was out shooting wild pheasants and rabbits when the gang struck. He could not stay around Provo, so he

moved on and came to Salem where he got to know Dan and was allowed to sleep in his office most nights as the kid had nowhere to stay.

Dan liked the young kid and would often stay up talking to him for hours. 'You always carry that rifle around?' he asked him the first night they met to which the youngster replied, 'yep, it gives me the best kind of protection, though it didn't stop those murdering toerags from shooting my pa and ma, who were not carrying one, my dad was a simple farmer, maybe if he had been carrying a gun he might, they might …both be alive today …well …who knows?

The kid buried his head in his hands. Dan said to him,

'You do know don't you, ...that one of these days, you going to have to decide if you're going to use it on another human being, what then?

'Then' said young Tommy, 'I hope it is someone trying to kill me, I will have no hesitation in shooting him down.

Dan often found himself thinking that the kid might even make sheriff one day, hopefully in the not-too-distant future. As things stood, he was always following Dan around, almost like his son or even deputy. Dan liked that but encouraged Tommy to take up a part time job, at the general store.

Which he did.

It was at the general store that Tommy got to hear about this new man in town looking to buy up any property for a fair price, but as it was only a young town, nobody was willing to sell, fair price or not.

It was then the killing started.

Tommy did not know it then, but he was hearing about the man called Ray Barnes. Jacob Mac Callister the 3rd was looking to expand his empire, and Salem's fine reputation had come to his attention. That monster they call a human being was never one to miss an opportunity to make money, even if it meant innocent folk getting killed for it.

It started with old Joe Forrester. A man that raised his family of four partially on his own after his wife passed away from a very bad fever.

Old Joe lived about ten miles north of the town and had about 500 acres of good feeding land. He used to keep cattle and horses and sell them to the army the day after every Christmas, had done for about forty years, then he lost all heart when his wife died.

Ms Coburn, an elderly spinster lady used to come and help Joe when his wife got sick, stayed on to help raise his four young kids to grow to be fine young people, but as soon as they were able, they moved to Provo where they married and settled down, leaving Old Joe and Ms Coburn alone on that fine big ranch. Ms Coburn died in her sleep two years before old Joe was murdered. Shot in the back while he did what he still enjoyed doing every day, out walking on his land.

The Silver family were next to go, forced out by Mac Callister's gun happy crew of killers. When the timid man said no to Ray Barnes pitiful offer, the message was relayed to his boss who then sent his bully boys in to do whatever it takes to make the poor man sign a bill of sale.

Because he signed it, he and his family were allowed to live but forced to move on. This was how Dan got to know what was happening in his beloved town, and two days later he came face to face with the evil Ray Barnes.

It was on his regular trip to the bank on the Monday afternoon when he literally bumped into the killer as he came out of the manager's office. Ray looked him up and down then smiled as he said, 'Excuse me ...sheriff, my fault, sorry' as if butter wouldn't melt. **Dan asked the bank manager,**

'Who is that man, John?' he looks dangerous to me' 'Oh' replied John, 'he is just a businessman looking to buy up any unwanted property around here, seems a nice enough fellow'

Dan said to him, 'well. if looks could kill, I would be dead now, he looks more of a gunman than a businessman, he looks to me slimy, somethings not right about him'

'Naw! Said John, 'You should not judge people with the first glance, Dan my friend, take me for example, people used to take me for a preacher man, there are similarity's I guess but they were always surprised when they met me next time in the bank when they came into my office looking for a loan, you know the old saying, you should never judge a book by its cover'

Dan said to him, 'John, I am a good judge of peoples character, I may not be always right, but I am never wrong, and I tell you John that man stinks to high heaven and I am not referring to his smelly cologne'

It was however the deaths of the McCarthy family later in the same week that caused outrage in the community. They were all six of them murdered in their beds when their house was set ablaze in the early morning. A man coming home from another town saw the house on fire and raised the alarm. He also described seeing a man resembling the one and only Ray Barnes.

'Are you sure it was him?' Dan asked him the next day. 'You know it was dark at that early hour, I mean how can you be so sure?' the man replied, 'it was not dark on account of the flames reaching so high, I could see plainly with the brightness of the fire, I tell you sheriff, if it wasn't him I saw then, it was his twin brother'

That was good enough for Dan and he went searching for the killer. What man, or woman for that matter would set fire to a house full of people? One as young as three years old. He found him in the hotel lounge eating dinner and drinking wine. 'You are under arrest for the murder of Dan Mc Carty and his family last night at their home in Greystone's' not five miles from here'

Ray Barnes said to him in reply while wiping his greasy chin with a napkin, 'Tut ...tut ...now sheriff, can not a man enjoy his dinner in this one-horse town, without been harassed by the local one-handed sheriff, and then been accused of some grisly crime, I mean what grounds do you have for this wild accusation of yours?

'You will find out soon enough, now get up drop that gun belt and let's go, I'm taking you in' and Dan with his gun on the beast took him out across main street and passed the stranger who nodded his head in agreement with Dan.

When Jacob Mac Callister heard about the things that was happening in Saleem he got two of his toughest most experienced killers to go there with the intension of taking out sheriff Dan Gayle, and anyone else that stood in the way of breaking out Ray Barnes. He only sent two men because he laughed when he heard the sheriff had only one hand.

Two days later those two men were dead and when he heard that he sent six more. They were already halfway there.

Two days later Dan was talking to Tommy standing outside his office, 'I know what you're thinking, and the answer is no, you're too young for this kind of work, 'Tommy was adamant and said to Dan,

'I know you can shoot, sheriff, and so can I, so what is wrong with me helping you, I am almost a grown man now, so deputise me, and let me help you,'

Dan replied, 'Look Tommy, I know you mean well, and if I need you; I will call you, ok? but at the moment I don't need you, so please stay out of the way, I have enough to worry about without having to worry about you, ok?' Tommy left Dan's office in disgust and disappointment.

John Dillon the bank manager said to Dan the next morning. 'I know how you must be feeling, and I have tried to get some men together to stand with you, but all I got was, 'My wife is expecting our baby I cannot risk anything happening to me, or my mother isn't well, she needs me more than the sheriff does, sorry, and other unlikely excuses, I am sorry Dan, but it looks like you're on your own on this one' as if he had helped with the other two gunslingers.

Dan said to him, 'it's ok John! I am the sheriff after all, and I do get paid to help keep law and order in this town, don't worry, anyway, I have you to help me, don't I?' John said almost choking, almost swallowing his tongue, 'Eh …I am a man of …figures not eh …bullet's Dan, …I am sorry, but I cannot help you, …this town would be lost without me' then he made his excuses and left, as Dan knew he would.

Ray Barnes was laughing at Dan saying stupid things like, they will be here soon sheriff …you will need more than one hand to deal with these ruthless men sheriff?' then he began to mock Dan saying stuff like 'you want another hand sheriff?

And 'two hands are better than one left hand ha …ha …ha, at least you won't have to let your right hand know what your left hand is doing, hahhaah'

Dan just ignored him, but Tommy stuck his rifle in Ray's face and told him if he did not shut his stupid mouth, he would shut it for him. Ray Barnes shut his stupid mouth as the look on Tommy's face told him he would do it too.

Molly was talking to Dan in his office one day later and she said to him, 'Oh Dan I can't wait for the day when we can both sleep in the one bed, it seems so far away but it is only two weeks, O' how wonderful to be in love and be loved by the one you love, oh dear that sound poetic doesn't it darling? and I do love you Dan, you're the most wonderful thing that ever happened to me, and to think that if those two bank robbers had not decided to rob the bank that day… 'Dan barged in saying, 'They would still be alive darling, but yes! it is wonderful to be getting married to the most beautiful woman in the world, I mean that darling, have you sorted the dress yet? and all that goes with it?' Molly replied, 'this time tomorrow everything will be done and oh …Dan, I simply cannot wait any longer so if you want to stay the…' again Dan barged in saying, 'Oh Molly, I do, like yourself long for the moment, but also like your good self, have been brought up in the Christian tradition with Cristian values of waiting until waiting time is over.'

He was a man with a way with the words, even if sometimes he fell all over them.

The simple act of kissing can and often does save the moment. It can also lead to having babies when one should rather wait.

Captain Jack Lowey had been in the army in Fort Worth all his life. By now he should have reached lieutenant Colonel but a bad patch with the Colonels daughter did him no favours, but he was still doing the job he loved best.

For years now he had been coming to Salem to see his old friend Joe Forrester, checking over all the horses before his old friend them sold to the army. They would often spend an evening drinking whisky and going over the old days when the Apache Indians were on the warpath.

Those were the days when men were real men, when men had balls not goose bumps all over their bodies, back and front, at the first sign of trouble.

Many a time Jack had to spend the night at Joes house

after downing one drink too many. Yes, he was looking forward to seeing his old friend. He was only two hours away from Salem and could not wait to have a hot bath, a few drinks, and later catch up on all the news.

John Dillon the bank manager came into Dan's Office the following morning and said to him, 'Dan, I have been thinking over what we discussed the other day, in terms of deputies, and it just is not right that you should have to face this dangerous gang alone, and I got to talking again to some of those lame ducks I told you about, and they at last agreed in principle with me on that score, but when it comes down to it, who knows if they will even show up, but you now have my full support, for what it's worth, at least I will back you from a safe place, if that is ok with you sheriff?' Dan was delighted to hear him say that, even if he didn't mean it. It was good to feel that someone even cared about his predicament. Besides, he knew he needed all the help he could get, imaginary or not, and time was running out fast.

As John was walking back out Ray Barnes said to him. 'Dead man walking' and he laughed until he heard John say back to him, 'Yes! and I will be walking to the gallows when they hang you, good morning to you, do have a nice day'

Later that morning Jack Lowey entered the sheriff's office and introduced himself to Dan.

'Yes! I remember you now, welcome back is it that time already? 'It is, and I just can't wait to hook up with my old pal Joe Forrester again, we two go back a long way' Dan told him the sad news and when Jack asked him if he knew who was responsible for the killing Dan nodded in the direction of his prisoner.

Jack got up and went to attack Ray Barnes, but Dan held him back saying, 'steady on Jack, he is my prisoner now, he has been swindling homesteaders out of their homes, he is working for someone called, Jacob Mac Callister the...'

Jack cuts him off and then says to him, 'the 3rd, 'I have heard that name before Dan ...in fact just before I left the fort there were army men setting up an investigative team to go looking for and bring to justice this man Jacob, and his side kick Ray Barnes, there is even a huge reward for anyone bringing either one of them in dead or alive' Dan nodded in the direction of the jail and says to Jack, 'There is the one called Ray Barnes and the other one is not too far away, in fact he is in Provo but his gang is on its way here to break this rotten apple out, as we speak' Jack looking at Tommy lying there says to Dan, 'Who is the kid?' Dan replies, 'he can talk ...ask him and he will tell you ...if he has a mind too, kids these days ...huh? Tommy sits up saying, 'I can hear every word you say, and I am not a kid, I am a man, well ...almost a man ...and you are going to need me to do some of you dirty work for you' Jack says to him, 'Killing scum like that is not dirty work son, in fact it is one's solemn duty to kill such as these, but only of course if one had the authority to do so, and the facts are proven, hello …my name is captain Jack Lowey I hav …' Tommy sits up and says, 'Yeah! I heard you the first time, no need to repeat it again, I am Tommy Tucker Mellick … time trust and motion, soon to be sheriff Dans deputy, only he just doesn't' know it yet'

Later in the afternoon when Molly brought Dan and Tommy's dinner to the office, she saw the captain, she blushed and said shyly. 'Oh,' I only brought enough for two, I am sorry Dan maybe …if I get another …plate then you…' Jack stood up, introduced himself then said, 'That is quite alright my dear, I have rather overstayed my welcome …sorry sheriff, Thomas, …mam, I will get back to you later Dan, if that's ok?' Dan said it was and Jack left. Tommy said to the other two, 'God, only my mother called me Thomas! Molly smiled but then that was when she said to Dan, 'Then the rumours are true Dan! oh, dear, how can this be happening …we are getting married soon, and now you might be…' Dan took her hand and said to her,

'Now. stop that darling! nothing is going to happen to me, this is all part of the job, I mean if nothing ever happened in this town, I would not be the sheriff, would I? so don't worry, everything will be fine, I promise you' Tommy got busy stuffing his face when Dan and Molly started kissing, and the clock was ticking away. Dan saw the man who had pointed out Ray Barnes to him the other day and offered to buy him a drink in the saloon, which he gladly accepted as he was a man of poor means and spent many a night sleeping around the General store. As they were drinking Dan said to him, 'As soon as we finish here, I want you to come with me to my office' the man looked surprised and said to him, 'Why! What have I done?' Dan laughed at him and told him about the big reward he was due for helping him catch Ray Barnes, he said to him, 'I just need you to sign a piece of paper, so that when the time comes to pay out, you will get the money and no one else ok?' the man named Simon Ward, simply said, 'I'll drink to that'

Molly said to him later 'Are you sure everything is going to be ok Dan, I am really worried about you, I love you and want to take care of you, but in our new home and not in some doctors surgery somewhere, or worst in the horrible graveyard out there, these men that are coming, they are killers and don't care who they kill, they don't even care for themselves darling, I can't help worrying I don't want to lose you Dan' Molly began to weep as Dan took her hand and said, 'You're not going to lose me honey, I have no intention of letting anyone shoot me, or hurt me in any way, so stop your wailing and worrying girl, we will be getting married this day new week, isn't that enough for you to be worrying about? She said to him, 'Yes, but that is a different kind of worrying, darling, getting married isn't going to get you all shot up or even killed, darling I love you so Dan you do know that? that is why I worry about you,' he kissed her gently on the lips and said to her, 'Look I am not going to face these outlaws alone, I have men here willing and able to back me up, so stop you hissing and keep on kissing me honey, I like that, I really do' and she did, kiss him again and again, until Tommy got up and walked out of the office, shaking his head sideways.

Meanwhile not fifteen miles away the outlaws were busy drinking coffee at the side of the road, Mac Callister was with them, he had come to see for himself just how fast this one-handed sheriff really was. He wanted to be the one that unlocked the jail cell and free his old friend Ray Barnes, to terrorise and scare people out of their homes. He was also eager to meet the bank manager, after all he was the one that would be keeping his money safe and sound in his bank vault. Money that would be mounting up day by day.

Another reason was the coming elections, Ray Barnes would, he considered, make a fine sheriff of this fine town he would have been hearing so much about lately. Relaxing with his coffee and big cigar, the fat man sat back in his horse-drawn buggy and surveyed the land that he hoped to own any day now, and the twelve gunslingers he had riding with him would make sure of that, even if they had to kill everyone in the place.

'Can you really face down as many as twenty hired guns sheriff? I mean you with only one gun and all, are you sure you don't need an extra hand, …ha…ha …ha, I'm sorry I know I should not be laughing but you just have to see the funny side to what's about to happen any day now' Ray Barnes said to Dan as he was getting ready to go to the meeting the towns folk had arranged to discuss the upcoming situation. He replied, 'Forgive me if I don't join in the laughter, but I will when this is all over and you'll either hang or rot in jail for the rest of your miserable like, you and that murdering swine you call a boss'

'Well!' said Ray, 'I would not be too sure about that, from tomorrow on he will be the boss of this whole town, only you won't be alive to see it, you'll be moving on to that cemetery up on that hill yonder' I will make sure of that,

'Oh yes! Dan said to him, 'and how will you do that from inside that cell, even if you were free out there with those fancy guns of yours you wouldn't stand a chance, so don't waste your breath with your fancy talking, you're as good as dead anyway.' later that evening a meeting was called in the town hall, it was opened by the mayor who was also the back manager.

As mayor of this great though small city, I call this meeting to order. On this day Sunday October 21, 1899. At precisely six –thirty-five pm. This meeting is now open I call to the floor the Reverent Don Brown who will blest and will be our MC. The reverend a small man in stature but with a voice like a bull frog.

'Friends, brothers and sisters in the Lord Jesus Christ, in this crisis as in any crisis there is only one Saviour and that is Christ the Lord, if we put our trust in him and in each other we will not be shamed and…' some man on the floor stood up and spoke up. 'It is not the thought of been shamed I am worried about Reverend, it's been shot,' everyone in the hall nodded their heads in agreement with him and one or two even laughed'

The Reverend continued saying, 'I was about to say brothers and sisters in the Lord, that we will not be put to shame or disgrace, which actually means' he was looking at the man that interrupted him, 'if we are not put to shame nor disgraced, then that must mean we win this battle between good and evil, evil has no place in our modern society, and besides our wonderful sheriff Dan, is the man for this job, but he needs our help, so can we have a hands up to see how many will help him in his hour of need, and I am not talking about drinking to his good health, my friends, my brothers and sisters in Christ, if we want this town to survive and thrive, then we must be prepared to fight for it, if necessary to die for it, for our way of living, our children and our elderly folk, a tree grows better if it's is watered daily but only if its planted by a nearby stream, my brothers and sisters, let the people of this fine town be that stream, let us give life to each other, and pray for those who think that they can come here and take our way of life from us, so hands up, who will stand on the path of life?' again the man stood up and said to all there,

'It is not life I am worried about, but the loss of it, there are men coming here to kill or drive our sheriff out of town and break that killer out of jail, I for one will stand with the sheriff, Dan there, a good and upright citizen of our fine town, no one has the right to just come here and take over, we are peaceful people …but we will fight for our freedom as our forefathers fought the Apache, …who by the way …owned this land,…long …long before we did, but these bully boys and drifters have no rights to our homes, our business and our town, not to mention our wives and our daughters' the whole place went into an uproar with the thought of those killers and filthy drifters even looking at their women folk, in that dirty vulgar way.

And every man there from young to old swore he would defend the town with the sheriff. And even back in the jail house Ray Barnes sensed a feeling of sheer dread, filling every ounce of his being.

Saying and doing is one thing but saying and not doing is quite another.

Jack Lowey said to Dan that same evening, 'I have sent a telegram to headquarters requesting an urgent dispatchment of soldiers, I am waiting for a reply but even if they were sent tomorrow, they would not get here till Saturday at least, and from what we are hearing those outlaws will be here by tomorrow afternoon, if not sooner,'

'No Matter' replied Dan, 'if those good towns men are true to their word, we will have more than enough support' Jack replied saying,

'It has been my experience Dan, that people such as you saw earlier are mainly full of talk, they allow themselves to get carried away with raw emotions running wild all over the place and even the weakest one there will say things he will regret as soon as the meeting is over,' he paused to catch his breath and take a drink from a glass of water then said.

'It is just the way some of us humans are, especially if there are women present, so while it is commendable what they said, when it comes right down to it, well, I for one will be more than surprised if even two shows up, do you have anything stronger that this?'

Dan poured him a whisky and Tommy asked him for one, but was refused, Jack said to him, 'are you not going to have one Dan? you need to relax man, let yourself chill out, all this must be bearing heavily on you, a couple of drinks are not going to hurt you'

Dan replied, 'Whisky is the last thing I want or need right now, I have to keep a clear and steady head, if they do come tomorrow, then I want to be ready and sober, I don't want to go shooting the wrong people, now do I?'

Jack laughed on hearing that, and said to Dan, 'As if you would, mind you, you just might be a better shot, who knows?' but seriously sheriff, you must have a plan for everything and anything, and speaking of plans, do you even have one?'

Dan said to him, 'The only plan I have at the moment is that tomorrow or whenever they show up, I will not be running for cover, but will decide on a spur of the moment plan, when I see what the true situation I'm facing is,' that's the plan oh, and the other plan I have is not ...to run for ...re-election.' All three of them laughed at that.

Dan poured Jack another whisky and Tommy another glass of water. At eight am the following morning Jacob Mav Callister came into town with six men left and right of him. He went straight to the bank and when he found no one there he sent a man up to the mayor's house and by gunpoint had the mayor brought down to his buggy demanding to know where the bank manager was.

'I am the bank manager' said a shaky John Dillon, ' the fat man said to him, 'and I am Jacob Mac Callister, and I have a business proposition to put to you' John said to him sharply,' 'the bank does not open before ten, so I suggest you come back and maybe then we can do business, but not before that, so if you don't mind, I am going back to bed' Jacob said to him, 'Ah! but I do mind and as your incoming mayor I demand you open this bank right now or you won't see your precious bed again' he nodded to the gun who hit John over the head, so he had no option but to open the bank, just as they were about to go in Jacob stopped him and told him to look around. He did and he saw Jacob's men all holding torches and waiting for the order from Jacob to or not to burn the town down.

Once inside Jacob produced a sheet of paper and told John to sign the bottom of it. He refused saying, 'What on earth is this?' Jacob replied saying it is a contract between your good self and I the next bank manager and owner of said bank. 'This is an outrage, how dare you come in here and show me such a false document,'

Jacob's face reddened somewhat, and he said to John. 'If this document which is a legal document by the way, is not signed by the next five minutes then, Mr Mayor, this whole town goes up in flames, inhabitants, and all, so sign dam it!

Dan woke up to the sound of running boots and when he opened the door Simon was standing there breathless, 'there are here sheriff, those men, they are here and the big fat man in the white suit is with the bank manager, and I don't think they are playing chess' tommy had heard everything and was standing behind Dan then rushed past them and was gone into the darkness of the morning.

Dan cursing himself for not been ready for an early morning attack, said to Simon, 'wake up as many folks as you can, but stay out of sight of those men out there, you didn't happen to count them did you Simon?'

'I did there are twelve gunmen, that fat man and his driver, that's 15, yeah? Dan looked at him and pitied him then told him to go quietly and do what he could to try and warn the others. Then all hell broke loose when the outlaws started to burn the stores, and the one who came to burn the sheriff's office was the first one to die as Dan put a bullet between his eyes.

Two more shots rang out and Dan saw two more outlaws fall in front of the bank, and the outlaws began shooting all over the place. Dan through the flames saw Tommy with his rifle on the roof of one of the stores next to the two that were now blazing with the flames lighting up the cool October morning, and by now all the people in the hotel were up and running in all directions and Dan thought of Molloy and hoped she was alright.

Molly had in her rush to escape the flames had in fact fallen down the hotel lobby's stairs and broken her right leg. Dan was now out on the street running between the burning buildings and shooting outlaws like he would fish in a barrel. Dan himself had taken a bullet to his right arm and another to his left leg, otherwise he was okay. The fat man said to John.

'You hear that Mr bank manager?' that is my men tearing up this town, I had hoped to avoid this as it means that I will have to rebuild, but rest assured it will be rebuilt bigger and better, with a huge gambling casino bang smack where this bank is now, now sign it and be gone before I have you shot' John picked up the piece of paper and tore it in two saying, 'You hear that? fat man! that is our 'Sheriff' and his deputy shooting you men like the rabid dogs they are in the street, and soon the whole town will be here armed to the teeth, what will you do then? you miserable excuse for a human being, begone yourself, before I have you shot,' the fat man panicked and ran to where he told his buggy driver to wait, up the laneway behind the bank.

Out on the street the killing continued with Tommy picking off his targets with ease from the rooftops that were not burning and Dan ducking in and out of the alley way's doing likewise, normally Dan would never shoot anyone in the back but this time he made a few exceptions and within an hour the shooting stopped. In the morning air now warmed up slightly from the now burnt-out buildings were the bodies of the slain gunmen lying all over the place, and in the stillness of the morning Jacob Mac Callister the 3rd came out from behind the bank with him and his driver been held captive by John Collins with a gun to the fat man's head. With John saying, 'I wanted to put a bullet in his miserable brain, then thought he may not have one and besides, a lifetime in a small cell will give him more time, in fact forever to repent his wicket ways'

Simon Ward was busy counting the bodies on the street and when Dan asked him how many there were he answered, 'there are nine sheriff that leaves four missing yeah?' Dan pitied the man and said to him, 'Yeah 9 and 4 are 12, seems like 5 of them got away, but no matter now all that remains now is to bury these 8 and the lock up the two on the cart and that makes 11, yeah, we should be okay now, thank you Simon, you did great man' then turning to young Tommy Tucker says to him, 'and young man, it was fantastic the way you took those men out, you have indeed the makings of a great sheriff and I for one would be proud to be your deputy'

Tommy said to him, 'Now can I have a whisky?' Dan says to him calmly and sternly, 'No! you cannot have a whisky, there will be enough of us wobbling down the aisle tomorrow, as you near enough kin to her now Molly wants you go give her away, if you don't mind that is?' Tommy was over the moon with that and said to him, 'What does that make you then, my dad, my uncle, or my granddad?' thinking of Molly, Dan ran to the hotel to see where and how she was and he found her two doors down in the doctors house getting her leg plastered, otherwise she was ok and when she saw Dan come in through the door she tried to get up and run to him but the doctor stopped her, saying, 'you want to break that other leg woman? lie still,' Dan knelt beside her and hugged her and kissed her and said, 'I love you so baby thank God you're okay, are you still good to go tomorrow? She replied to him, 'Why! what's so special about tomorrow?' then they embraced as the doctor smiled and looked on the happy couple as if they didn't have a care in the world. The doctor never married.

End

The Big Girls Brigade

Was a club formed by big girls for big girls; To get each other healthy and fit by going for long walks eating smaller but more nutritious meals while at the same time with some supplying a service, while for others it simply meant having a few laughs.

The hours were 10 am to 4pm, except bank holidays, and if it did nothing else it got some of the girls out of the house for a few hours every day. The club was based on Fortunestown Way opposite the Lidle store in Tallaght area. It consisted mostly of foreign people in the main, as every nationality was welcome. The fee was 50 euro every six months or 100 euro a year.

Mary 67 was the founder of the club; Madge 57 was the chairperson of the club, in charge of fees and funding plus activities was Elenora, the most glamorous of the three big girls, with a body more sculptured for want of a better word.

Joan 43 was their first member; she was part time at first but quickly entered the spirit of the club and became a full member. She also introduced other friends and neighbours to join and soon there were well over fifty members, all having a laugh at first then getting down to the serious side which of course was losing wight.

Among the fifty was a young lady called, Merinda 32; with a smile that brought light into whomever came close to her. Okay her large breasts might have had something to do with it, at least as far as the men were concerned, and one or two, three or four, of the other women in her club.

They went swimming, dancing, ice skating and even rowing up and down the local rivers. The local lads got to know the swimming days and would shout out encouragement to them as they got on the bus hired especially for the occasion, with the odd joker often shouting out, 'Tsunami warning' or for the less educated, 'Tidal Wave' which means the same thing. More or less. Doesn't it?

Some of the girls developed strong feelings for each other, and got to playing little games in the pool, but more serious ones in the changing rooms, for example when no one was looking a woman called Jane 42; a fine beautiful looking woman would lift her bra and show her breast to her secret girlfriend name Susan 43, and would both play with each other if there was no one else there at that particular time.

Another woman called Mira 39; struck up a relationship with one of the lifeguards on duty and would often get her own kind of exercise in one of the men's changing rooms where she did a lot of sucking and blowing, and the lord knows what else.

Another girl Anna 47; because of her widening experience in the ladies' club began to give massages during her spare time outside the club hours, but they were everything but holistic.

Then there was Stella 41; the queen of the club and the most outspoken of the fifty. She would often come out with the most outlandish and shocking phases, like, 'Who wants to be blown up first?' or 'who is the best breast baby in the shop window?' or 'if it was any bigger, you'd get a job in the County Council as a shoveler in the gardening department,' stuff like that.

Laura 38; a fine-looking woman with boobs to die for, had a special trick which put her out there on her own. She advertised herself as a cleaner but when she got there, she cleaned out everything that was not nailed down, and that even meant the woman and her husband if he just happened to be there, at the same time, which by some strange coincidence, he always was.

Then there was Cheyenne 40; so, called because of her Indian looks, maybe because she was an Indian, all the way from India. She was a smallest in stature but very well thought of by the other girls, especially Jane and Susan when the two of them would invite her over every other Wednesday night for a threesome. With coffee and chocolate biscuits for afters, as well as be fore's and in between moves that got so hot and steamy they had to takes breaks every ten minutes or so.

Then there was Lilly 57; the gypsy woman, told everyone their fortunes whether they wanted to hear it or not. She too has beautiful breasts that could hypnotised any man in thirty-seconds or less. She made effective use of them as well, for while they were watching her glorious boobs bobbing up and down, they were not, repeat not, watching their wallets.

There were other girls too that had moves and secrets of their own, like Christina 49; every time she ran short of money she would go into her neighbours and flash her boobs and he would gladly hand over his last 20 euro, or if she needed a little more give the old pensioner a BJ, and it was not blowing the paint off his hall door. He always had a little extra money under his mattress for just such an emergency.

Then there was Justin 52; with her stern looks and long legs that went all the way up to her, well, her backside. She was always complaining about how cold she was, even if it were just a little bit windy. Then Stella well known for her one-liners would often say to her, 'If you kept your pantie's on and your cave door closed, your big mouth shut, you'd stop letting the central heating out, you would be a lot warmer, you might even smile more, darling'

So, these were the main ladies in the club. The doers in all that was going on, while the rest were there just to lose weight and keep their husbands from looking at more slender women and hopefully to stop them for straying from home.

Mary's husband said to her one rainy Monday morning, 'You're not going to that club again? I mean here I am in bed on my day off and I have this big empty bed and you are there and I am here and I don't want you there I want you here beside me, doing rude but beautiful things to my overworked body, and all you want to do is go out in the rain and please other women, I mean what am I to think? That you don't love me anymore? is it just because I am a little on the generous size down there? or is it because you're saving yourself for someone else? You can tell me, I can take it, if you can take the pain, so can I'

She undressed completely and got in beside him running her hand down along his back until he turned over and began waving his flagpole from side to side. She covered him with her mouth and slowly began slowly moving her head up and down, they had been doing that kind of stuff for the past forty-odd years yet neither of them ever tired of it, she was as a master craftsperson using all her skills to shape her invention, and he loved every second of it, and when he was ready to explode he gently moved her up until she was sitting on top of manhood and he was playing with her boobs lovingly making her soft nipples rock hard.

She gyrated on him as if she were dancing which of course she was dancing, not around, but on his flagpole, and it wasn't over until they both hit the heights at the same time, when the pleasure bomb exploded, and as she was once more getting dressed she said to him, 'Well now darling, you've had your breakfast, time for your little lie on and if your still awake later on you can do me at dinner' but he did not hear a word she said as he was sound asleep.

Jane could not wait to see Susan again, she had slept over and they had the most wonderful evening together, so much so that they both slept in late, and just was Susan was getting up Jane pulled her back down in the bed and began passionately kissing her, and feeling her breast, then kissing her nipples before gently running her hand down between her legs and began massaging her gently at first, then furiously make Jane cry out in ecstasy while she pushed her body upwards, singing Susan's praises as she did so.

Activities list

Mary got there a little later that she thought she would and as she got to the door the manager of the whole development came up to her just as she got out of her four-year-old Nissan Juke and said to her sarcastically,

'Good afternoon, Mary, my …my …but you are an early riser, I have a plan here that might be off some use to you, I was doing nothing last night and I thought of you and here I am, I know you probably have your own list of things to do, like Bingo and such but I thought you might branch out a bit, you know ...make life a little more challenging and so forth, don't thank me just yet, put it before your members and see what they think, okay? again, good afternoon'

If he had not been the top man in the place, she would have told him where to stuff his list, if life wasn't challenging enough for god's sake.

She gave the list without even looking at it to her treasurer Elenora who just glanced at it and said, Mary where did you get this piece of ass paper? Mary told her and she raised her eyes to the ceiling and said nothing else, then like Mary she too went to the kitchen to have her morning cup of coffee and half a dozen small but delicious cream cakes.

By half past ten all the big girls brigade were present and with two exceptions were accounted for. Mary began to tell them about the list, 'I have photo-copied it for each one of you to see for yourself what you would or would not be interested in, take your time and remember you are not obliged to do anything you don't want to do, when you do decide just put an x in whatever box you want, yes or no, it is as simple as that...' one of the younger girls Joana 45 stood up and said, 'Mud wrestling, what the f...k is that?' Mary said to her,' it is wrestling, in mud, you know, that mucky stuff' another big girl named Nora 49 stood up and said, 'Will we be naked? because it we are then I'm all for it' everybody laughed. Mary said to them all,

'Remember, it is to raise funds for the club' another big lady, though not as big as the last lady that spoke said, 'What do you mean? Are we to do this mud wrestling in front of people, like outsiders, cos if we are then I am out, no way Hosea, am I showing my naked body to anyone,' a woman called Tina 43 jumped up and said to her, 'You showed it to me, then realised what she had just said and sat back down blushing like mad.

Mary coughed and said to them, Paul the manager said that if we raise enough money, we could turn the very large back garden into a mini pitch and putt course, and charge people five euro to play nine holes, that should bring in a few euros a day' someone said up to her, 'How long will it take to play nine holes Mary?

Another lady called Claire 39 replied saying, 'My husband spends all day playing with his little white balls, if we have a person playing the course and it takes her, five or six hours to finish it then we won't be making any money at all, another butted in saying, it was Shelia 73.

'Not if we are butt naked, they will be round that course like bees to a honey pot, and we should charge the onlookers ten euro for the pleasure they get from eh, urging on their favourite player,' there was a long silence in the room.

Another girl called Mona 47 possibly the biggest lady in the club, said, 'I like the beauty competition, it would give us girls a chance to maybe have one every year, you know like those skinny women have, I mean beauty is in the eye of the beholder, or failing that we could do a naked Calendar and charge people for it,' again there was a long silence in the room. The she said before sitting back down, 'Well! I think it is a wonderful idea, so there'

Eleanora said to the hall, 'The slides in the playgrounds are out for obvious reasons and so is the poll dancing, so pay no attention to those two, okay? I think it's time for a little break, ok ...coffee and cakes are already laid out, but take no more than four each or one or two of you will be laid out, by the chef ok, back in fifteen'

When they returned twenty-five minutes later Mary said, 'I didn't like that sliced soda bread, it was too thick, almost twice as thick as normal.' the Irish lady called Mahanmaid Hasheem 49 stood up and said to Mary,' Why were you looking at me when you said that?

Are you implying that I am thick just because I am Irish, even though I am of dark skin? Mary was flustered on hearing her say that and replied, 'Of course I was not implying anything of the sort, Mahanmaid, we have a strong no racism policy here as you well know, and as for your dark skin, well we are in a coloured neighbourhood, as you can see if you look around you, we have lots of beautiful black women here, and besides, there are black Irish people in Ireland,

Mahanmaid she to her,' Yes! I know there is, but they are not here to defend themselves, so I will do it for them' there was a long silence in the room, it was as if someone had just died in front of everyone there. Mary feigning a headache said she had to go home early and lie down.

When Mary had gone Elenora carried on saying, 'Plus we have the monthly day trip to the Hellfire club up the Dublin mountains, on Tuesday, and as you know the hills are a little steep up that way so we will get the bus up and have a picnic on the devils table as usual, but this time we will bring our umbrellas, so we don't get piss... on, eh ...drenched like the last time, when all ten of us had to shelter under the devils table, and ya'll know how that feels, I was expecting to see the devil's hoof underneath that table and I know I was not exaggerating when I said I felt something like a foot feeling around my bottom, it was very scary, though at the same time it was nice, but that is not the reason I'm going this time, in case anyone is thinking it is' again the long silence.

'How much is developing the pitch and putt course going to be?' asked Janet 64.

Elenora replied, 'We don't know yet, but it is going to cost twenty-five grand.

Then Phillis 72 said to all there, 'why don't we hire out some spades and develop it ourselves, I mean it would be a lot of fun, all we need is a few bags of sand, an inexpensive plastic swimming pool for the water feature and bobs your uncle, I mean, how hard can it be? 9 small holes in the ground, 9 little wooden panels to show what hole it is ...and an arrow pointing the way to the next hole, simple'

'Shut your Hole!' a girl called Shauna 39 shouted. Elenora said to all there, 'Actually that is a very good idea, my husband is a landscape gardener, he will map out the way to go, and tell us where to put the holes ...eh'

'Shut your hole' Shauna called out again, she seemed to have a fixation on holes for some reason, then she said, 'And how much is this husband of yours going to charge the club? you been treasurer and all, Elenora was caught out on that one but steadied herself and spoke up, 'I don't expect him to do it for free, he is after all a tradesman, but I would not say it would amount to much, maybe five-grand, that's all, which is a big difference to twenty-five grand'

Then she said, 'Can we have a show of hands for those willing to give it a go, we are not bound by it, it is just to get an idea, to feel the mood so to speak, all in favour of the proposal, and don't forget the benefits of doing it ourselves, losing weight toning our bodies, sweating out all those bad toxins ...'

'And digging holes!' said Shauna.

Looking around the room she says, 'Mmmmm ...that is about 50-50, so we need to do a little more work on this one, we will wait until the other two ladies turn up tomorrow or one or two of you here now don't turn up tomorrow then we'll see what the others think, ...okay girls that is enough for the day, see you all tomorrow'

Then next day just after everyone had tea and scones for breakfast one of the ladies Kathrine 59 said to Elenora at the table.' I watched the game last night between Ireland and Scotland and it was brilliant with Ireland winning and going into the women's world cup for the first time, so I was thinking, how about us here forming a rugby team? who knows in a couple of years we could be in the women's rugby world cup' Elenora said to her, that sound great Kath, but in two months we would all be dead, imagine us trying to run round that huge pitch, I don't think the others would go for it somehow,'

'Well said Kathrine, 'if you were on that pitch and suddenly a wild bear or a sex maniac came at you wouldn't you be able to run like the hounds of hell, I know I would, and so would every woman here' Elenora said to her, 'You have a point there Kath, but I still can't see it happening,'

'Well how about Sumo wrestling? that could be fun, and those suits they wear are simply beautiful?' Elenora pretended not to hear that and jumped up from the table knocking over her glass of orange juice in the process.

Mary asked the two ladies why they hadn't shown up yesterday and why the two of them were black and blue and sporting double black eyes?

'Because' said Hillary 47 'she called me a hippapotm ...eh a ...hipapot, eh ...a fat Hippo!' Mary looking with disgust at the younger Mary asked her why she had been so rude?

She replied, 'because, she called me a fat Rhinoceros! and we both ended up mud wrestling in the sand, that is why, that stupid cow there with the biggest udders that no cow would ever be ashamed of'

The younger Mary went to go for her again but our Mary, the eldest one, did not want to get caught between the two rather large ladies so stepped aside and let them get on with it, there was a hell of a scrap with three of the partition walls getting knocked out of place and the wooden tiles popping up all over the floor, when it was over ten seconds later on account of the ladies running out of steam Mary the older one said to the two of them,

'Well, we will have no more discourse in our club, bang each other's tits together and then forget about it, life is to short' and they belly banged each other and agreed to let bygones be gone. As was the custom in the club.

Then everything went a bit sour when Paul the manager of the small industrial park- com- community centre, came into the club to complain to Mary as she was talking to Elenora in the middle of the hall and began to give out stink because someone in the club had parked in his car space.

A small thing really but WW 1 started over the killing of one man. Okay he was a particularly important man, but one man, nonetheless.

So, tempers began to rise, and sparks began to fly and insults galore where hurled at the big girl's brigade. Jesinta 46 not her weight, which was quite a lot as she was rather on the heavy side, was practising her mid-air rope dancing and when she heard the abuse her friends were getting, she swung herself onto a nearby ledge then hurled herself in the direction of Paul and when she got almost over the spot where he was standing, she let herself go.

She came down like a ton of cement on the poor man killing him instantly. The ambulance was called and as was the custom in any case of death, so were the guards.

Sergeant Jack Slasher arrived first on the scene with his sidekick Snodaigh 'Snottser' Mc Gill and as they were looking over the body Jack said aloud enough for all to hear as there was by now a large crowd of people gathered, some drinking coffee and eating cheesecake while others were just staring at the dead body, it's not every day one sees a dead body.

'Stand back, this looks like a murder to me, stand well back,' then to his sidekick Snottser he says, 'Better get forensics out here man, this looks suspiciously like a murder to me,'

Snottser pulled him aside and whispered gently in his ear, 'Hold on a minute, Jack, this is an accident …no doubt about it, now you and I know how much of a rollicking you got off the Super the last time, are you sure you want to do piss him off again?'

Jack said to him, 'Ok, you're right …let us go over the facts of this case again then, that man is dead, and it looks like he was hit by a 40-ton truck and trailer, look at his face …the way his eyes are looking upward in terror and those glasses of his …how did they end up between his teeth? which are at least four feet away from the body, I tell you man …I smell foul play here, and I have seen more than my fair share of dead bodies, I mean I see the wife every morning noon and night, ah no, …that's not fair…scrap that last remark,'

Because it was a community centre with lots of onlookers and the press there, the Superintendent himself decided to tag along and show his face. The guards after all had had a terrible trashing in news lately. With them ramming cars all over the place just because a few joyriders were out having a smashing time.

When he was told how the terrible accident had happened, and the conclusion that his sergeant had come too, the Super told his two men to get the f…k back to the station and that Jack was suspended for two weeks, pending a review.

A review that found that the girl that landed on Paul purposely and she was later jailed for ten years to life in the women's prison in Wheatfield.

Sadly, though, all the negativity caused the big girls brigade club to close. Most of them however still can be found there every Friday night at Bingo with the men's wrestling club thrown in at the ten-minute fight during the fifteen-minute break.

End

YOU

With the prison system all over the world in a complete state of chaos, the heads of very government department of each country in the world were summoned to a top-secret meeting in New York. Its whereabouts to the public unknown, and any leak to the local media would be severally and instantly punished. Such was the crisis the world found itself in and if it were not solved in the very near future would severely dimmish its chances of ever been solved.

It started with the head of the Department of Justice speaker Colin mac Flintlock, and he addressed the meeting as follows, 'Ladies and Gentlemen what you are about to hear will astound all of you, disgust some of you, horrify most of you terrify all of you, but we the American Government have decided that in the current situation, drastic measures for drastic situations and in truth these drastic measures are, and will be, our only option.

As of this day next month the 12th of May in the year of our Lord 2037, the prison and the court system in the United States of American will cease to be as the world knows it now to be, there will be mayor changes to the way the system works, for example, we in this country will no longer tolerate the principle of if there is doubt leave him out, no, and all the human rights activist in the world will not make one of us change our minds,

We have in short and by we, I include all off you here in this gigantic effort to change our system which is simply overwhelmed, we have in short come to a brick wall that is far too high to get over and much too wide to go round, we have in short, a new order coming …and coming very soon as dated above.

In this new order, we will not only be changing the lives of prisoners but ourselves because for far too long we have been way too easy on these people. Most of whom are better treated than the hard working innocent person out there will ever be, the money we save will be used for better health care for our people, there will be more employment and better employment for those who obey the law in terms of living standards, better homes and environmental issues not to mention security in our places of work in our homes and on our streets, in a few moments we will have some people go into more detail of what's in our program, and you will be shocked to the core, but I tell you we need to be shocked to the core to make this happen, and make this happen we will, with or without your approval, though we do hope you come on board with us on this,

As you were told on the way in, when they collected your phones that this is a top secret meeting and must not be told to any other member of your government and or departments until we have discussed every detail, crossed every T's and dotted every I's and all are agreed on the one system, thank you for coming and please pay attention and do not, I repeat do not keep interrupting the speaker, there will be plenty of time allotted for discussion later on, thank you and now I give you the Inspector of Prisons in the US, Mr John Devlin'

He was a big man 6 foot 8 or 9, white haired with a hard complexion. Far too heavy for his height at roughly one hundred kilos which is 220 pounds with a gravelled voice.

'Ladies and Gentlemen, I does not give me any great pleasure to address you here today, as what I am about to say to you will be hard for you to bare, but I will tell you this, it must be said, it will be said and it will be acted upon, no one likes been hurt, been taken advantage off no one likes been a victim,

No one in this world wants to be raped murdered crippled or left vegetated, robbed of their life-savings, and so on, for far too long we in this country have been way too soft on criminals, but no more, now we will as the good books puts it, take an eye for an eye, (Matthew 5;38;39) and we will go even further and will not hesitate as before by putting those who murder innocent people to death, not in five, ten or twenty years' time, but within a few days of been proven guilty beyond doubt, an eye for an eye and a life for a life, no longer will we tolerate children gunning down children in their classrooms, we will consolidate and strength the right to defend oneself but will tolerate no more gun lobbying full stop.

So, it follows that we will no longer tolerate gun super stores selling automatic rifles to anyone other than army personal, and even then, ladies and gentlemen, a very comprehensive check must be done, and will be done, we must be strong in our beliefs, and confidant in our actions, every immigrant entering our country must be doublecheck then checked multiple times again before he or she is even allowed on our streets.

And this applies to all immigrants whether they come from the north south, east …or west, we quarantine animals for God's sake, so we can protect our animals, and ourselves, then we go and sell guns to foreigners who are not in our country five minutes to go out and kill our people, enough, I say, time to tell it like it is,

No more pussy footing around these serious issues if you want to break our laws then you must know that there will be catastrophic consequences and you will be caught and held to account, and no amount of money will save you if are found guilty, no more 12 men juries, no more lawyers, just a competent person to state the facts and just two honourable hard working people to sit in judgment, rotated every month so no one can get intimidated or frustrated, no long debates, just simple and very fast justice.

If you steal you must know that you will lose not just your freedom but you hand, when you are caught and you will be caught make no mistake about that, if you assault anyone you will be assaulted by that person's family or friends, practical justice my friends, is personal justice, no more very expensive prisons to run, no more very expensive courts houses to run, just some small, very small, court houses in every city village and large housing estate, instant justice for everyone. If someone deserves to be shot that someone will be shot end of story,

Now I know what you have just heard is overwhelmingly alarming and draining so we will take a two hour break during which time you may have dinner in any of the four dining rooms, just try to let what you have heard sink in, and do not rush to any conclusion until you have heard the full conference, thank you for your attention, enjoy your meal'

There was an uncanny silence before and during the meal and when everyone was back in their seats the next speaker as every bit as blunt if not even more so continued by introducing himself,

'My name is Albert Armstrong, I am the director of human resources in the state department, I am a family man and I love my country and hate what these criminals have done to it, let me start by saying, I believe that every man woman and young adult deserves the best system we can give them,

we are not after all a third world country, where its everyone for themselves, no, it is here that there is one law for us and many better laws for the ones that doesn't care a fig about you or I, the law as it stands in this great country of ours is an ass, it needs kicking out and replacing with a more humane law, simply put ladies and gentlemen, an eye for an eye and a life for a life, as the good book tells us to do,

We here in America want and give the best to all our people, even to those who take advantage of our generous nature, by being against every decent thing we have to offer and by deliberately attacking us as we hold out our hand to help them to stand back on their own two feet, take that beggar the other day in Orlando,

When some kind stranger takes pity on him and gives him a ten-dollar bill, what does he do, he jumps up, head butts the man, then knifes him in the chests and takes his wallet, leaving that kind stranger now fighting for his life in hospital, at your expense I might add, this is only one tiny example of how good and honest people are treated now in our beloved country by those that could not care less.

And I know it is the same old story where you guys come from, well no more, that beggar and thousands of similar criminals instead of been put out of their misery is now costing the taxpayers in this country billions of dollars every year.

Well, no more! as of the 12th of May which is one month from now, there is going to be a massive change in how we treat criminals in this country. Instead of prolonging that beggar man's miserable life he will be speedily tried and if found guilty which he will be, he will be put up against the nearest wall and shot, so to be so blunt but it is time to be blunt,

It's as simple as that, instead of spending thousands of dollars treating a drug addict, that drug addict will be given a shot of drugs, again free from the state's coffers and with mercy and compassion be sent on his or her way to the promised land, as for the drug lords and pushers they will receive the same treatment, an eye for an eyes, a life for a life, and I know that most of you are thinking that we are revolving backwards but can you put your hand on your heart and genuinely say that our civilisation is the best we ever had?

I think not.

I kid you not, our future depends on these drastic measures we take right now, this very moment, yes, we can build a space colony and send all these horrible people up there …but at what cost and for what reason, to prolong their constantly scheming miserable lives? I think not, nor will you if you are honest with yourselves, if one is sentenced to death in this country and it can take anything up to twenty odd years for that one sentence to be carried out, it will cost the state anything up to 500,000 dollars, tell me, honestly, is this justified? I think not, my friend, please remember why we are here today,

It is not to be cruel to these cruel people but rather to show them mercy and the easy way out, thereby saving the state billions of dollars and putting that money to where it really belongs, to the aid of all those hard working honest people all over our country and the world and to make their lives more rewarding and full-filling, can't you see the logic in all of this?

It is not oppression, no …it is the total opposite to oppression, it is true freedom of expression to spend one's life in doing good for the community and freely giving back what is freely given to make one's life more fulfilled and might I add mor enjoyable. But all this takes true understanding of the reality of our world and what it has become, a haven for those that steal kill and maim thousands of our citizens here every single year, in every country of the world, not to mention the many benefits to all, because of this very firm but necessary action,

The benefits to all of this will be easy living, no more living in fear, no more crime, no more spending small fortunes on securing our homes and places of business, a world where our children whatever their colour or creed, can walk the streets in safety,

Take a paedophile for example, if one of your children is taken say, your five-year-old son or daughter, and you know what is happening to that little child, do you not feel utter revulsion, don't you want to take revenge on that disgusting person? She paused to let her words sink in then said, 'don't you want to see that horrible person hang? Be honest with yourselves, it is alright … just as long as it is someone else's child, but when it's your own, don't you want to rip him or her to pieces?

I know I would, a bullet is far too good for such gusting terrible people. Rest assured in the new order all such horrible crimes will be a thing of the past, the sordid and sorry past of the American people, thank you for listening and I wish you all goodnight'

The following morning when all is seated and the second session begins it is opened by a woman called, Mary Mc Clusty treasure of the city's financial district. A well-known and much-loved member of the local society and indeed much further afar.

She after introducing herself to all there says, 'Some of you know me, most of you might know off me, what I do here in New York city, so I can assure you that I am not going to fill your heads with quantum physics so when I talk about money in this meeting I am talking about billions of dollars, trillions of dollars of taxpayers money, for example to run one local penitentiary it cost this city 2 billion dollars every year, 2 billion dollars of hard working people's money.

And there are now four such prisons in this city of twelve million people, now to those people who don't value money and believe me that are some that don't that may not seem like a larger sum of money, but you just try counting eight billion dollars, huh, that is eight billion dollars that could be spent on our health system, free health care for everyone, free school meals and bus trips for our children, a better pensions for our elderly people, and then think of the money we save from our hospitals, with better health people will live longer, thrive better and life for everyone will be so much better, no one will feel the need to steal from his neighbour, no one will feel the need to take what does not belong to him …or her, our daughter will be able to walk the streets at any time day or night because they will not be afraid to be outside after dark.

Storekeepers will be able to open 24/7 if they want, which in my humble opinion they won't have to because as wages increase so do their profits. People will be able to go abroad for longer periods of time and not have to worry about running out of funds, as everyone will have a specially designed credit card. Life in general my friends with be so much more enjoyable for everyone, and this is not a dream, a sneaky kind of election pledge, no, this can and will be achieved in the very near future…'

One member there from, the United Kingdom the right honourable Sir James Johnson stood up and yelled as there was no microphone provided, said to her, ' you ARE living in a dream world, what you are proposing is a totalitarian government and we have been fighting against such a government forever, do we not condemn such governments that are enslaving their people in various parts of our world, it simply will not work,'

A security guard told him to sit down and be quiet and been the gentleman that he was he did what he was told.

Ms Mc Clusty replied with some enthusiasm saying in answer to his statement, 'Of course we are not totalitarian in our approach rather the opposite in fact, because most if not all of our politicians will be of the same ideals and frame of mind, there will be elections every two years where most members will have a chance to govern and there will be no more need for a president but there will be a dozen well-chosen people to take up those responsibilities for we all know what one man can do, not mentioning any names but he thought he held the trump card and did whatever he wanted.

Furthermore, the good people of our great American nation can and will still have their rights and nothing will change in that regard, life for the most part will continue with the exception of and exclusion of the criminality brigade, our honourable English gentleman will no doubt remember the great fellowship that his people showed in getting together to help each other and they're country after the war ended in 1945, that is the same kind of community spirit we are seeking in the new order.

Now please, I know that most of you will have many questions to ask me and the three other speakers and you will have plenty of time after the dinner break which is as you know by now is two hours give or take a few minutes, thank you and see you all later, oh, …by the way …when you do return to your seats you will be giving a number, it will save us time and effort as there are so many of you here that will have multiple questions to ask us, so please do not be offended by that …thank you '

When everyone returned there were now four seats on the stage, with the Reverend John Williams of the church of the Latter-Day Saints saying a prayer which he began as soon as the people that taken their seats and were paying attention.

'My brothers and sisters, we have come here not to do the work of the devil, no …but to do the will of God, to make life better and richer for his people, what you are hearing here today might sound draconian, but is anything but, for today is a day of new visons …new hopes for the future …a era is dawning and one we here are all a part of,…eh, yes number 4, you have a question for me?

'YOU don't mean to tell me Reverend, that you are advocation this mass murdering scheme that these people are intent on committing, if they get their way? I mean didn't the Germens think the same way in the concentration camps in Poland? getting rid of the sick the lame and the elderly, and other poor souls and even mere children, by every horrific means those evil monsters could think off' the Reverend held up his hand and spoke.

'My dear man, you are totally off the planet when and if you compare these four lovely people to the Nazi regime in Germany in the 1930's, the people you just mentioned were totally innocent of any crime and so did not deserve any kind of punishment:

Now if I may finish my prayer,

Heavenly Father, we ask you to be with every person in this hall today and in the coming days weeks and years ahead, difficult decision must be made, let their faith in you and humanity prevail with the outcome of a glorious Holy race, in Jesus, name …Amen. Number ten said to number 1A the Justice senator,

'When you say put them up against the wall and shoot them, you didn't actually mean that did you?'

Number 1A replied, 'I most certainly did, it is the quickest way and less painful for the person being shot, now here's the thing, good and honest people of the world, we are not going to just go in there and terminate everyone, no …we will open our prison gates on such and such a day to allow most of the prisoners free, but only one condition that they never commit another crime again, oh I know what you're thinking but we will have them sign a form to state that fact, if they do commit another offense, they will face the harshest penalties, no trials no excuses, no mercy, an eye for an eye and so on,'

Number ten said back to him, 'You do know that when you use that phase you are only using half of it, in fact if you bother to read it and you should know this reverend, that it is all about showing mercy to one another, so why not practice what you preach senator?'

'But we are showing mercy and compassion number ten, when we obliterate crime from our communities, and rid the world of the evil that is so prevalent in our society today, people killing their families while they sleep, how sick is that, school children gunning down other defenceless children in their class rooms, where they should be safer than anywhere else, no number ten, we simply cannot offered not to do this, and we will do it, no matter what is decided here today and in the coming months, just let me say this, anyone who is not for us is against us, and anyone who is against us, need not turn to us in their time of great need, be it food, goods or any other kind of help, now some of you are thinking, that is blackmail but to be honest, we don't really care what you are thinking, because if our new order is to succeed then we have to be tough as nails, '

Number 4 stood up again and said, 'There you go again, number 1 A, that is exactly word for word that Adolph Hitler gave to his generals before they began their blitz screen campaign into Poland and elsewhere, I rest my case'

Senator Mac Flintlock replied angrily, 'How DARE you compare me with that evil monster Hitler! we have absolutely nothing in common, I resent that aggressively number 4 and any more remarks like that one and you're out of here, on the plane home, comprehend?'

Number 23 said to number 3 A, 'All I understand is that you guys and you madam what to turn the world our world upside down, first you want to put all the criminals up against the wall and shoot them then you want to release them now, you want to hang the worse of them, really sir, it is all a bit shady to me,'

Then number 3A retorted saying, 'Then take off those blooming shades sir, if what I say is gibberish to you, you may go, and don't forget your copy of this conference on your way out, look, ladies and gentlemen, if anyone here wants to jump ship then jump, but remember this night when you land in rough seas and do not look to us to pull you back on board,

Any more questions? Everyone stood up at the same time but number 3A picked number 52, yes sir what would you like to ask me please?

'If I may be excused sir, I badly need a washroom?' number just nodded in his direction then said, 'you sir, the Lord is my shepherd number 23,

'I would like to ask the panel if this new order is the same new order that past presidents and world leaders have spoken about, and will there be an army presence on the streets in case of riots?

All four speakers looked at each other and number 3A just said, number 57 please folks I am getting tired so make it short and simple,' number 57 asked him, 'A two-part question sir one, will the Russians be taking part in this new order? And two, will we allow them to take part?

Number 3A replied, 'One, would you like them to take part, and two, if they ask us nicely, we may allow them to take part, does that answer your two-part question sir? Of course, they may answer with nuclear weapons, but that is a chance we have to take, two hours later after many dozens of stupid questions like 'will the circus still be coming to town? Number 1A called a break and everyone got up and hurried to the dining rooms to an early dinner. When they returned Ms Mc Clusty or number 4A was the speaker and she started with a few questions of her own, 'let me ask you a few questions if I may please, before you decide on whatever way you want to go, ask yourself this, what would you do if your father was murdered on his way home from work?

What would you do if an intruder broke into your home and snatched your adorable child? What would you say if you saw a man been hanged for the colour of his skin? And what would you do if your beautiful daughter was gang raped in the park by a bunch of drunken slobs? How far would you go for revenge?

The reverend shouted, 'Revenge is mine! sayeth the Lord' he was told to shut up and sit down by security.

In all honesty folks what would you do people if your 76-year-old mother was mugged while going to pick up her pension?

Well, each and every one of these questions are easy but at the same time hard to think about, but we the government in America have made it easy for you to answer, we have giving you all the choice of not having to answer at all simply go with the flow with wh…' 'Big brother is doing,' shouted someone out loud,

'Really people' said number 4A, 'if that is your attitude then we are wasting our time here even though we have taken the time to reassure you, we have been given the grace to take your opinions on board, so I call this conference to order and to end, thank you for coming and don't forget to take your DVD with you when you leave and shut the door on your way out,'

Well! what would YOU do my friend? Would YOU even vote, be honest with yourself, what way would YOU vote, yes or no?

End

SAVING LITTLE JOHNNY

A short play by tom warner

A family home in a large housing estate in Dublin 24.

The cast,

Ma Mac Clennon………… Suzy 55

Da Mac Clennon………….. Big John 59

Son……………………….… little Johnny 15

Next door neighbour…. Rita 45

Guards………………… Jack and Julie 40+39

Bully boy……………. Tommy Tucker 16

EBS cashier………… Kathleen 35

   In the bedroom of the Mc Clennon house.

Da says to Ma… 'Bring me up some breakfast will you babe, I want to lie on,'

Ma replies saying… 'Ok darling …God, I remember the days when it was me you wanted to lie on…'

Da… 'Give me two eggs and four sausages, three slices of toast with marmalade and a big mug of tea, and I will fulfil your every wish my love,'

Ma… 'My days of wishing are long gone, so they are'

Da… 'Nonsense my sweet, your just as sexy as ever'

Ma… 'That reminds me, your due you eye test tomorrow at 3pm, in Specsavers'

Da annoyed… 'Ah for f…k …sake …I forgot again, I am meeting Tommy at the Square at that time, ah sure, I can do both, sure how long will it take?

Ma… About an hour, a little less, so don't miss it or I will not be the only one getting headaches'

In the kitchen with Rita the neighbour from next door…. Sitting at table drinking coffee.

Ma… 'I see you got a new car Rita, what is it?'

Rita… 'It's a car, a Nissan Jukebox or something like that'

Ma… 'It is a lovely colour, what colour is it?

Rita… 'It's a bronze colour, Suzy that's all I know'

Ma… 'It's lovely whatever colour it is, so it is,'

Rita… Well, no …Dick head has got a rise, so he has, and what is seldom is wonderful,'

Ma… 'I suppose he will be taking you out for a ride in it, and I don't mean to the shops, hah …hah …hah'

Rita… 'Well! He will have to show me what to do, its

been that long, 'that long,' do you get it? I hope I get it and soon, and nobody bleeding else gets it, hahahaha, are you still off the auld smokes, how long has it been now Sue?'

Ma… 'Too bleeding long …it's only been two weeks, but it feels like two years, so it does Rita'

Rita… 'I know I remember when I quit, I was like a dog without a bone, like a mad thing I was, but he was happy as I had something else to focus on, hah …hah if you catch my drift Suzy'

Ma…'God what's wrong with men of those days, Rita? when you meet first, they would walk the earth in hail wind and snow just to spend ten minutes with you, then you get married and three months later they barely know you'

Rita… 'Ah sure that's men for you, I've been married to that man for twenty-five years and he still doesn't know me, and I still don't know if he is just plain stupid or is getting fed somewhere else'

The family dinner table at the Mc Clennons.

Ma to little Johnny; Mrs Taylor told me she saw you down at the square today, I hope you are not back shoplifting?

Little Johnny… 'Of course, not ma, do you know how hard it is to lift a shop? hahahhh,'

Da smirking… 'Don't be a wise ass son, nobody likes a wise ass, and you ma, don't be believing everything you hear about our little Johnny, people say all kinds of thing just to have something to say, anyway he gave it up, like I said he would, I told you he's grow out of it, didn't I babe? Like I did,'

Ma… 'Like 'you' did Big John, like you did! you only gave it up last year and your nearly 60 years old, I hope we don't have to wait that long for our little Johnny,'

Little Johnny…to his parents…' I do not do that stuff anymore, I might want to, but I do not do it, cos their all watching me, I swear to you ma and you da, I have not done it in ages'

Da to his son…'When I was your age son, I could clean out a shop in under an hour, mind you that was the middle of the night, up the drainpipe, through the skylight, and bobs your uncle, now a days, everything has a tag on it, but still where there's a will there's a way'

Ma, 'Don't you be encouraging him big John, you should be praise him for giving it up, I don't want the guards knocking at my door in front of all the neighbours,'

Ding Dong…The hall door doorbell.

Da…'Speaking of the devil!

    Ma goes to answer it and it is the guards, Jack and Julie

Jack… 'Is the young fella in Mrs? you know the one with the light fingers?

Ma replies, 'He is and has been all day, we are just having dinner,'

Julia… 'We just want a quick word with him Sue, we won't take long'

    Ma brings them into the kitchen where the lads are finishing their dinner,

Jack says to little Johnny…' I saw you this morning down the Square, some people said you were swishing in and out of the shops like a ghost, now there was no reports of anything taken but the day is not over yet lad'

Da kicks in saying, 'Now there is no need to threaten my son like that guard, he is past that sort of thing'

Jack… 'The only thing he is past is his dinner John, and I am not threatening him, just warning him,

Da… 'Well okay then, but he is doing well, and I myself never listen to what other people say'

'Julia… 'That is good to hear John, he is a fine-looking lad I wish I were that good looking, okay …sorry to mess up your dinner, Sue'

Ma… 'Sure the hunger has gone off me now, so it has, I'll show you out'

Later that same evening when all was quite with the world Ma and Da were chatting by the fire in the sitting room.

Ma… 'I hear another house has been robbed on the Avenue, only their gold jewellery was taken, and no doubt was sold to one of those money for gold shops that are springing up like mushrooms all over the town,'

Da… 'Little fucker's, in my day it was money for drink, now its money for drugs, they would rob the bleeding eyes out of your head, and come back later for the glasses,'

Ma… 'Sure, what's the difference? Isn't alcohol a drug?

Da… 'Now, you know what I mean love?'

Ma… 'I wish we would win the lotto, we could move out of the estate, give little Johnny a better life, he deserves one,'

Da… 'Now don't be running down this place, Suzy, I remember the day you moved in, high as a kite you were with happiness, it is not so bad here, just one or two rotten apples, but they will grow out of it, or be taken out of it and locked up in prison,

Ma... 'I don't want that for our Johnny, he is a good kid really, keeps to himself, doesn't have many friends if any at all, I never see him with anyone, do you?'

Da... 'I saw him a couple of times with that Tommy Tucker f…ker, big lump of lard,'

Ma... 'What did I tell you about cursing in this house, I don't want little Johnny picking it up, there is no need for it, so shut your gob or I'm off'

Da... 'Little Tommy Tucker, the mammy's little f…ker, where are you off too daring? off to see the wizard, the wonderful wizard of Oz,'

Ma... 'Sometimes I wish I had him adopted, saved him from all this…'

Da frustrated... 'All what! Christ you're starting to get on my f…king nerves Suzy, you'd think we were in a concentration camp for God's sake, this is our home, our home, and okay it may not be Buckingham Palace but its clean and tidy, and we want for nothing more or less, so shut the f…k up and stop reminding me how successful I am not. Okay, I'm off to my f…king bed, I suppose the ride is out of the question? again, it's been almost four months now'

Ma... silence.

Da... 'Thought so, well, the devil makes work for idle hands, good f…king night'

Then he says to himself but making sure she hears him, as he is leaving the room... 'f..king woman, flying solo again tonight'

What neither of them knew that little Johnny was sitting in the darkened kitchen listening to every word they said, especially the word 'adoption.'

Little Johnny was in bed, but he was not sleeping. So, she wanted to have me adopted did she now? All that crap about her wanting to give me a better life, is that all it is, crap?

I wonder though, had I been adopted by some wealthy people I would probably be in boarding school by now, with those fancy talking rich kids, ah no, better where I am, at least here I can get away with the odd mitch from school. And they do love me …don't they? He turned over and went to sleep.

There was nothing little about little Tommy Tucker. He was a big kid for his age, 15 almost 16. A big bully a big liar, a big thief, that is what he was doing in the kitchen of number 27 at two in the morning, going through the little egg cups and other likely places looking for gold rings and such valuables. He heard a noise upstairs and waited to hear what happened next, whether someone was just using the loo, or in this case coming down the stairs, 'coming down the stairs,'

The big bully panicked and hid behind the kitchen door, after a very long few seconds a young man entered and was hit behind the head with an old-fashioned ornamental iron that was lying around on top of the fridge, and the young man went down never to get up again.

Next morning in the Mac Clennon kitchen.

Rita says to Suzy while drinking a cup of coffee… 'there was another house done last night, they must be important there are guards all over the place, going door to door Sue,'

Ma… 'Sure there is no one that important on this whole estate, I hope no one got hurt Rita'

Da comes in and says…'Did you hear the news? young Danny Moran got himself killed last night someone broke in and wacked him one,'

Rita… 'Oh no, and he is, eh, was such a lovely boy, who'd want to kill him for God's sake? He never hurt a fly,'

Da… 'Well! whatever it was that killed him, it wasn't a fly'

Ma… 'Well thank God our little Johnny was tucked up in his bed all night'

Da… 'Well, he wasn't there when I looked in at 7…babes, though his bed was still warm, I felt it, just in case,'

Rita… 'In case of what John, has he been taking to taking nights out?'

Ma… 'He spends an odd night over in McKenna's place, you know how nervous she is? and he likes helping her out, so he does'

Rita… 'Oh yeah, I forgot about her, poor things a nervous wreck, scared of her own and everyone else's shadow, well, it is coming to something, I mean breaking into houses is one thing but murder! that's a first for this estate …poor kid'

Ma… 'Yeah and he is eh was, only little Johnny's age, you have your breakfast dear, I don't think you have'

Da ready his paper says no, and Rita says to Ma… how did you know that Sue?

Ma nods towards the sink and says… 'Lovely clean drainer, I love him dearly and I mean that Rita, cos he costs me dearly, but he is not the tidiest person in the house'

Da just continues reading his morning paper shaking his head.

Rita… 'It's terrible so it is, that young man murdered in his own house, Sweet Jesus! are you on strike or what? Why are allowing all these terrible things to happen? there is not a night goes by without someone's house been broken into, are you alright Suzy, you've gone white as a sheet?

Ma… 'I am Rita thanks, something just flashed across my mind, that's all, another cup of tea?

Rita… 'Talk about something flashing, I foresee a knock on your door Sue,'

The front doorbell rings and Sue goes to answer it and it's the two guards Jack and Julie.

Jack…'Sorry to bother you Suzy we won't come in, as we are doing a door to door about that murder last night, and we were wondering if you or indeed little Johnny heard or saw anything suspicious?

Ma… 'Ah, now guard, how could I or anyone else for that matter see anything when we are fast asleep?

Julie… 'Is little Johnny in? can we have a few words with him please?

Ma… 'He is not here at the moment, guard but he knows nothing about any murder, I can vouch for that…'

Jack… ' I do wish you would call me Jack Suzy, we just need to talk to him, you know how kids hear things that adults don't, even if it's only silly little things, like so and so had a black eye last night or cuts and bruises to his arms or legs, the slightest thing might help us catch this killer, who knows he might even kill again, so we will come back later, hopefully he will be in then okay Suzy?

Ma... 'Do guard, I will keep him in after dinner, you are welcome to come back then,'

The guards thank her then leave and she closes the door.

Back at the dinner table in the Mac Clennons kitchen.

Ma dishing out the dinner, says to little Johnny, 'The guards were here earlier, wanting to know if we heard or seen anything that might help them catch whoever it was that killed that young man...'

Little Johnny cut her off saying, 'His name is Danny Moran ma, don't be afraid to say his name'

Ma... 'I am not afraid son, it just sounds better not to mention his name, less personal, I mean if that had been you little John, I just don't know how I would cope,'

Da agitated... 'Well it wasn't him babe, so stop worrying about something that hasn't even happened, bloody Irish, always worrying about something or other, I blame those bloody Brits the legacy they left us, I mean what's the point of worrying about money you haven't got for God's sake, its ok to worry about money you have got, but to worry about money you haven't even got, beats me'

Ma... 'Oh yeah! since when did you ever had to worry about anything? You needed something you just took it and thought nothing about the poor sod you took it off, he or she might have had to work all week for that wallet or bag you snatched, anyway I was the one that worried myself sick about the money we never even had, to pay the rent, to put food on the table, to put clothes on our backs, I tell you John, you haven't got a clue'

Da getting angry... 'Ah for God's sake! will you let me have my dinner in peace, always dragging up the past, that stuff is all behind me now,'

Ma... 'It's only behind you because you were caught too many times,'

Da... 'Well! I done my time, and I have changed you know that babe, so why keep bringing it up and in front of the wee lad as well?'

Ma... 'I keep bringing it up in front of him because hopefully he will listen and not turn out like you John, that's why'

Little Johnny... 'Why were the guards looking for me ma?'

Ma... 'They just want to know if you knew anything, they think this man might kill again, so any little bit of information might help get him caught, I told them I would keep you here till they came back, so when your finished here don't go back out, they are coming back later on just to see you'

Little Johnny... 'I don't know anything now, and I won't know anything then either ma'

Ma... 'I know son, but they will ask you just the same, so finish your dinner and go to your room son, I will call you when they come,'

Little Johnny goes to the fridge and takes out some yogurts then leaves the kitchen.

Da getting angry… 'It's coming to bleeding something when a man can't have his dinner in peace, seems like those coppers are always knocking on our door, what's for dessert?'

Ma… 'That's because they 'have' always been knocking on our door big John, and whose fault is that? certainly not mine, there's yogurts in the fridge, that is if little Johnny has taken them all, after all like father like son'

Da…'Why did you marry me, Suzy?

Ma…' because I had too'

Da…' Yeah, but…besides that, why did you marry me?'

Ma…' Because I loved you'

Da…'And do you still love me?'

Ma… 'I am still here, aren't I?'

Da… 'That's not the same thing and you know it'

Ma… 'I thought that you would have changed your ways by now John, but you still gambling and only God knows what else'

Da… 'So, you don't love me then …is that what you're saying'

Ma…'I didn't say I didn't love you, only that…'

Da jumps up from the kitchen table and slams down his paper saying. 'It's what you haven't said that speaks volumes to me, you know as well as I do that you are never lost for words, yet, you can't say those little three words, well, that just fucking great, I burst my arse to keep this house going and that's the thanks I get, well screw you,'

He throws the paper into the air and leaves the kitchen then slams the front door leaving Suzy in tears.

Little Johnny comes into the kitchen see his mother in tears and goes over to her and hugs her tightly saying, 'He is never going to change ma, you know that as well as I do, did he hit you?'

Ma... 'No son ...he wouldn't hit me, well, he did only once when he was drunk but I walloped him good and left him in a heap on the floor bleeding from every hole in his body, well ...almost every hole in his body, now little Johnny sit down and listen good to me, your father is a thief, he steals to pay the bookies wages, he will lift anything and everything of value, but inside if you can dig deep enough he is not a bad man, he is like those drug addicts you see hanging around always looking for an opportunity to make some easy money...

now Johnny darling, that is why I am always in your face...and now I am begging you, yes begging you not to follow in his footsteps, the only money worthwhile having is the money you earn from your own hard work...how would you feel if I was working every hour of the day to pay the mortgage and keep a family well fed and dressed and some gutless wonder attacks me on my way home on a payday and takes every cent I got in my purse, what would you do in those circumstances?

Little Johnny...'I would break every bone in his body ma, so I would, and then some'

Ma...'I am so glad to know that you'd care enough, can't you see how that person who was robbed and maybe even beaten for his or her few pounds feels, scared and empty

...that is why I don't want you to get into trouble like your father did and go to prison for years and when you come out no one wants to know you, and then 'you' are left feeling scared and empty, can't you see that darling, I am only trying to protect you from all of that stuff, you are a good kid and I love you so much, and you will find a job you like please God and meet a girl and fall in love and have kids of your own and all will be well with your world, but if you live outside the law, family or not you will always be looking over your shoulder, Johnny ...do you know what I am trying to say darling, if I am shouting at you it is because I love you and want what is best for you, yes it is a hard world out there but it is also a very beautiful world if you give it a chance, don't be like your father, taking what doesn't belong to him, but work for what the world gives you, you will find life so much easier if you stop fighting it'

Little Johnny jumps up into her arms and says, 'I'm sorry ma, I wouldn't hurt you for the world I love you too, and I promise I will never again lift anything from anybody, I told you I gave it up and I did, so stop crying ma, and stop worrying about me, and Mrs Mac Kenna's brother came over to see her the other day, and told me when I leave school I can go work for him, in his newspaper company, he said I will start at the bottom and work my way all the way up the ladder until I become his best reporter, isn't that great ma, you will be so proud of me then won't you ma?

Ma hugging him as tightly as she could say's to him, 'I am already proud of you son, the way you help that old lady, not many people can do that or even want to do that, so yes ...I am mighty proud of you my little Johnny, and I love you to bits'

The doorbell rings and it the two guards follow ma into the kitchen to see little Johnny.

Jack…'Well hello there, young fella, and don't worry, we only come to ask you a few questions about the young man who was killed the other day…'

Little Johnny… 'Danny Moran, his name is Danny Moran…why is everyone afraid to even mention his name?

Julie… 'Did you know him, Johnny?

Little Johnny… 'Of course, I did! he only lived down the street, everybody knew him'

Jack… 'How well did you know him son?'

Little Johnny…'Well enough guard why? You don't think I killed him, do you?

Jack…'Of course not son, but you do want us to catch the killer, don't you?'

Little Johnny…'Yes, we all do, he shouldn't have died the way he did'

Julie… 'In what way did you know him, Johnny?

Little Johnny…'Well we weren't pals or anything, he used to give me rides on the back of his motorbike, maybe twice, three times a week, it was a lot of fun, so it was,'

Jack… 'Ah yes, his motorbike! And where did he keep this motorbike of his son?

Little Johnny… 'In his garage, I suppose, or maybe out his back garden, I don't know I only seen him on the road with it, if he saw me, he would stop and give me a ride home, he was good like that, so he was'

Julie… 'Were you ever in his garage John?'

Little Johnny… 'No, I just told you that, I just assumed that was where he kept it, that's all,'

Jack… 'Did you ever go joyriding in stolen cars lad?'

Little Johnny... 'Once or twice, maybe three times'

Julie... 'And what made you stop, joyriding I mean?

Little Johnny... 'Because it was bloody stupid, they were so reckless and it was so dangerous, so I stopped doing it, I am not a fool,'

Julie... 'We know that Johnny, and we are not saying you are, in fact, we commend you for that and as for the shoplifting, that was only very minor stuff, and we notice you have either stopped doing that as well or you have gotten very good at it, either way we salute you son'

Ma... 'Now guard, he has stopped doing that and my boy is a good boy,'

Jack... 'I know he is Sue; I have known that from the first time I met him, he is a good lad, but we have to ask these questions,'

Julie... 'When was the last time you saw young Danny, John?'

Little Johnny... 'The day before he was killed, I was on my way home from Mrs Mac Kenna's house and he stopped and gave me a lift, that was the last time I saw him, guard'

Jack... 'Did he mention anything to you about him selling his bike son? or swapping it or anything like that?

Little Johnny... 'No, he loved that bike, so he did, no, he never said anything like that, why do you ask me that Ms?'

Julie... 'Because that bike has gone missing young man, it is nowhere to be found, and maybe whoever killed him took that bike and made his escape on it, now he lives not ten houses down your street, one would think that if a motorbike was started such a short distance from this house one could hear it from here, did you hear it John? cast you mind back John did you hear it that night?

Ma… 'That means nothing, whoever took it simply walked it away then when he was far enough away, he would start it, don't you think guard?'

Jack… 'That's a fair point Sue, thank you Johnny, that's all for now son, if you hear anything or see that bike around, please let us know, will you do that son please?

Ma… 'We will guard, wont we darling?'

Little Johnny… 'Yes! We will ma'

Big John comes into the kitchen and says, 'What's going on?'

Jack… We are finished here John, we were just asking the young lad some questions,

Big John… 'Yeah! well the next time you come into my house, you better have a warrant, coming here all hours at night,'

Ma to Da… 'I told you I invited them round after dinner so shut your gob and behave yourself, and where have you been all day?'

Da stormed out of the kitchen and went marching up the stairs in a temper.

The guards thanked her and left, with Julie saying to Jack,

'Interesting reaction, don't you think Jack?'

Jack… 'I do girl I do'

The next day Tommy Tucker bumped into little John down the street.

Tommy Tucker... 'I saw the police at your gaff last night, what did they want? have you been stealing again?

Little Johnny... 'No, I haven't and mind your own business,

Tommy Tucker... 'It is my business to know what's going on, on my patch...'

Little Johnny... 'Your patch, this isn't your patch, who do you think you are? the Godfather, so feck off and mind your own...'

Tommy Tucker grabs little Johnny by the coat and pulls him up closer to his fat face saying, 'This is my fucking patch, and nobody does anything dodgy round here without my permission, and if they do ...do anything without paying me, then they get what Danny Moran got the other night, and that goes for you too arsehole, you got that...?

It was just too good an opportunity to miss.

Little Johnny headbutts him and Tommy Tucker goes down like a sack of spuds.

Little Johnny... 'The next time you try pulling me into your face your better try cleaning your teeth first, you got that fart head.

Tommy Tucker with his nose broken and bleeding heavily mutters something to little Johnny that sounded like, 'Okay, ok …I'm sorry …just leave me alone'

Meanwhile Suzy is down in the EBS office in the queue for a cashier, ten minutes later she is facing Kathleen who gives her a warm welcome by saying to her, 'Hello Sue, I haven't seen you in ages, where have you been hiding yourself? Are you going on holidays, somewhere nice?

Sue replies to her saying… 'The last time I had a holiday was when Big John was in prison, that was the one and only holiday I ever had, gives us a withdrawal slip there, I want to buy my little Johnny a new suit, he deserves one, so he does, he has been so good'

Kathleen's face reddens somewhat, and Suzy notices and says to her. 'What's wrong, have I said something wrong Kathleen?

Kathleen shifts uneasy on her seat and says to Suzy.

'Your husband has been in Sue, last week, he emptied the account, I am sorry but there is nothing left'

Suzy… 'But …but, there was over fifteen hundred in it, he can't have taken every penny, did he?

Kathleen… 'He did Sue …it was a joint account; I had my suspicions but there was nothing I could do…I'm so sorry'

Suzy was crestfallen and just turned away before Kathleen could see her tears.

She met Rita in the mall outside and seeing how upset she was Rita brought her into a nearest coffee shop and bought her a coffee and a coffee cake. Suzy told her what had happened.

Rita… 'That miserable old toerag …that tight arsed skinflint, how could he do that to you?

Suzy… 'I really should not be surprised, he has been doing it to me for years, dipping into my purse when he thought I wasn't looking, I caught him red handed once and you know what the lowlife said to me. He said 'you silly cow, I am not taking anything out I am putting this fifty in, and you know Rita, I couldn't really prove that he wasn't…a long pause. Then she says to Rita,

'I was saving that money for Christmas, oh …I should have known …how stupid am I?'

Rita… 'You are not stupid, he is the stupid one, here blow into this, she said giving Suzy a few tissues. Then continues.

'I have a few grand I can lend you a grand or two, Suzy and I'll be in no hurry to get it back'

Suzy… 'Ah bless you Rita! thanks but no thanks, I have been in tight spots before and gotten myself out, I will just have to do it again, it's just that, well I trusted him with that money …I mean he knew it was for little Johnny when he left school in a couple of years' time, to help him if he wanted to go on to college or go abroad to get a job, and sure God is good, there is still time, I will get a cleaning job, they are always looking for good cleaning women and they don't come much cleaner than me, I haven't had sex for over four months hah hah hah.

Later that evening when little Johnny heard what his father had done, he wanted to bash his head in.

Ma… 'You can't do that darling, he is your father and technically he could do what he did, he did nothing illegal, just sneaky that's all, what did he need so much money for that's what I would like to know'

Little Johnny…'He maybe my dad but he is a toerag doing what he did to you, and did you hear what I did to that big bully Tommy Tucker?'

He told her thinking it might cheer her up and it did somewhat but when she heard the bit about her darling little boy getting what Danny Moran got, she immediately took him down to the garda station, not wanting the neighbours to see them coming back to her house.

Jack and Julie little Johnny and his ma were sitting round the table in one of the interview rooms.

Ma… 'Tell them what you told me son,'

And little Johnny told them everything that Tommy Tucker had said to him earlier in that day, he did not however tell them about him headbutting him.

Jack nodding to Julie who got up and left the room.

Jack… 'We'll have him in here in no time, you did good son, you really did, and you too Suzy for bringing your son in here, maybe now we will get to the bottom of this killing, sooner or later someone always lets something slip, and bingo, burst the case wide open, so hopefully it happens this time too, do you need a lift home darl…eh, girl?

Ma… 'Eh …no thanks guard…we will take a taxi home; about time we had a bit of luxury in our lives eh son?'

Little Johnny… 'Bang on ma, from now on nothing but the best for my beautiful mother'

Jack… 'You 'can' call me Jack Suzy, I have been calling you by your first name for ages, I don't mind, in fact I would be delighted if you would,'

Ma… 'Ok, thanks then …Jack

Their eyes meet holding a loving gaze and Suzy leaves the station a little brighter than she went in.

Little Johnny… 'Is he a married man ma?'

Ma… 'How would I know son'

Little Johnny… 'I saw the way he looked at you, and you him, and just wondered that's all'

Ma blushes and little johnny says to her… 'Do you want him to be married, ma, cos I don't know much about all that lovey duvvy stuff, …but I do know he fancies you; do you fancy him ma? it's okay I won't tell da'

Ma… 'I'll give you a belt around the earlobe little man, come one let's get the bus home'

Little Johnny… I thought we were getting a Joe Maxi ma'

Ma… 'I know …I just said that to impress Jack, sorry son'

Little Johnny… 'So, its Jack now is it, and you wanted to impress Jack, so you do fancy him then'

Ma… 'Well! He is rather good looking has a steady job, and can keep you out of trouble, what's not to fancy?'

Little Johnny… 'Well ma, da is not going to like that, so be extra careful, won't you, you know a rat can smell trouble from miles away, you do know that don't you?'

Ma… 'I do son and I also know a cat can smell a rat from miles away as well, you do know that …don't you son?

Little Johnny… 'No, I didn't know that ma'

Ma… 'There's the bus son run ahead and stop it please; these shoes are killing me'

Within the hour Tommy Tucker was in the same interview room that little Johnny and his mother was. Also present were Jack and Julie.

Jack… 'So little Tommy Tucker, what do you know about Danny Moran's death, or should I say murder?

Tommy Tucker… 'Who?'

Jack... 'Now let's not play games son, it is getting late, and I need to go home, even if it is to an empty house, where were you the night that Danny Moran was knifed in the stomach?'

Tommy Tucker went white in the face and said, 'What! he was knifed, you mean he didn't die from a bang on the back of his head?

Julie... 'No! he did not, he was knifed in the chest, so if you know anything you better come clean and tell us, what's all this about a bang on the head, were you there that night? You were ...weren't you ...there that night, what were you doing there?

Tommy Tucker... 'Okay I was there that night, I was robbing the place but I swear to you and to God almighty, I know nothing about him been stabbed, I swear I don't ...I wouldn't do anything like that, I was only after a bit of gold jewellery, I was in the kitchen when he came in and I hid behind the door, he didn't see me, then I hit him over the head with an old iron I found on top of the fridge, I didn't even hit him hard just a tap so he would bend his head and I could escape I swear I didn't do any more than that, he fell to the floor and I legged it out of there pronto'

Jack and Julie left the room for a few minutes and Jack said to Julie... 'That kid is telling the truth, everything he says matches up with what the coroner says, and if he hid behind the kitchen door he could not have seen the blood on Danny's shirt, I believe him, he didn't kill Danny, I don't think he has the guts to do anything as deadly as that, but we do have him on breaking and entering, and he is a proper little burglar if he is responsible for all the other houses been robbed, at least that is something, lets grill him a bit more'

Jack... 'Now you are going to jail for breaking into all those houses on your estate, robbery with violence is a serious offence Tommy, maybe be a ten-year sentence, how old are you?'

Tommy Tucker... 'Sixteen next May, so you can't really touch me ...can you copper? ok ...I might get juvenile detention for a few months then kicked out, so don't threaten me guard or you will be the one in trouble'

Julie... 'So you know how to play the game sunshine, then how about us delaying this case for say a year or two, a file might go missing and we will ask the judge to delay the case until it's found only it turns up two years later, then we nab you again and hey presto, you are charged as an adult, how does that grab you big boy?

Tommy Tucker... 'You can't do that...can you?'

Jack... 'We can and we will if you don't cooperate'

Tommy Tucker... 'I told you everything I know, what more do you want me to say?

Julie... 'Okay, so you were there at the house, and you must have been there when he was stabbed, have you anything else you want to tell us about?

Tommy Tucker... 'Like what?'

Jack... 'Like someone moving a motorbike for example'

Tommy Tucker... 'A motorbike!

Jack nods to him and he looks from Jack to Julie.

Tommy Tucker... 'I know nothing about a motorbike, except...'

Jack... 'Except what?'

Tommy Tucker... 'If I tell you, will you go easy on me, I mean speak up for me in court?'

Julie... 'We can't promise you anything, but we will say how much you helped us solve this terrible crime,

Jack... 'And the judge is an old friend of mine, so who knows he may go very easy on you'

Tommy Tucker... 'Ok well, I heard about a man that bought a motorbike off another man...

Julie... 'Name of this man that bought and the one that sold?

Tommy Tucker hesitated.

Jack... 'You must help yourself now, young man, you are in serious trouble with the law, and only you can get yourself out of this mess you are in, names ...and if possible, addresses'

Julie...'Don't worry, we won't say who told us, so there will be no comeback on you, I promise'

Tommy Tucker... 'Okay then...the man who bought it was Frank Wilson...'

Julie... 'And the man who sold it to him was?'

Tommy Tucker...'John Mac Clennon'

Jack took a deep breath and looked at Julie and spoke up. 'I knew it, I knew that mangey bastard was involved, I just knew it, now Tommy, I am going to ask you one more time, are you sure it was him?

Tommy Tucker... 'Very sure, my dad saw him on it way over in the village of Nass... he knows him very well... he wouldn't lie about a thing like that,

Julie...'Why didn't your dad come and tell us about it?'

Tommy Tucker... 'Because they go back a long way, anyway nobody said anything about a motorbike until tonight, so how was my dad too know?

Although no one in the room could see it Jack was rubbing his hands furiously to himself. He had been after that low down skunk for years and now here he was, getting ready to send him down for the rest of his miserable days, and that feeling was good, but how to tell Suzy his wife and son little Johnny, true it would be hard to do but he was looking forward to it immensely at the same time. At last, his chance had come.

Ding Dong... Suzy's doorbell rings and when she answered it she was surprised to see Jack and Julie and two other guards with them. She brought them inside to the sitting room where big John was sitting watch television. He jumped up when he saw the guards and said to Jack...' I hope you have a warrant cos if you don't out you go...'

Jack... 'We have a warrant, a warrant for your arrest for the murder of Danny Moran,'

Big john was speechless.

Suzy gasped and said...'Surly not Jack, not murder, he is a thief, but ...no murderer, not my husband?'

Two of the guards held big John and were leading him out to the squad car.

Jack... 'Sorry Suzy, but yes, he killed that young man that caught him in his garage stealing his motorbike, and sold it to some man in Nass,'

Little Johnny... 'And you can prove that eh, Jack?

Jack...'We can son, sorry, but we have to take him in'

Little Johnny... 'Take him and good riddance ...huh ma?'

Then he goes over to her and wraps his arms around her waist and lays his head on her breast saying, 'Don't worry ma, life can only get better from now on, that snake will get what's coming to him, we can sleep easy now mum, you don't have to worry, I will look after you,'

Ma... 'I know you will darling, I know you will, thank you, my precious little Johnny boy,'

When they were at the front door Jack says to Suzy... 'And I will too if you let me Suzy, look after you I mean, I know its early days but if you let me take you out and I will spoil you rotten girl, I have fancied you for years'

Suzy... 'You're not married then?'

Jack... 'No, my wife died ten years ago from breast cancer,

I live a lonely life and I would be more than happy to have you in it, I am not pushing you Suzy, please say you will think about it girl'

Suzy... 'After the trial, then we'll see Jack'

Jack... 'That is all I want to hear, after the trial then, how does a trip to Paris sound?'

Suzy… 'Sounds good to me, yes, I will look forward to that Jack and thank you'

Jack…'It will be my pleasure girl; I suppose the rid…'

Suzy cutting him off quickly… 'Yes! it is, out of the question, at least until Paris then we'll see'

Jack…'Goodnight then darling'

Suzy… 'Goodnight Jack, sleep well,'

And for the first time in a long time Suzy Mac Clennon slept the sleep of dreams.

End

OLA

Holiday Palace Apartments in Malaga Spain, 2nd day there of a 7-day break. I was walking along the edge of the pool wondering if I would get in or not as it was late October and the water was cold, it was a nice 29 degrees outside and I had been in the day before, but it was cold, and I was on two minds whether to get in for a swim or not.

There were two ladies a few metres up ahead of me talking away and as I approached them, they separated to let me pass. The one on my left stepped back as did the one on my right but the one on my right took a step too far back and fell into the pool. She came up gasping and struggling so I had to go in and help her out, but had I known then what I know now I would have let her drown.

The water was very cold, and she was shivering so I carried her up to my apartment which was not too far away so she could dry off and get warm.

She was and still is a beautiful looking lady with an amazing body for a woman of her age which I guessed to be around sixty or so, with the most beautiful breasts I've ever seen. I did not know it then, but I found out later that she made sure that I had seen her boobs and to be honest they made my mouth water. Her long legs also my heartbeat faster.

After I made her some coffee and sat her by the heater in my sitting room, she felt warm enough to introduce herself to me saying, siento raheho tener que hacerte bucear oh, eh excuse me, you are English, yes?

'Ola, I am so sorry for making you dive in and save me like that, I am such an <u>estupido,</u> eh, how you say in English? a silly ass, let me introduce myself, my name is Countess Felisa Fermina Fonda and I am here to visit my distant cousin whom you saw me talking to down by the pool, and you are senor, masculine, eh?

Not having much Spanish, I realised she was asking my name, Thomas Bell Cree, the 2nd, well, it sounded cool enough as I thought I was talking to royalty.

She explained to me that the woman she was talking to by the pool would go find her chauffer and tell him what happened, and he should be calling here at any moment to take her home to her mansion eh, somewhere I could not even pronounce, but it was on a high hill somewhere by the sea. I got that much.

Two hours later she was still waiting and by now her clothes were dry enough to wear though she did borrow a vest of mine to put on under her dress, to warm my chest up she said. Another hour passed before she said to me, 'Can I use your phone Thomas as mine is in the car?'

I did not have a phone as I am a writer and I left all that stuff at home, like laptop and phone, just so I could get a little peace and quiet away from the hustle and bustle of Dublin. I told her that and she said, 'Okay, no problem, if you would like me to take you to dinner across the road there is a fabulous restaurant I know very well, it is very expensive but well worth it, I will treat you to a wonderful meal it will be my way of thanking you and I can use the phone there, what say you?

How could I refuse such a wonderful offer with such a beautiful lady, and I told her so and she smiled and showed me a bit of leg and I could feel myself blushing as she rose from her seat.

So across the road we go into this fancy glorified cafe and when the top waiter sees her coming, he runs over to her and says, 'Good every countess, it is a pleasure to see you, you haven't been here in quite some time,' then looking at me say's 'good evening senor, welcome to our little restaurant, I do hope you have a lovely evening though I do expect to be kept on my toes as the countess is very choosey about what she eats, please follow me...'

The countess is already on her way to a seat she had chosen even before he finished his sentence. 'Shall we have Champagne Thomas darling, Oh I do love champagne, don't you darling' she calls the waiter over saying 'Alfred, please bring me a bottle of Armand de Brignac, and a menu thank you dear' then turning to me says,' Well thomas darling isn't this just the loveliest of eating establishments, I come here whenever I am down this way, though I must confess it is best suited for lovers,'

My face reddens and she notices and says, 'Why darling you are blushing, oh how sweet, in this day and age,' then she makes me blush even more when she says, 'Do you not have a lover, Thomas? if not then you can imagine I am your lover, for this evening anyway, would you mind that darling?'

I had been trying so hard not to keep watching her almost bare breasts heaving up and down and her last remark nearly floored me. The waiter brings the menu a fancy golden two-page sea food menu that shouted to me to run but I could not run no matter how expensive this night was going to be, after all it was the countess treating me, wasn't it?

She says to him after he was left standing there for almost three minutes. 'We will start with 'the Buddha Jumps over the wall' soup please

Alfred, followed by some Coffin Bay King Oysters, not too many dear and don't forget my champagne, is that okay with you Thomas darling?' had she ordered cow dung with cold custard it would have been alright with me as I just could not take my eyes of her beautiful face and revealing breast cleavage.

I was hooked lined and snookered by her charm and her beauty. Little was spoken during the meal, but I did notice she drank more than I thought she would, and when the meal was over, she even indulged in a little song called 'I love you because' by the late great Jim Reeves.

It was nice but she was no singer, but I did like that way she kept glancing over at me. I hate seafood and despised it even more after struggling to eat those slimy oysters but I made the effort to please her.

When she called Alfred over by clicking her long slim well-manicured and adorned with expensive looking gold and diamond rings finger's she says to him. 'Please be a dear and put it on my account, plus a ten% tip for you darling, you are a brick, so you are dear'

He was gone five minutes and came back a little red faced saying, 'The manager is out countess, and will not be back till morning, so we cannot put it on your account without his permission, he gave very strict orders as there have been some very bad cheques passed here in the last few weeks, I would lose my job if I went behind his back and did so, I am so sorry countless, but there is nothing I can do'

She frowned and said to me, 'Darling, Thomas, is it okay for you to pay Alfred, he will give you a receipt and I will reimburse you tomorrow at the latest when my chauffer arrives with my purse, and I have decided with your permission of course, to spend the night at your apartment, I am too tired after all the excitement of the day to travel home, will that be okay with you darling?

I nearly had a heart attack but managed to say to her, 'Of course countess, it will be my pleasure to please you in whatever way you see fit,' did I just say that? Or was I hearing things? No, I just said that'

So, I handed over my gold credit card to Alfred as she fell into my arms and the feel of her slender body in my arms nearly drove me wild with passion. I never even glanced at my receipt I just shoved it inside my jacket pocket.

I say nearly but I managed to control myself and held her waist as we walked slowly back to my place, with her still singing 'I love you because.'

She had a shower and she called me in and we made love under the silver waterfall and it was terrific and so exciting and when we finished, we made love on the sofa, and it was wonderful and when we finished, we made love on the bed on the floor, and we shared everything part of each other, and it was fantastic and when morning came she was gone and so was my gold credit card.

A neighbour said she left earlier that morning in a white pickup driven by a man that fit Alfred's description precisely. I felt such a fool as I watched her after been arrested with Alfred a few weeks later, on TV.

She had scammed the wrong man when she scammed some high fluting mayor or other. She was no countess but a two-bit actress from some little town up north. She was very good at what she did, she was very beautiful and very forward in her love making and I was very foolish for falling for one of the oldest tricks in the book

And I loved her dearly. I got a bill from the credit card company at the end of the month for well over 20,000 euro. Enough said.

End

STAR SHIP

The Captain of Star ship Arthello Captain James P Smirk, is in his quarters when his intercom comes on, 'Captain, can you come to the bridge please'

Captain… 'Be right there Mr Hughes'

Two minutes later the captain arrives at the bridge 'What is it Mr Hughes?'

The navigator Mr Hughes replies… We are not sure captain, but we appear to be in some kind of iron cage'

Captain… 'Have you been drinking Mr Hughes?'

Navigator… 'No sir, not since this very early this morning captain sir'

Captain… 'And what did you have this morning and in what amount Mr Hughes?'

Navigator… 'One glass of orange juice captain, and two cups of coffee sir'

Captain… 'Okay Mr Hughes, was there anything else in that orange juice or coffee Mr Hughes? Because quite frankly Mr Hughes, you are not making any sense at this particular hour of the morning, now steady yourself and sit down and explain in terms that I can understand,'

Navigator… 'Captain, we …seem …to …be …in …some …kind …of …wire …cage, sir'

Captain… 'How is that possible Mr Hughes, this is a Starfleet exploration super modern Star ship, we simply cannot be contained in a birds cage, as you put it, Hypothesis Spook'

Spook… 'It is highly unlikely that is what is happening captain then again it is only your perception of what is happening, it might be what is happening in your mind yet in reality, it might be something else entirely, captain'

Captain… 'Can somebody, anybody tell me in plain English what is happening on my ship, please'

Spook… 'Well captain Smirk… let me put it this way, just before we called you to the bridge, we felt a kind of tremor going through the ship, all proximity alarms sounded at once and when we checked our proximity in space, we found ourselves under and over, from east to west, yes sir, from starboard and aft in between what can only be described in our memory banks as an iron cage, we that is you, and I and our navigator Mr Hughes here, try to ascertain what is happening, which is you will agree captain, is quite logical,'

Captain… 'I agree nothing of the sort, Spook, there must be an alternative explanation for what is happening and I for one intend to get to the bottom of it, whatever it is and whatever it takes, am I making myself clear Spook, Mr Hughes, what do the other crew members of this ship have to say about this frightening situation we find ourselves in and that question applies to you also Mr Spook?

Spook… 'There are no other crew members on this ship, captain, you left them all behind when we landed on the rock, near the planet Shuto last November, don't you remember captain?'

Captain… 'Ah yes, I remember now, they each and every one of the 500 of them said I was suffering from the Corona virus 679, but I proved them wrong, it was them that had the virus, that is why I beamed you and I and Mr Hughes here back on board and left them isolated back there on that rock as you put it Spook, now to our present predicament, can you elaborate further please?'

Spook… 'Well captain Smirk, the ingredient that make up this iron so called cage is one we haven't seen in millennia, it is one of our, sorry, your great …great …great …great ancestors used when they first developed a brain, it is called I believe, steel, and our laser weapons are not made to recognise steel so are useless against it'

Captain… 'Aha, YOU, are in error Mr Spook, our ancestors first discovered bronze then copper then gold, that is why they started killing each other, Mr Hughes, can you not plot a way out of here? I am beginning to feel claustrophobic in all this space'

Navigator… 'The ultra-strong magnetic field that these irons radiate are playing havoc with our senor's captain, it will take me two years to figure out a way of getting past them without taking up too much of your time captain…'

Captain… 'There is something wrong with what you just said Mr Hughes, but I will deal with that later, now is the time for action, and as you three know, I am a man of action.'

Spook… 'Three captain! there are only two of us, plus yourself, that makes, eh, three, but you were talking to the two of us, so that means you sir are in error when you say the three of us, that is not logical please explain sir'

Captain… 'Well, there is you Spook, and there is you Mr Hughes, and there is that huge hairy thing standing in the corner over there, what is it Mr Spook?

Spook… 'Oh that, yes that is a Zillyman captain, we found him on board two weeks ago, we did not inform you at the time as you didn't seem interested in anything on board this ship, a rare error of judgement on our part, sorry captain, '

Captain… 'A Zillyman! what the f…k is a Zillyman, Mr Spook'

Spook… 'I am not familiar with some of that language you are using captain, but we don't know what it is, yet, but we are working on a way to communicate with the creature, we should have found a way by the time we finished this fantastic, but outrageous journey captain, in about ten years' time'

Captain… 'But you just told me it was a Zillyman, Mr Spook, so how can you now tell me you don't know what it is?

Spook… 'Well yes captain, that is because it looks so silly man, get it, Silly man …Zilly…man, oh never mind'

Navigator… 'CAPTAIN… we are picking up some rather strange tissue on our picking up tissue radar screen captain sir,'

Captain… 'What is it Mr Hughes?'

Navigator… 'Well sir, it is tissue! almost identical to human tissue sir'

Captain… 'Have you been sneezing again Mr Spook?'

Spook… 'Not for two days now captain, I picked up a slight cold from somewhere sir, but it seems to have gone now captain Smirk, thank God'

Captain… 'Thank God! I thought you were an atheist Mr

Spook?

Spook… 'I was until you caught the virus captain, then one day I found myself praying to an unknown entity which logic tells me could be the God of all human life sir, you were in such a state captain, I would have even prayed to a Zillyman, if I thought he would save me,'

Captain… 'Do you want me to leave you out there alone in the vastness of space? Mr Spook, because I will, I promise you I will if you mention that I had the virus again, do you read me?'

Turning to face the navigator.

Captain… 'Now Mr Hughes, what do you mean human tissues? there are no human beings out this far west, so how can there be human tissues out here this far south? huh, explain that to me and Mr Spook here, please'

Navigator… 'Incorrect captain, as you have been incorrect for the whole of these past two years when you beamed most of the crew down and left them there on that huge rock, leaving only myself and Mr Spook here to cook your meals and wash your bed clothes, the human tissue I speak of is here your human tissue captain, and we myself and Mr Spook here before we became eh, become infected with your virus, have come up with a plan to keep you contained for the next two years in a iron cage up here in the vastness of space where you can do no harm to any other poor unsuspecting soul, human or alien, but first you need to dress up in one of those fancy suits they gave us all those years ago when we began this voyage to where no man, woman or child has ever gone before, so be a good chap and go to the space stores and suit the f..k up,'

Captain… 'And if I don't? this is space mutiny you know, I could and will have you dismissed from your post, if I ever get back to earth, which seems unlikely now, and I don't believe that either of you will ever get another position on any Starfleet ship, not even a renegade one, the kind those space bandits use, most certainly not on any ship I may be the captain off, that's for sure,

Mr Spook…'captain, that cup of coffee you just drank contained a sedative that will put you to sleep any hour now, then Mr Hughes here and my good self, will undress you then dress you up in a space suit, the kind of one we keep here in the space store room, for just such an emergency, we will then beam you into that cage, the coordinates which Mr Hughes here will calculate any moment now and hey presto, we will be rid of your very annoying smile and kind of idiotic sense of humour for the foreseeable future'

Navigator… 'We are ready Mr Spook,'

Mr Spook… 'Then beam him into that cage Mr Hughes, anytime you're ready'

Navigator… 'There he goes Mr Spook, oh dear, we forgot to dress him in that space suit we keep in the space stores for just such an occasion Mr Spook, he won't last long out there, what will we do now Mr Spook?'

Mr Spook… 'Is there anything you want to do now, Mr Hughes?'

Navigator… 'Not really, we could try beaming him back aboard Mr Spook'

Mr Spook… 'I would not be logical or indeed ethical for us to do so, as he may be brain damaged for want of too much air Mr Hughes, not that anyone would notice the difference, no leave him as he is, he was a danger to the crew of this fine luxury spaceship Mr Hughes'

Navigator… 'We have no crew on board this very spacious spaceship Mr Spook,'

Mr Spook… 'Oh, really Mr Hughes, then who are all these people on the bridge Mr Hughes? there must be well over forty people on the bridge Mr Hughes, and don't tell me they are all Zilly men'"

Navigator… 'No sir, Mr Spook, some of them are Zilly women, we should have a good time with those, if we can find a few million razors'

Mr Spook… 'Logical Mr Hughes, very logical, warp speed 300 please, due west then northeast then southwest, and back to west southwest again thank you'

Navigator… 'Aye …aye, Captain Spook, warp speed 300 it is sir, oooooh, if I were a rich man'

End

Train

Every wonder when you see a train load of people passing, where they are going or what their life is like? If the answer is yes, then here are just some of those people.

The night train from Houston Station in Dublin to Collins Station in Cork is very fast, the journey takes under three hours, and as everybody knows, a lot can happen in three hours.

The man with the large leather bag seemed to be very anxious as he lit another cigarette and stepped back into the shadows, he was a tall and heavy man and the glow from his cigarette as he inhaled lit up his stern face.

He was a bank manager in a well-known Irish bank but for now he was taking a well-earned holiday break. He was also taking as much of the banks money as he could stuff inside his large brown leather shoulder bag, plus bundles of notes filled every pocket in his very expensive and very altered black leather coat.

His name is Thomas Watts and he had worked at the bank since he graduated from Trinity College in Dublin, almost thirty years ago to the day. he was fifty-seven years old, married with four children, two sons and two daughters, all married now with children of their own.

Four weeks ago, he had caught his wife in bed with her lover and after much soul searching decided enough was enough and he was going to spend the rest of his life in style only thing was she had also cleaned out their joint bank account and left him penny less.

The other thing was she and her lover were now fertilising the newly dug flowerbed in his massive back garden in the leavy area of Foxrock.

He had a brother in Cork named Robert, and he invited him down to his little farm just outside the city in a place called Ballinhassig which just happened to be on the main route to Cork airport, from where he planned to fly out to some far away foreign land where the sun shone for 12 hours a day and where money brought the most beautiful of women knocking on your door. No matter how awful you looked or how fat you were.

The train was late. And the longer he waited the more nervous he became smoking one fag after another. A fact that did not go unnoticed by another man in the shadows. A very thin and tall man that had many troubles of his own.

Lisa Morgan was a beautiful looking woman in her day. Not so this day as just hours before her husband a drunken bully and wife beater had beaten her black and blue and left very heavy bruises all over her body.

She had her twelve-year-old daughter beside her called Cherie and she was excited about going on a train journey with her mum. Lisa held Cherie's hand very tightly as her daughter was the only comfort she had in her life. John her husband had become very jealous of her beauty though she never gave him a reason to be. He just assumed she was shagging every man she met, though she never went outside the door most days.

The only time she did was once a week to do some shopping. Her jealous husband was drinking most of their money and listening to the other men in the bar running down their wives and putting all sorts of dirty thoughts in his head. He would not however hurt her anymore as she had split his head open with axe she had been chopping logs with to keep the fire going so they could have a hot meal at least once a day.

She wasn't sure she if she had killed him or not and she didn't care if she had. She took what money he had left which amounted to enough to get herself and her daughter on the train to her sister in Douglas where she could find time to heal and recover from her sorry state. The train was late, but she didn't mind just as long as it arrived.

She had just enough money to buy two small bottles of mineral water and for the taxi fare to her sister's house near the Douglas shopping centre where they had arranged to meet. She was getting cold as she was wearing only a heavy jumper, she had grabbed on her way out the door, thankfully little Cherie had managed to bring her coat.

Other than that, they had only the clothes they were wearing. No luggage, no money no one to turn to here in Dublin, but she did have a sister at the other end of the country that loved her. It was this fact and her little girl that kept her going, plus the fact that she was now free from the consent threat of been beaten by her late husband. She truly hoped that he was late, but she wasn't too sure about that either.

Young Johnny Sullivan was an 18-year-old heroin addict. Spent every penny he had on the drug. Robbed everything that was not nailed down so he could to pay for his addiction. Left his family of four siblings and his mother and father with large debts he owed the drug pushers around the area where he lived of which there were many. Too many. He had been beaten several times before and would be again if he did not pay up. He mugged old ladies and even men on walking frames to get his money for a fix. Shoplifted from every store in town multiple times before he was caught and sent to prison where he learnt new tricks of the trade like how to rob houses and even money lenders that called to people house's every week to collect their money.

It was this that got him to where he was now, standing in the rain in Houston Railway Station waiting for the next train to Cork to arrive and get him to safety. The train was late, but there was nothing he could do about that. He had made another very bad mistake. He mugged an old lady coming out of Bingo two nights ago. That old lady was the mother of one of the drug pushers he owed money to, and he was caught on CCTV doing it. Now here he was as usual, standing alone but not too far from where Tom Watts was standing, still in the shadows smoking like a trooper.

Father Moran was a catholic priest from the parish of St Tomas's in Darragh in Dublin, he had been a priest for many years and had been like most priest though the agony of the sex scandal in the catholic church not just in Ireland but all over the globe had placed a heavy burden on his shoulders.

He had heard many a sad confession but nothing like the one he heard last night just before he got ready for bed, there was a knock on his door and when he opened it there was a man standing there in great distress. He was clutching a plastic bag to his chest. The priest having taken pity on him invited him in and offered him tea and biscuit's and sat him down to warm himself by the electric fire before asking him what the matter was as the man was visibly and virtually shaken in his shoes.

When the man had drunk the tea and eaten one or two of the biscuits and warmed himself by the fire, he turned to Fr Moran and said to him. 'I need confession Father, I done a terrible but to my mind a justifiable thing, I am sorry it is so late, but I just could not wait anymore'

Fr Moran said to him. 'I understand my friend, but it is rather late, and I am so tired, could it not wait till morning?' he was also a little bit frightened by the man as he was in the hallway alone with a complete stranger at this very late hour. A man he didn't know from Adam but then again, he might not be a church goer as most of his parishioners were now not coming to mass anymore. The man was adamant about getting confession and Fr Moran decided to hear his confession if only to get him out of his house so he could go to his nice warm bed.

So, he went to his little oratory and got his purple shoulder vestment and lit a candle and sat beside him and began by saying the blessing over him. When he had finished the man began to confess. 'Bless me Father for I have sinned …it has been a few years since my last confession …last night I killed a man, I drove up to his hall down and when he answered the door bell I ran him through with a long butcher's knife, …straight through his throat I stuck it …forgive me father but …I went there to cut his balls off but when I saw him I just lost it and nearly decapitated him …you see Father my son told me that this man …this so called human being had been sexually abusing him for months …while he was supposed to be teaching him Taekwondo …you know, judo kind of fighting …but the bastard took advantage of him and well you can guess the rest …I saw red and well I took that evil man out of the game …for good …he won't be assaulting anymore children I cut him up good and proper …did I tell you I am a butcher by trade? no well …I am and I can do things with a knife that very few men can …I pulled him outside and did him good, the local dogs eat well last night'

Fr Moran felt sick to his stomach but managed to say to the man. 'And what about that man's family, they did nothing wrong, so they did not deserve the pain and misery you inflicted on them, imagine the horror that they woke up to this morning'

The man interjected saying, 'Oh …he had no family Father …these kind of monster usually live alone …this one lived in a big house while decent ordinary folk are homeless on the streets of Dublin and all over this country Father …it is a scandalous state of affairs …so it is, anyway, I cleaned up the mess …it just took me a few moments as I came to his house prepared and ready for anything'

Fr Moran said to him, 'And this man, that you say you killed and chopped up, is he known in the area, I mean would I know him for example, what is his name?'

The man bent down and opened the bag at his feet and took out the man's head and held it up to Fr Moran face and said to him, 'Here he is …do you know him, Father?'

So here he was now poor Fr Moran, on his way to Cork City by train to visit his old friend now retired Fr Bill O' Donnell after the Bishop have given him a few weeks off. The train was late as usual but no matter, what's another ten minutes or so? no point in losing the head over it, is there?

End

Marie Mc Donnell

Maria Mc Donnell was born and reared in Cork; she came from a large family but not a poor one. She went to Cork University College on her twenty first birthday and studied hard to be a veterinarian. She loved animals of all kinds and especially the ones no one else cared about, like abandoned dogs and horses, she loved horses.

She had to leave college because she got herself pregnant in her second year by one of the senior men there and he spread that word that she was an easy lay and soon everyone was pointing the finger at her, so she had to forgo her final two years and swim with the rest of the fish in a sea of hard knocks and sharks and dog eat dog.

She tried her hand at almost everything after giving her child up for adoption. Even prostitution. Though after been beaten for the fourth time she quit and went to Dublin where she got a job as a cleaner in an old people's home. Some man there saw her and offered her a better job looking after his mother over the south side in Ballsbridge, a leafy area of Dublin.

It was great at first then the man started making sexual advances towards her and she didn't like that, so she left there and found a similar job elsewhere but that didn't last long either and after going hungry for a few weeks of living on the streets, on her twenty fourth birthday she found herself talking to another man and he knew someone that needed a woman to take care of his elderly mother.

This was in the days before the carer occupation became professional. Today it is very professional. Back then however it was anything but. Of course, the man said she would have to tidy up and get some new clothes to wear before she went to the house where she would be working, after all no one turns up looking like a tramp needing a job, but he said he would be happy to buy new clothes for her. Much to her surprise he did just that without looking for any reward of any kind.

And when he took her home to his house so she could shower and dress herself up he said to her, 'Now if anyone asks you where you live, just give them this address, I think they won't, but they might, it is by the way a live in job, this man is a businessman so doesn't have a lot of free time, and besides that he travels a lot.

What is in it for me? I hear you asking yourself and well I will tell you, two years ago I was where you are now, though I was a crack cocaine addict, been through it all, the stealing the mugging the shoplifting and even beat up other addicts that couldn't pay their pushers, just to get my fix, I went into rehab for twelve months and came out clean, but with nowhere to live but on the streets, just like you are now, then some kind lady took pity on me and got me into a hostel she worked at, and I haven't looked back since.

To be honest the longing is always there in the background and to be truthful I am using you as a tool to keep me focused. Don't worry I am not going to use you for anything else I promise you, go see this man, he owns the hostel by the way, that was how I heard he is looking for someone to look after his mum, now he cannot know you live on the streets or else he won't give you a chance to even say who you are, but like that lady two years ago I see something in you that reminds me of me, so I want to help you, do you accept that?

You do then? good, let me take you to his house and I will wait outside in the taxi and when you get the job, which you will cos I know he has been looking for the right woman these past few weeks, as I say when you get the job we will go for a meal and celebrate. I don't like people who lie but in this case you have to lie and make up some kind of story, this job can save your life and put you back on track, just say something like you looked after your aunt or grandmother for the last four or five years of their life so you have plenty of experience, I'm sure you did that at some point in your life,anyway, even if it was only to one of your siblings, I mean how hard can it be?, okay you might have to do some unpleasant duties if she is bedridden, but it just has to be better than living on the streets, what do you think then Marie?' and don't forget if it gets too hard for you at times, you can come back here and rest. Marie was gobsmacked at his kindness. God must have sent this man to help her, she could find no other explanation.

She could not believe her good fortune, because here was a young man, a handsome young man, that really did care about how she was, and was prepared to go out of his way to help her get back on her feet. Manna from heaven indeed.

It turned out that she was also a Godsend to the businessman who had been searching so long for the right woman to look after his precious mother while cleaning the house at the same time. She was good at it too, polishing the furniture and mopping the wooden floors and such like, she was window cleaner, a washer woman, a great all-rounder kind of woman, she could cook too and did cook for two and three whenever he came round which was every now and then as he was a very busy man. He paid her above the odds and even threw in the extra odd twenty every other week and soon she had her own bank account with her own hard-earned money mounting up in it.

At last life for Marie Mc Donnell was good and getting better every day.

The old lady was very nice and quite easy to get along with and made no special demands on her other than the ordinary things like a special shop or go to the post office to pick up her pension money which was once a week. Marie was still working there up to the week the dear old lady died which was years later.

Now I know you are waiting for the bad news. Like that young man turned up one day and robbed everything that wasn't nailed down, that he turned up with a large van another day and cleaned out the contents of the house, well he didn't do anything of the sort. In fact, he was very good to Marie and in time they fell in love and even got married and raised a nice family of four children three boys and a little girl, and as I said she worked there until the old lady died and left her a good sum of money, and they all lived happily ever after. So, remember if you are going through a tough time, there are much better days ahead for you, don't give up hope and rob yourself of a bright future. Amen.

End

The Little Robin, The Logger The Moma Bear and The Child

Shirly McKenna had stopped at her local petrol station two miles from her home in Wisconsin. It was an isolated spot where she and her husband Don decided to live, away from the hustle and bustle of city life but only two miles away from the city proper, as Don worked in the city as a bank manager in the local branch of the Wisconsin bank, he loved living in the countryside where he would hunt rabbits and small deer and squirrel and such like.

There was a large wood beside their property that went on forever and Don spent many an enjoyable time stalking deer and one time even wolves that had come a little too close to his house for his and his wife's comfort.

Shirly filled up the tank and went inside to pay for the gas, leaving her four-year-old son in the backseat of the car. While she was inside a man seeing the keys still in the ignition jumped in and drove off, with Shirly still inside the gas station store, when she realised what had happened, she screamed the place down crying out,

'My baby, my baby …that man has taken my baby' the police were called and they put out an APB on the car, a dark blue two year-old BMW, 'Don't worry mam,' the officer said, 'he won't get far, I would say as soon as he spots that child in the backseat he will stop and leave him somewhere where he can be found, I will follow that road in a few seconds and see if that is the case, don't worry, mam, I am sure it was only the car he was after, I am sure of that, he won't harm the child, if indeed it is a he, we are now checking the CCTV camara's and then as soon as we know who we are dealing with, i.e. a male or female, then the search begins in earnest , you should have that little boy safely back within the hour, I am sure of that mam'

When the man that stole the car heard the child in the back seat he nearly had a heart attack and pulls a right turn off the road up into the forest entrance where he takes the child from the car and leaves him by the gate, there were always forest workers coming and going, so someone was bound to find him very soon, the man reverses the car and heads back to the main road where he puts the foot down and gets as far away as possible, heading north away from the city.

Meanwhile Shirly phones her husband Don and tells him what happened, he tried to reassure her that such cases are quite common, and everything always works out with the missing child returned unharmed,'

'But that was three hours ago Don! if he had been dropped anywhere someone would have found him by now, oh, darling, this is like living in a terrible nightmare, my worst fears have been realised, I cannot believe how stupid I have been, what was I thinking? O' God! Please, my baby, ...my baby'

Don put down the phone saying he was on his way home and told her to try to calm down. How could she calm down? Their little darling is missing and only one person knows where he is, and he is not telling anyone, for obvious reasons.

Officer Peter Johns was waiting outside for Don and when he drove up into the driveway the officer got out of his car to meet him saying who he was and that 'I am reluctant to speak to your wife alone sir, she is very irritated ... understandably so and I don't want to upset her any more than I have to, but now you are here she may calm down a little, long enough for me take a statement from you sir,'

Don replies saying to the officer, 'You know more about this that I do officer, my wife just told me on the phone, that is why I am here, to help calm her and do whatever I can to help resolve this terrible situation,'

The front door opened, and Shirly runs out straight into Don's open arms crying her eyes out. They hug each other for a long time before Don says to her, 'Try not to worry too much darling, there is still time, if he is out there, if he has been dropped off somewhere, then we will find him soon,'

Shirly still sobbing says to him, 'How? It will be dark soon! What if he was dropped off and nobody has seen him, oh darling he could be wandering around out there lost and terrified,'

The police officer says to both to them, 'We have a lot of people out looking for him, so hopefully we might get lucky and find him, we might even have good news soon,'

'And what if you don't have good news soon officer?'

Cry's Shirly, 'What if he is out there alone in the dark and cold, he is only four years old,' the officer replies, 'Let us not jump to any conclusions mam, that man in the car might have even brought him home to his place, he might be at this very moment nice and warm and getting fed in this man's house, not every car thief is a horrible person, some of them are very caring human beings with kids of their own mam, so try and relax at least in the short term, please, this man might just have wanted to get home, and that was the only way he could,'

Don still hugging his wife says to her 'He is right darling, no point in making this anymore terrifying as it already is,'

Meanwhile just moments after the car thief dropped the child by the forest entrance the little boy whose name was Michael had walked into the forest and got hopelessly lost to the outside world.

He did however find a little nook to shelter in and soon he was curled up fast asleep in a pile of dried leaves. The forest came into its own in the dark as all kinds of furry little creatures began foraging for food and bits of twigs and leaves to make their little homes warmer for the oncoming winter.

Wolves and even bears were on the hunt for food, and they knew the area very well and where they would most likely find food, the river was not too far away and there was fish galore, but bears don't fish in the dark as their eyesight is not too good.

When the child woke early next morning there was a little robin perched on his shoe. He laughed as he tried to pick it up, but the little bird flew up and landed on his hand chirping merrily away as if it was trying to console him. Then it flew away and the little child shivered in the morning sun.

The Mc Kenna's got no sleep that night and Shirly still sobbing went to make breakfast, she was looking out the kitchen window when a little robin landed on the outside sill and seemed to be staring at her.

It began chirping away and even did a little dance around the outside windowsill and Shirly felt something stir within herself. She remembered her mother telling her about little robins and how some people thought they were spirits of loved ones coming back to reassure them of their wellbeing.

Of course, she did not really believe it, but it gave her some comfort as she watched the little bird hopping about and singing its little heart out.

By now it was all over the news how little Michael had been taken in the car and the police wanted the public's help in tracing the car and the little four-year-old boy.

The man that had taken the car had seen the news bulletin and thinking that the child may have died after been out in the cold overnight became really scared and it was a week before he got the nerve to phone the police and tell them where he had left the child several days earlier.

Meanwhile the little boy was heading towards the river, with the little robin fluttering before his tiny face doing its best to get the child to turn around and away from the danger. It was a fast-flowing river with more than its share of hungry crocodiles that were sunning themselves on the riverbank and were just waiting for lunch to arrive, and they didn't care what size or shape it came in.

Big Joe Mac Cortney was a logger for the Wisconsin Logging Company, and he was sitting on a tree trunk having his lunch when a little robin few down and landed beside him. Big Joe was well used to seeing little robins do this and he picked a little piece of bread and placed it in front of the tiny bird.

The little robin began to flutter, chirping and dancing round in circles making a nuisance of itself causing Big Joe to say to it, 'Okay, I get it you don't like bread, that's okay ...little fella...I have some meat here, there you go, enjoy that ...it's not every day you get to eat cooked meat, ha, ha,' but the little bird kept up his squawking and dancing so much so that Big Joe finally got the message, this little fellow is trying to tell me something.

The wolf had also got the message. There was food to be had around here, and sniffing the ground began to follow little Michael's trail.

Shirly kept phoning the police station looking for any news. Surely someone out there knows where her son is, and surely every mother in the country knows how much I am worrying about my little child, my little baby blue eyed boy, but why is there no response? The reward of 50,000 dollars should have helped but nothing, not a sight or sound of her little darling.

Not a word, as if he had simply vanished from the earth. How can such a small child survive on its own, if indeed it was on its own. Oh God! please let him be found soon, please God ...Blessed Mother ...you know what it's like to lose a son, help them to find my son ...my precious little baby, please God, please'

Meanwhile the little robin kicked up such a racket that Big Joe began to follow it as it flew from branch to branch threw the forest until at last Big Joe knew what all the fuss was about because there in the clearing was the little boy Michael, cold wet from his soiled diaper sitting on the cold, cold, ground, and not a moment too soon as the wolf had found the child also and now it was a matter of who got there first.

Big Joe or the wolf.

Then out of nowhere came a female black bear snarling and growling at the wolf and as there was a kind of standoff as they began snarling at each other. Big Joe crept forward and was just about to run the last few metres and grab the child when the bear sniffed the air and turned to face him. Big Joe having worked in the forest for most of his life had heard how fast these bears could move so he stopped dead in his tracks.

The large black bear looked at him then at the child and said something that sounded almost human, a bit like a cat miaowing but this was no cat, this was a wild beast with the strength of a Rhino and the cunning of a mountain lion, and here it was acting so human. Big Joe picked up the child and the bear looked him in the eye again and then causally walked off in the opposite direction.

The little robin was singing sweetly on Gig Joes shoulder as he realised that this was the missing child that the whole country was searching for and talking about and he had found him alive and well, if somewhat cold and hungry, and eh, smelly.

Shirly was in the shower when the house phone rang so Don answered the call. 'He has been found safe and sound, we have taken him to the hospital to be checked over, but he seems to be okay' said police officer Johns with delight.

Don ran up the stairs and when Shirly heard him running she thought he had got bad news, her heart was bursting in her breast as Don said to her gently, 'They found him darling! they found our little Michael, he is okay, they have taken him to the hospital just to check him over but he is alright darling he is alright' and the two of them hugged each other and both cried with relief.

Big Joe claimed and received the large reward that he donated to the local hospital, and he made as much again if not more from the television and radio shows that wanted to hear his wonderful story.

Everybody wanted to hear the good new even the man that stole the car in the first place cried with happiness at the finding of this precious child. People were phoning in telling similar stories like the time a bear saved their child from falling over a high cliff and when they looked again at the bear it turned into a man with angel's wings. There were lots of stories like that coming in from all over the country, some even from Canada and as far away as Australia with similar tales of joy.

Meanwhile Shirly and Don were so happy that their little wandering star was back healthy and happy that when Don got to the hospital, he left the keys in the car, they were in such a hurry to see their child, and when they came back out two hours later their car was gone. They just fell into each other's arms laughing and crying and so happy they were a family again, thanks to Big Joe the logger the wonderful mother bear and of course, the little robin.

End

White Suit

Little johnny robins was an ordinary looking Joe soap. I say ordinary because one would not look at him twice if one saw him on the street, and like most fifteen-year-olds he was a good kid with no confidence in himself despite been a talented guitar player. He was very good in school in terms of results, but his main ambition was to be an accomplished guitarist.

He was well on the road to fulfilling his dream. His first step in reaching this began when he got the opportunity to play alongside two other musicians on stage at his local club and it went very well despite the fact that Johnny played sideways, meaning that he did not have to look directly at the audience.

A thing quite common with first timers, and it often took months for artists to overcome this normal trait.

This went on for week after week and if one was following him in any way, one could see he was getting more and more confidence as he began to enjoy his playing with the band.

He did however always dress in dark clothing that did not do his image much good. Till the day he went a bought himself a white suit, after all it did not do Elvis any harm, not that he was trying to be Elvis, there was and is and forever will ever be only one Elvis Presley.

When he got home with his white suit and tried it on something magical happened to him. His whole demeanour changed and for the better. He loved that suit and when his girlfriend and future singer with him and his band saw him wearing it, she was overjoyed at his confidence as was everyone else in the family who saw him wear it.

The first time he wore it on stage he wowed the house down. Not only did his whole manner change but he also became much more confident with his guitar playing. In short, he had finally arrived on stage, and people began to take notice of him as he faced them and played his heart out. He got to know other young players and in time they became a band that worked well together.

Then his girlfriend Marie, began to write some songs and after a while she too became quite good at it and soon enough they all gelled together to become a very good middle of the road band called 'Spirits' at first playing only hits of the stars then doing the odd one or two of Marie's songs that went down very well, and slowly but surely began to make a name for themselves, as more and more young people began to know of them. Their young drummer Adam was particularly good.

Because they were so young, they could not play in pubs and any club that served alcohol but only in school halls and theatre houses, but this gave them the time they needed to really get to know one another's musical skills that only helped them even more to become one family of great musicians. This band that was now looking great and sounding great would soon be ready to take on the world, all they were waiting for was a good manager. Could that be you by any chance? Watch this space.

End

Three's A Crowd

Henry Rawlings and Patricia Nolan were school time friends and in time became boyfriend and girlfriend much to the annoyance of Patricia's parents. They thought that Henry was not good enough for their little girl, but Patricia would not give him up, firstly because he was a handsome blue-eyed boy blond hair young man that most of the other girls at school would flock around him as if he were already a film star and secondly, because he was very athletic on the running track in their last at Mercy's high school in Mulder County in Chicago. He also came from a very rich family that lived on a huge ranch ten miles outside the city.

He was an only child.

Henry was besotted with Patricia. He loved everything about her but was rather the jealous kind that kept her many male friends at a safe distance, and at one time even had the nerve to punch a young man to the ground that he had seen talking to his girlfriend for longer than the minute he allotted her in his own mind.

Patricia had shouted at him, 'We were just talking Henry, there was no need for you to do that, can I not even talk to people anymore? you broke his nose, now you might have gotten yourself suspended from school, you idiot'

He did not like being called an idiot and he got in her face so much that she feared he might hit her. She stayed away from him, and she did not answer his calls for two weeks but gave in on the last few days as he persisted in saying how sorry he was and that it was only because he loved her so much and that it would not happen again. Her trust in him however had been forever shaken and things were never the same with him again. He was not suspended from school as his father was a member of the school board.

Patricia was always uneasy in his presence and would look for and used every excuse not to go with him and this really took off the time he deliberately turned on one of her girlfriends when he saw them kiss each other on the cheek the way good girlfriends always did.

Calling her a lesbian and making rude gestures every time he saw them together, and to prove she was not a lesbian to the other people at school she went out with another boy called Tony that had asked her out before but was afraid to go out with him on account of Henry's bad temper. Henry did not like that at all and promised her if she did not go back to him, someone was going to pay.

She did not give in to his threats and avoided him at every opportunity. This did not go down well with Henry who got angrier every time he saw her. It began with her receiving rude texts on her phone and even some hate mail in her post box calling her all kinds of racist whore's and the like.

One day she drove out to his parent's ranch to try talk some sense into him. She found him fixing some heavy boards to the outside of barn door and when she asked him what he was doing he simply said, 'These doors need strengthening, as if you were interested' she tried to be civil with him, but he wasn't having any of it and made it quite clear that she was no longer welcome on his property.

So, she just walked away feeling very unsettled and hurt at the way things had worked out between them as she still had a soft spot for him.

The following week she became quite ill, and the doctor told her she had a bad case of flu, and she was to rest for the next few days and drink plenty of fluids but to mainly rest, which she did having no one else to look after her in her apartment.

When she felt well enough to return to school, she found that Tony too had not been seen at all the same time that she was out and thinking that he may have caught the flu off her or vice versa she thought no more about it.

Until she got a note in her post box saying, 'the missing dog is in the barn'. At first, she thought that this was some kind of joke, and then the more she thought about it the more she thought that this was the work of Henry and his childish schemes.

Her mind began to work overtime thinking that Henry had hurt Tony in some way and the more she thought about it the more scared she became as Tony was not answering the many phone calls she was making to him. As the days went by the more frightened, she became until she just had to go out to Henry's ranch and challenge him on the matter.

He was waiting for her as if he had been expecting her and when he saw her drive up, he went out to meet her and he was pleasant enough even inviting her into his home to have some coffee and a chat. She accepted with some reservation when they were inside having coffee, he said to her,

'You do know I still love you and wanted to marry you, so imagine how I felt when you dumped me for that 'black' fellow, that really got me in the gut, and I will never forgive you for that, not even if you fell to your knees this very moment and kissed my feet, what's the matter …are you feeling sleepy now girl? am I boring you with all my heart felt sorry for nothing feelings, well tough shit, you made me suffer and now it's your turn, as well as that dog in the barn that you call your boyfriend, oh, that's got your attention now hasn't it, my lovely Patricia…baby?

Well too late darling, but I do have a surprise for you, I do want to see you back together with your 'coloured' friend, so if you can stay awake long enough, I will take you too him in a moment just as soon as I take from you what you have denied me these last few years'

Then he punched her full in the face and she fell to the floor where he stripped her naked and had his way with her. She could still understand what was happening despite feeling so sleepy and unable to resist him, so she just had to lie there and let him do what he wanted to do to her. He did a lot of unspeakable things to her, but she had no choice but to lay there and take it. Then she fell asleep, but not fast enough.

The next thing that she remembered was waking up in the barn with him sitting there smoking a joint and just staring at her, every now and then he would reach over and twist her nipples so she would come to quicker as she was still rather sleepy and naked and badly bruised and very cold, and surprisingly hungry after all she had just been through. The barn doors were wide open which indicated to her that there was no one else on the property that could or would come and help her.

Then his mood seemed to change as he got up and picked up a blanket lying nearby and placed it on her shoulders whispering in her ear, 'Now I did promise you a surprise didn't I darling, well here it is!

And he stood up and went over to the left side barn door and slowly closed it, revealing Tony's naked body nailed hands and feet to the back of it, she fainted at the horrible sight, but he was ready for that also as he put some smelling salts to her nose and watched her slowly recover.

'Now!' said he as he watched her terrified face and he laughed and said, 'He is not so handsome now darling is he? are you sorry now that you didn't marry me and have my children, we could have lived happy ever after on this fine ranch with a big house of our very own, ha ...ha ...ha, you stupid cow, aren't you sorry now darling, your toy boy Tony here is not in a position to come to your aid, but don't worry, you will be joining him soon enough ...darling and he threw her on the ground and raped her again and again until he could no longer do so and he fell in a heap by her side staring into her battered face.

She managed to spit in his face, and he jumped up even more angry than before and dragged her over and shut the other half of the barn door and then nailed her to the back of it, first one hand then the other in the places he had already marked out for her, and when her hands were nailed, he lifted her feet and nailed them to the door saying,

'Now I know I said I would reunite you two together and don't worry I am about to do that in a moment, you can even kiss him goodbye which was more than you did for me, bitch'   then he opened the right hand side of the door that he had fixed the hinges on some time before so that it opened in then folded out until it brought the two of them together so that they were face to face with their noses touching but Tony was already dead.

Patricia was in such pain that she could not even scream and seeing her boyfriend left hanging there she knew she was about to die and she was feeling so bad that she would welcome death, but Henry was not finished yet as he began sprinkling petrol over the two of them and he waited for the horror of it all to sink into to his former girlfriend and when it had he lit a match and set the doors ablaze and watched from a safe distance standing outside sniggering to himself as the whole barn burnt down leaving nothing but a pile of ashes and twisted metal hinges and bent nails. When he was satisfied with the result the last question, he asked himself was, 'That new girl in school, what is name again, Noreen, yes, the lovely Noreen, I wonder if she has a boyfriend?

End

GEHEIMNISSE (SECRETS)

A Railway station somewhere in France on Wednesday 29th May 1940 during WW 2.

A line of German soldiers of various ranks minor lined up on the platform being addressed by their commanding officer Major Von Beck: 'Soldaten…nien, soldiers… I vill speak in English so that those vho listen in on our conversation… ja…. vill hear every vord I say, I vant them to hear me, ja… this morning, vell… very soon now, a train vill be stopping here ja…on that train vill be many American captured soldiers being transported to de homeland, these Americans came here to do some secret mission ja… but ve stopped them in their tracks… ja… vhy…because they talk too much… do these Yankees, they love to hear themselves talk ja…und… they have talked themselves into our hands ja… und ve vant them to talk some more ja, ve vant them to tell us everything about their mission ja… Aufmerksamkeit…*pay attention*… if even one of these prisoners escapes from here, ja… even one, your lives von't be vort living, you all wissen, eh *know*… me… you vill all be sent directly to the front… I Major von Beck… promise you this, und I keep my vord, so be alert at all times,' he looks down the tracks and sees the train inching along. Then back to his men and says to them, 'Hier kommt der Zug, so… *be goot soldiers and do your job… ja…be ruthless*'

The train pulls into the platform and the soldiers immediately stand in line at the back of the trains wooden car guns drawn and pointing towards the door. One German soldier seeing a greenhorn standing beside him shaking in his boots and says to him. 'Haben Sie keine angst …dass dcese Jungs Sie nicht verletzen konnen also entrpannen Sie sich' meaning …*'don't be afraid, these guys can't hurt you, so relax'* the door was opened and out came twenty-two American soldiers looking all dishevelled and scared.

They had heard all about the German brutalities and knew that life for the foreseeable future was going to be anything but pleasant. Captain Michael Collins says to his men. 'Remember your training, we will be not here for long guys, so mums the word' all his men nod their heads in agreement and are frog marched into a nearby old disused army barracks where they are addressed by the Major.

'Velcom to der Plaza hotel, ja, weil, eh…because, that is vhat this place will seem like vhere you are going, ja…ve know about your dirty geheimnisse, eh… little *secrets*, und believe me you vill tell me everything I vant to know, I eh…erinnern Sie sich daran, *remember that ve already know ja, ve have vays to make you speak that even the Gestapo how you say,* Katzbuckeln, eh, kriechen, *cringe,* ja… that is the vord I looking for, cringe…

So do not be stupid, like most Americans, save yourselves from many hard, eh, hardships… up tell us vhat ve vant to know, ja… no need to eh… schlichten, settle down, your vorries begin right now, ja…' he calls out 'stabskapitan'… *staff captain*…More German guards enter the large room with vicious dogs and unleash them and urge the dogs to attack the prisoners which they do viciously. The prisoners run this way and that but some of them are badly bitten on the legs and arms. This goes on for five minutes after which two of the dogs lay dead on the floor. 'sehr gut…ja… *very good,* but vhat vill you do when there are thirty dogs, ja…denk daruber nach.. eh…*think about it, you have two hours,* ja…' then turns to the guards and says,' bewache sie gut' *guard them well.*

So, it went on and on for three days with the prisoners been savagely beaten, nails removed, and testicles burnt with hot irons but not one of them told the Major anything. The Major been a very stubborn man finally slammed the table and told his adjutant to get a firing squad ready. And when it was ready, he took great delight in lining the men up against the wall and even more delight when he saw how white their faces became. Thinking that the prisoners were now at breaking point he himself took control of the machine gun and was about to pull the trigger when Captain Michael Collins stepped forward and addresses the Major. 'Herr Major, …*dumach einen groBen Fehler… you are making a huge mistake and will pay dearly for it.*

Wir sind keine Amerikaner, sondern Spezialagenten… SS-Einheit Spezialkräfte Schutzstaffel

' *We are not Americans but special agents… SS unit special forces* 'Schutzstaffel'

Der Fuhrer's *handpicked personal bodyguards, sent here to impersonate American soldiers,* mitdemziel Partisanen und Saboteure giftbag zu nehmen, *with the aim of capturing partisans and saboteurs that have been killing our soldiers by the hundreds every single day…*' Having realised his great mistake, the Major opened fired and killed every one of the prisoners. No prisoners, no story telling. His men were left almost paralysed by the brutality of it and the young greenhorn that was shaken at the railways station actually did wet his pants.

Two days later Colonel Peter Schmidt arrived at the camp with his Lieutenant Colonel Michael Gurz and marched into Von Becks office and demanded an explanation. 'Why have you killed these brave soldiers of the 'Schutzstaffel'' the Majors mouth dried so much he could hardly speak. He said almost coughing. 'But… no one told me Herr Colonel. How vas I to know that these men ver not real Americans?'

The Colonel slammed his fist down hard on the Majors desk then threw down a yellow paper wallet containing photographs and credential of the slain men. Von Becks face turned ghostly white, …'weil es Ihnen von unserem Top-Mann-Kapitän Collins gesagt wurde. ' *You were told by our top man captain Collins. We have witnesses to that fact.* '

Wir haben zwei Jahre damit verbracht, diese Männer auf

diese Mission vorzubereiten und sie sogar absichtlich hierher geflogen, um ihr amerikanisches Flugzeug zu crashlanden, um die Partisanen in die Irre zu führen, und es dauert kurze Wochen, in denen Sie alles vermasseln... Sie sind eine Schande für diesen uniformierten Bürgermeister, der es abnimmt...' English Translation.

We have spent two years preparing these men for this mission and even flew them in here... deliberately crash landing the captured American plane to mislead the Partisans, and in two short weeks you fuck it all up... you are a disgrace to that uniform Mayor... take it off the Major clumsily removes his uniform after been stripped of its decorations including its iron cross.

The Colonel nodded to his second in command and the Lieutenant Colonel escorts the Major out to where the prisoners were mowed down.

Facing the same machine gun that he used to kill the prisoners the Major has one more humility to face, the same little greenhorn that wet his pant has now been directed to open fire on the Major. He does but is shaken so much the Colonel and his lieutenant have to dive for cover. The Major however lies dead almost floating in the blood of all the prisoners he had killed only two days before.

The Colonel on the other hand says to his second in command pointing at the little greenhorn that is now vomiting all over the place. 'Senden Sie dieses für weitere Schulungen ya.' English Translation.

Send this one for more training... yes.

End

Check Mate

The CIA office in Washington, top secret meeting between its top operatives. There are three members in the room.

Agent number 1 addressing the meeting.

'Good morning gentlemen, we have brought you here because we have a very important mission for you, you may or may not know that you guys are the best we have in our department, and come very highly recommended, in short, there is no one else, as most if not all our agents have now been caught or killed now,

It has come to our attention that the Russian have developed a new weapon of mass destruction, and with that madman at the helm it is quite possible that they will use it very soon in you know where! the only thing is precisely when, we desperately need to find out when and where and quickly, before we find out the hard way,

It is a newly developed spy plane, nothing new there, but this one is equipped with missiles, nuclear missiles …four in all and from what we do know is that the Russians have built this plane for very specific reason, and I assure you that reason is not good, that much we do know gentlemen, now we have devised a plan to take this plane from its hanger …its whereabout we will reveal to you in a moment and fly it to German where we will then dismantle the larger parts and ship them back to the states where we will put it together again and take a proper look at it, as far as the Russian are concerned a rogue operator will have taken the plane to sell it to their well-known terrorist in Africa or elsewhere.

Agent number 2 will fill you in on the plan, he is by the way a Russian double agent, a very fine one too …I might add,

Agent number 2… Thank you, number 1, now gentlemen, this plane is housed in hanger in a very large industrial area off the coast of Siberia, yes, I know what you're thinking …but get this so do the Russians,

It is guarded round the clock by the president's own security service, two heavily armed guards at the front that circle the building continuously until there replaced by two more, this circle is forever surrounding the building at all times, but we already have some of our guys watching them as we speak,

The pilot of this plane will have myself along with him to explain the controls in the cockpit, why? because hah …hah we don't want him blowing himself and the plane up right there and then, it might be bobby trapped but we don't think so, anyway having started the plane we can then inch out onto the runway, there is CCTV cameras watching the building but one of our guys will take them out at the appropriate time, so we can take off without anyone seeing us,… as they have also found a way of silencing the engines… yes agent number 3, you have a question for me?'

Agent number 3… 'yes number 2, who will take out the guards? one …and two, who will take out the plane?'

Number 2… 'Ah, don't you worry about that number 3, it will be taken care off, any more questions no, …good then let's get this show on the road, shall we? and good luck to you guys'

The meeting was closed discreetly, and the agents went off in the way they do and met up the next day at the usual place for a final briefing.

Having been briefed they then separated and made their way by plane to a secret destination in a secret nearby country and from there made their way by truck to Siberia. The truck contained machine parts and was heavily invoiced by top officials in high command in case they were stopped anywhere along the long route.

The invoices were forged but were so good that even those who would have signed it would have difficulty telling the difference between them and the real ones. The CIA had planned well and many hours later the truck pulled into the industrial area and then the plan began in earnest.

Two of their agents number 5 and number 6 crept up on the Russian guards dressed in the same uniform and when they got close enough they sprang into action and killed the guards by knifing them in the chest and dragging them out of sight of the CCTV cameras while the third agent made his way to the building housing the camera's and cut the power and phone lines and when the guard inside came out to find out what was going on, he too was killed by having his throat cut.

Meanwhile agent number 2 along with agent number 4 the pilot had made their way into the hanger and found the small plane as predicted and once inside the plane agent number 2 told agent number 4 what the controls were and once the engines were started a blue light in the cockpit screen came on and agent number 2 said to agent number 4, 'Shit' and when agent number 4 asked agent number 2 what was wrong agent number 2 replied to agent number 4 saying, 'It has its full missile load on board, we were not expecting that, no matter, they are not armed so we should be okay,' the plane moved forward towards the small runway, where it silently took off into the cold night sky and away westward to Germany as planned.

Everything had gone as planned and back at headquarters in Washington all the top brass were very pleased and gave themselves and their wonderful network of agents a huge pat on the back.

Back in the Kremlin the powers that be were also patting themselves on the back. So far so good.

When the plane landed in a secret landing strip in Germany it was immediately surrounded by dozens of special agents and escorted to a specially built hanger in a nearby industrial estate that was near completion and almost ready to be opened for business.

The powers that be in Washington had flown over to see for themselves what the nuclear plane looked like as they had just built one of their won and when they saw it …it became very clear to them that their design have been used by the Russians who then replaced the two short range missiles to four long range nuclear missiles under the wings , just like an ordinary missile weapon system but these were weapons of mass destruction.

The American's were stunned at the sight and ordered that the plane be dismantled at once and flown back in crates to a site in Texas where it could be reassembled and studied and the findings giving to the Department of homeland security after all it was weapons of mass destruction that had got America involved in Iraq not too long ago, and look what a mess the CIA had made of that, so this time everything had to be spot on, no fuck ups whatever.

And so, when the cargo plane landed in Texas its precious cargo was immediately taken to a private hanger and reassembled, all the top brass were there shaking hands and congratulating themselves on a job so superbly and beautifully done, and agent number 2 sitting in the cockpit saw a red light come on and light up the compartment, he said to agent number 1, 'Shit' and agent number 1 asked him what the matter was? agent number 2 said to agent number 1 'Noka' which was Russian but which means goodbye in English and the four nuclear bombs exploded wiping out the hanger, every building nearby and most of Texas causing a massive wave of radiation to spread through most of the nearest states in America. They were indeed weapons of mass destruction.

Meanwhile back in Moscow the head of the powers that be, a certain lunatic president whose name shall remain nameless in case it offended the Russians simply said because he was a simple man, in very plain English, 'Checkmate'

End

Puss in boots

Stuart Randell had just moved into his brand-new home with his wife Shelia and two children two little girls Breda and Joan. He was a labourer on a lot of different building sites and had learned a lot of different skills in the past few years, in short, he was a handy man but the only thing that made him handy was the fact that he now lived on the property.

The family also had a German Shepherd dog named Matilda and a young kitten named Puss which everybody thought was a stupid name for a cat, but Breda and Joan loved the little beast that was always getting itself into trouble, and they named it Puss so that was what it was called.

John was not in the house one day when he heard something moving in the walls of his immaculate sitting room and when Breda came in looking for the cat, he put two and two together and got six.

His wife Shelia came in from the back garden and saw him cutting a small hole in the longest wall in the room and screamed at him to stop, 'It is just a dry lining wall,' he assured her, 'and Puss is trapped in between the boards, we need to get her out, don't worry, I can fix this in five-minutes flat, you'll never know the difference, I promise you babe'

She said to him, 'If that wall isn't fixed by the time I get home from mothers I am going to divorce you, that too is a promise'

Stuart knew she would be a least five or six hours away as her mother lived way across town and it took nearly an hour and a half just to get there. So, he had plenty of time, he waited one hour to see if Puss would show its little head in the hole that he had just made and when the little darling didn't, he made another small hole at the other end and when that didn't work, he made a big hole in the middle of the wall but that didn't work either.

Then he heard the same noise again in the opposite wall and once more he made a hole but a little bit bigger and he listened as he laid out a large bowl of cat food to see if that would entice the little kitten out, but it was of no avail.

So, he made a bigger hole but that didn't work so he made an even bigger hole almost taking the whole plaster board off the studs but there was still no sign of little Puss, then Breda came running down the stairs saying there was a strange noise in her bedroom so up the stairs he ran and yes he could hear it too so he punched a hole near the skirting board and when he looked over at Breda she had broken through the dry lining with his hammer only her hole was much bigger than his, no matter, he still had plenty of time before his wife came back.

When he got annoyed at her she went into Joan's room and heard the same noise, so she ran into her father and told him about it, by now most of the dry lining from the floor to about six feet up had been damaged or removed altogether.

After he kicked a large hole in Joan's room big enough for his little darling Breda to simply step back into her own room, he got into a rage and tore down all the other dry lining walls in both rooms but to no avail.

Still the sound persisted, and he started on the landing only to go all the way down the stairs kicking at the lovely freshly painted wooden balustrades as he went from stair to stair, breaking most of them in half, then into the walls on the ground floor knocking pictures to the floor that his wife had spent hours lovingly hanging up the night before. Now the hall was full of broken picture frames and glass all over the place. It looked like a bomb had gone off. It had, a human bomb.

Like a mad man he tore through the house following that horrible sound and if the truth be known if he got his hands on that little f..king cat, he would gladly have strangled it with his bare hands, that was if his darling little girl wasn't looking.

No luck in the hall downstairs so he started on the kitchen and tiled wall or not he knocked hole after hole in the walls but all to no avail, then he noticed that he was fast running out of time and he had better get moving on the repairs before his wife came back and murdered him on account of what he had done to her dream home, that she had lived in now for almost two whole days. F..k, I better order some dry lining boards, they won't be here on time but what the f..k she will see I mean business when they do arrive.

Then he heard it again and it seemed to be coming from the attic this time.

How the f..k, did that f..king little cat manage to get up into the f…king attic without using the f..king wooden stepladder? Why she simply climbed up the inside plaster boards dummy, cats can do that sort of thing.

Up Stuart went and the first thing he noticed was a hole in the roof and two squirrels running in and out of it so he quicky made a dash for the hole to cover it up, but his right foot went through the ceiling board and his left foot went through another ceiling board and the whole ceiling came crashing down into the sitting room. Filling the room with dust and debris.

It was only the beam that got caught between his legs that saved him from crashing down also, but the pain was awful. The house was in a heap and then he panicked as he heard his wife's car pulling up outside with her saying as she opened the front door, 'Darling, would you look at who came with me to my mother's house, little Pussy, what the f..k…'

Stuart is now living at his mother house which just happens to be in another state. A better state than the one he left behind.

End

www.ingramcontent.com/pod-product-compliance
Lightning Source LLC
LaVergne TN
LVHW061932070526
838199LV00060B/3824